The Christmas Tree Cottage

HOLLY MARTIN

CW00550739

CHAPTER ONE

Heath blew into his hands as he waited for their guests to arrive. It was one of the coldest Decembers he could ever remember, the icy wind tore in off the sea and moaned through the trees as if the fairy-style treehouses that usually looked so enchanting and magical were taking part in an altogether more sinister movie. A crow let out a squawk nearby, helping complete the eerie feel. Snow had been forecast though, which at least would add a Christmassy feel to the place and make all the treehouses look magical.

This year, Christmas at Wishing Wood, the luxury treehouse resort he owned with his brothers, was going to be special. There were only eight days until the big day and they had a lot planned. They had built a Christmas tree cottage for Father Christmas to meet all the children staying in the resort, plus there were plans for him to have breakfast with them on some days and read bedtime stories to them on others. A lot of the local children had signed up for the 'meet Santa' events too. They were even going to hold a Christmas market in the woods. He and his brothers, River and Bear, had hurriedly built several wooden lodges amongst the trees over the last few weeks and as of Saturday they were going to be filled with people selling their Christmas goodies.

Father Christmas and his wife were due to arrive any time now and they'd requested a field or stable, which was a bit of an odd request. As it happened, the resort did have a spare field with an old shelter at one end which his brother River had hurriedly repaired over the last few days. Heath wondered if Father Christmas was bringing his own reindeer.

Meadow, his ex-wife and the manager of Wishing Wood, had asked him to get them to park their vehicle near the back of the shelter. He chewed his lip as he thought. Vehicle was an odd choice of word. Not car or van. Was Santa going to turn up in his sleigh? Meadow had also asked if he would mind helping the guests for the next few days, which he'd happily agreed to although he didn't know what help they needed. When he'd quizzed Meadow, she'd snorted and then told him that Mrs Christmas would fill him in, making him wonder what he'd signed up for.

His phone beeped in his pocket and he pulled it out to have a look, smiling when he saw it was a text from Scarlet.

Looking forward to seeing you Saturday night.

He grinned because he was looking forward to it too. This thing with Scarlet felt like it had been a long time coming and he couldn't be happier he'd finally got a date with her.

Just then a clip-clopping made him look up and he smiled when a bright red old-fashioned gypsy caravan rolled slowly up the driveway, pulled by a spectacular grey shire horse that gleamed in the weak winter sun. What an entrance. It was just a shame there were no children around to witness Father Christmas and his wife arriving in Wishing Wood. His daughter Star and niece Tierra would have got such a big kick out of this.

The caravan was being driven by a young woman dressed in a green velvet cloak, her dark hair billowing behind her in curls as the wind caught it, though as the sun came out fleetingly from behind the dark clouds, he could see the hair was tinted with every colour of the rainbow, tiny strands of blue, purple, red, orange and gold cascading behind her in some kind of crazy wonderful dance. She drew closer and he could see she was incredibly beautiful in a wild, dramatic kind of way. If it hadn't been for the coloured hair, she'd be right at home standing on the cliffs in *Poldark* or some other windswept period drama.

She stopped the caravan right in front of him and flashed him a huge warm smile.

'Hello, so you're going to be my husband for the next week?' She looked him up and down and her smile broadened. 'Well I've had a lot worse, so you'll do.'

He frowned in confusion. Husband? Was she in the right place?

'It's Heath Brookfield, right? I'm Evergreen Winters.'

He smiled. She must be part of the act, maybe an assistant to Father and Mrs Christmas.

'Hi Evergreen, what a great name, very Christmassy and a wonderful dramatic entrance. If we'd known that Father and Mrs Christmas were going to arrive so spectacularly, we'd have arranged a proper welcome party. As it is you've just got me, so you can drop the act. What's your real name, I can't go around calling you Evergreen for the rest of your stay?'

Heath peered inside the caravan to get a glimpse of Father Christmas, wondering if he was already dressed in his full regalia and would come out ho, ho, ho-ing.

'You can call me Evergreen, as that's my name,' she said. 'I know, it's weird, the kids took the piss out of me at school, and with the surname, no one ever believes it's real. I was born in early December so my mum wanted something festive. Why she just couldn't have gone for Holly or Ivy, I don't know, at least that would have been more acceptable. I really like Evergreen though, it's different, unique, although most people call me Ever.'

'Oh I'm sorry, I thought it was all part of the show.'

'No show either, sadly. Although my friends, Joe and Daisy, your original Santa Claus and Mrs Claus, would have loved to arrive in style like this. No sadly, Joe broke his hip a few weeks ago and Daisy is at home looking after him, so you've just got me. I did explain all this to your manager, Meadow. I told her I would be perfectly happy to stand in as Mrs Christmas if she could provide me with a nice husband for the week leading up to Christmas. I told her I'd bring all the costumes and make-up to turn him into a convincing Father Christmas and she said that you'd do it,' Evergreen smiled, mischievously. 'I'm guessing she never told you that.'

'Wait, *I'm* going to be Father Christmas?' Heath asked incredulously. 'She said you would need some help for the next few days but she didn't mention that.'

'I think I'm going to like Meadow.'

'I don't think I can be Father Christmas… What do I have to do?'

'Chatting to children about what they want for Christmas, being jolly. I don't think it's going to be too hard,' Evergreen said with some amusement.

Heath shook his head in disbelief. At least the husband comment when she arrived now made more sense, although he wasn't sure that Scarlet would understand.

Evergreen must have noticed his hesitation. 'Well, if you really don't want to do it, we still have a day to find me another Santa, we're not meeting with any children until Saturday, but I'd hate to disappoint any of them if we can't find anyone else at such short notice.'

'No, it's OK, I'll do it. How hard can it be, right?' Heath said, knowing he was trying to convince himself more than her.

She grinned. 'That's the spirit. Now where would you like me to park my home?'

He blinked in surprise at that. 'Erm… just over there behind the shelter and you can put your horse in that field too so he can use the shelter if it gets too cold.'

She nodded and clicked the horse to move forward and her little caravan squeaked and wobbled its way up the path towards the shelter. Heath walked behind it. Up close it was a rickety old thing with some of the red paint faded and peeling. One of the window panes was coming away and the axel on the back wheels looked like it needed some work, the caravan shouldn't be wobbling to that extent.

She stopped behind the shelter and then stood up, flicked her cloak out behind her and made to climb down.

He quickly moved forward to help her and amusement filled her eyes.

'Well aren't you the gentleman,' she said, taking his hand and hopping down in front of him. She was a lot shorter than he was but then most people were. She had large greeny-grey eyes surrounded by thick long dark lashes and looking at her he felt something spark inside him but he couldn't put his finger on what that spark was. He watched the smile fade from her eyes as she stared up at him and then she stepped back, clearing her throat. Had she felt it too?

'I'm just going to put Thunder in the field,' Evergreen said, unhooking the horse from the caravan. She grabbed two bags from the seat, took Thunder's bridle and started walking him into the field.

'Here can I take those bags for you?' Heath said, falling in by her side.

She smiled up at him and passed them to him. 'Thank you.'

They walked into the field and she led Thunder towards the shelter. He watched as she gently removed the bridle, pulled a hay bag from one of the bags and hung it from the shelter wall. She pulled a small towel out and rubbed down the horse as Heath grabbed a bucket of water and brought that to Thunder too.

'Thanks,' Evergreen said, as she grabbed a blanket from the bag and threw it over the giant horse.

'Will he be warm enough here?' Heath asked. The shelter was closed in at one end but almost completely open apart from the roof up the other end.

'He's a Clydesdale, they're used to hanging around in the coldest conditions in Scotland. He'll be absolutely fine.'

Heath patted Thunder's back as he watched Evergreen tend to the horse. There was something so graceful about the way she moved and the way the cloak billowed around her was almost ethereal. She looked like she could be an elf queen from *Lord of the Rings* or any of the other fantasy books and films he loved so much.

'So don't take this the wrong way, but you don't look like the kind, elderly Mrs Christmas I had quite imagined when Indigo and Meadow came up with this event. Though I'm not the typical Father Christmas either,' Heath said as they walked back out the shelter.

'I have years of training in doing stage make-up. I could make you into a wizened old wizard or a terrifying orc or a hideous alien if I wanted. And yes, you're a lot taller and a hell of a lot more muscular than I normally like my Father Christmases to be but I can make you older, fatter and more cuddly.'

'Wonderful,' Heath said, dryly.

She appraised him for a moment as they walked back towards the caravan. 'You are a good-looking man. Are you single?'

Heath laughed at the open question. The women he'd dated were often a lot more subtle than that. But he liked her honest, up-front approach.

'That's one way of finding out,' Heath said. 'Don't beat around the bush, will you?'

She shrugged. 'No point messing around, trying to guess. Good to find out now if I can let my mind develop a full-blown crush on you or whether we're just going to be mates.'

He thought about it for a moment. 'That's difficult to answer.'

She climbed up into the caravan with ease, her velvet cloak fluttering around her. 'Why don't you come in for a cup of tea or coffee. We should get to know each other a little if we're going to be husband and wife for the next week. And then you can tell me why you being single is so difficult to explain.'

He followed her into the caravan and nearly banged his head as he stepped inside. He had to bend at the neck to avoid dragging his head against the ceiling.

Evergreen giggled and directed him to a small armchair that he had to squeeze himself into. He looked around as she filled a small kettle from a bottle of water and put it on the stove.

The place was so tiny it was hard to believe anyone could really live here. There was a small single bed up one end next to where he was sitting and above the bed was a shelf filled with books and a few cupboards, presumably for her clothes. He was sitting in an area that was the kitchen, dining room and lounge all in one. A small breakfast bar jutted out from the wall where there was one bar stool. The stove had two hobs, one of which was currently being used for the kettle, and there were a few saucepans and cooking utensils hanging from the wall. There were a few more tiny cupboards in this part of the room too. It was all very tidy with minimal clutter. Almost everything had an important reason for being there. Beyond the books there were no personal items at all and no photos of family members or friends.

He noticed that the paint in here was peeling too. The gas stove had taken several attempts before it had eventually lit and in the corner by the door a small pot was catching drips from the ceiling. In fact there were a number of patched-up holes in the roof.

He turned his attention back to Evergreen. There was something about her he found fascinating. He had never met anyone who lived in a horse-drawn caravan before. It was a unique way of life and he suddenly found himself wanting to know more about her.

'Tea or coffee?' Evergreen said, getting out two brightly coloured mugs.

'Coffee please. Although I feel like I should be the one getting you a drink, you are our guest after all.'

'Oh no, I'm just working here. I certainly don't need any special treatment.' She made two coffees and handed him a mug before climbing up on the bed and curling her legs under her. 'So tell me about the complicated business of being single or not.'

'Well, I met a woman, Scarlet, about a year ago and we spent the most incredible weekend together and I'm not ashamed to admit I fell a little bit in love with her. But when I told her I was married with a daughter she wanted nothing more to do with me.'

Evergreen wrinkled her nose. 'Ewww, you're one of those men, are you? How disappointing. I'm not surprised she ran away.'

Heath pushed his hand through his hair. 'It's not really

like that. I have a complicated relationship with my ex-wife.'

'Oh, I understand complicated family relationships. I had two mums, well sort of, three stepmums, two stepdads, nine half-brothers and sisters and four stepbrothers and sisters. And don't even get me started with all the grand-parents, the aunts and uncles and half and stepcousins. You'd need one of those massive tube posters to draw out my family tree. So go on, define complicated. Let me guess, your ex-wife never understood your need to sow your seed elsewhere.'

'My ex-wife, the lovely Meadow who set me up for this gig, is my best friend and I love her to bits, we were just never *in* love. We got married purely because she was pregnant and we raised our daughter, Star, together but we never had any kind of real relationship. Meadow was actively pushing me out the door to date other people so I wasn't exactly cheating on her, although we were techni-cally married at the time. Scarlet didn't give me the chance to explain all of that. She thought I was scum, which I can understand.'

'Well, if the two of you had such an incredible connec-tion, as you say, I think her stopping to listen to your explanation would have been fairer. When you meet someone special, you don't throw that away so easily. Unless it was just lust and sex.'

'I don't think it was that, it was one of those life-changing moments.'

Evergreen pulled a face. 'I have to say, you're not selling me the world's greatest love story here.'

'Well it was for me. I couldn't stop thinking about her.

Anyway, I bumped into her a few months ago, told her I was now divorced, and she seemed delighted.'

'Oh she sounds wonderful,' Evergreen said, dryly.

Heath hurried on. He clearly wasn't painting the best picture here and Scarlet *was* wonderful. 'We flirted quite a bit and the memories of that weekend came flooding back. She said she'd call me.'

'And did she?'

'Well no, but that's because she'd deleted my number after the misunderstanding, but fortunately I bumped into her again last week and we're going out for dinner on Saturday night.'

'Ah I see, so not really single, but not exactly in a relationship either,' Evergreen said.

'Well, I'm hoping she will want to move forward with that,' Heath said.

'Or at least revisit that weekend of hot sex.'

'I'm kind of hoping we had something more than that.'

'Did you have a ton in common?'

He wracked his brain for what they had talked about the year before but nothing really stood out. 'I'm sure we'll have plenty to talk about when we meet up.'

'OK,' Evergreen said. She didn't sound at all convinced, which annoyed him a bit. She had no idea what he and Scarlet had shared that incredible weekend.

'So are you single?' Heath decided to turn the tables on her.

'Oh me and relationships don't really mix. I'm really not looking for anything like that and I certainly don't stand still long enough to put down any roots. I like moving around, meeting new people.'

'So… this caravan is actually your home?'

'Yep. It's much better this way. I can just pack up and leave whenever I want. I have my clothes, a few books, Thunder, I don't need anything else. I tour around the UK taking acting jobs or make-up gigs whenever they turn up. Other than that, I have no responsibilities or commitments and I love it.'

Heath sipped his drink as he thought. She had no roots and no desire to have any. It sounded to him like Evergreen was running away from something.

CHAPTER TWO

'I like your home,' Heath said.

Evergreen tried to see it through his eyes. She loved her little home mainly because it was hers and no one could ever take it away from her but it was a long way off being perfect.

'Thank you. It needs a few repairs and a lick of paint and it could probably do with a new roof and some new wheels, but it's home. And I'm glad you like it, you're going to be very familiar with it by the time Christmas comes. We'll be in here for a few hours every day putting on your make-up.'

'Are you not going to stay in Christmas Tree Cottage while you're here? The plan when we built it was for Father Christmas to stay there. It makes sense for you to stay there instead. It's very comfortable. It even has a super-kingsize bed with a deep memory-foam pillow topper. I chose it myself. It's like lying on a cloud.'

'Oh no, I'll stay here. I've slept in here for eight years, it would be weird to sleep anywhere else.'

Although she couldn't deny the thought of stretching out in a super-kingsize bed was suddenly very appealing. Her own was too small and very lumpy.

'Really? You wouldn't want to take a few days' holiday in a luxury treehouse?'

She smiled. 'I know it's silly but I didn't have a home for a short time and this place has always been my haven. I know it's a bit of a crappy haven, it's certainly lacking in the super-kingsize bed department, but it's mine.'

Heath stared at her for a moment and she regretted sharing that, because now he was bound to want to know more and she really didn't want to get into it.

'I totally get that.' He shifted in his chair. 'But with the greatest respect to your lovely home, this seat is made for someone half my size and I can't even stand up in here without banging my head. If you don't want to stay at Christmas Tree Cottage, would you at least consider doing my make-up in there, for me?'

She let out a little sigh of relief that he wasn't going to ask her questions about what she'd said. He gave her a winning smile and she could see how a lot of women could totally fall for a man like Heath Brookfield.

'I could do that. Why don't you show me where the magic is going to happen?' Evergreen said, scooting down from the bed and knocking the side panel off the bed at the same time. It clattered to the floor and she quickly picked it up and pushed it back into position. 'That's always falling off.'

'You know, I could do some repairs for you,' Heath offered. 'While you're staying here, I could fix a few things.'

'Oh no, I wouldn't want to be any trouble.'

'It's no big deal. Building and fixing things is my job.'

'But I can't afford to pay you.'

'And I wouldn't expect you to. Consider it a Christmas gift.'

'I… always do my own repairs.'

Heath looked around and she knew he was thinking she'd not exactly done a great job. 'You could just say, thank you Heath, that's a lovely offer and I'm happy to accept.'

She smiled. 'I don't like being beholden to anyone.'

'There's no *beholding*. Look, if it means that much to you, I'll think of some way for you to repay me.'

She looked at him sceptically, folding her arms.

'Not that,' Heath said in alarm.

She paused while she thought. There were so many little jobs that needed doing and as the weather was getting colder it wasn't particularly pleasurable to stay here right now with the wind blowing in through the cracked window pane and the constant drips coming from the roof.

'OK. Thank you for the offer. But I'll owe you a favour. Anything you want. But I leave on Christmas Eve so all favours will need to be cashed by then, so you have seven days to think of something.'

'I'll make sure it's something big.'

She grinned and shook her head. 'Let's go. I'll take some of my make-up and prosthetics over now ready to use.'

'Here, let me help carry some stuff.'

She passed him a large toolbox and a bag and picked up a few things herself. Heath stepped back outside and climbed down, then offered out his hand to help her.

She took it, rolling her eyes as she hopped down. 'You

know I've been climbing in and out of this thing for eight years all by myself.'

'I'm a gentleman, as you said.' Heath gestured for her to start walking towards the woods.

'You must have had good parents who brought you up right.'

'I had terrible parents but that's a story for another day.'

She chewed her lip. She wouldn't wish what she went through on anyone and if Heath had gone through something similar that made her heart hurt for him. She had an overwhelming urge to tell him that if he wanted to talk about it, she knew what it was like and was happy to listen, but then he would expect that to be reciprocal and she didn't really talk about what had happened in her life with anyone. She'd found it better to keep it all locked away.

Something caught her eye and Evergreen looked up at the first treehouse, a real fairy house in the trees, with wonky windows and turrets placed precariously on jutting-out corners. It looked ridiculous and wonderful at the same time. Fairy lights twinkled in the setting sun, making it seem magical and other-worldly. Garlands of holly and ivy were interspersed with red ribbons as they wound around the balcony and balustrades of the staircase, giving it a festive feel. It just needed a sprinkling of snow to complete the look.

'These are incredible,' Evergreen said, stopping to stare at it.

'Thank you,' Heath said. 'They're a lot of hard work but I love making them.'

She turned to face him in awe. 'You built these?'

'Yes, with my brother River. My youngest brother Bear

did all the electrics so it's a team effort. I love working with my hands. There are thirty-two treehouses here for guests, three more that me and my brothers live in, the Christmas Tree Cottage and even a wedding chapel treehouse where we hold small wedding ceremonies. My daughter adores living in one. I love waking up here and seeing the sky through the window above my bed or walking to the balcony and looking out over the sea. It's peaceful and that's what we try to create here for guests to come and stay.'

'That's fantastic.' She spotted another one, decorated beautifully for Christmas. 'What a lovely place to live and work. So your ex-wife lives here too?'

'We live in treehouses next door to each other with a rope bridge between the two so Star can just come and go as she pleases. There's no set schedule, sometimes she chooses to stay with me, sometimes she chooses to stay with Meadow, just whatever suits her. Meadow is also now married to my younger brother Bear with a baby on the way, just to add another level of weirdness to our little arrangement. But honestly I couldn't be happier for them.'

Evergreen smiled. 'Sounds like a perfect arrangement.'

'My eldest brother, River, lives here too, with his wife, Indigo, daughter Tierra and their new son Alfie so meal times are often wonderfully chaotic and noisy but I wouldn't have it any other way.'

'I love the sound of that. I grew up in a big family and although I don't see any of my family any more I do miss them.'

She glanced round the woods and stopped dead as she

saw the Christmas tree. 'Is that… Christmas Tree Cottage?' she squeaked out.

'Yep, that's where you'll be working for the next week,' Heath said.

She stared at it in wonder. The Christmas tree was huge and right at the bottom, tucked into the lower branches, was a little red wooden house, with a white sparkly roof and Christmas lights twisted round the windows. Over-sized red and white candy canes stood sentry either side of the door. It looked like something out of every child's dreams.

'Heath, this is wonderful.'

'We wanted it magical for the children.'

'Never mind the children, this is magical for me.'

She hurried forward and up the steps to the house, smiling at the beautiful candy cane wreath hanging on the door as she let herself inside.

No expense had been spared with creating a full-blown home for Father Christmas. There were two big red squashy chairs, presumably for her and Father Christmas, and other red sofas and chairs around the room for the many guests they were going to entertain. A large dining room table that could easily seat twenty people was up one end of the room, decorated with a red sparkly table runner and white candles in gold snowflake-patterned candle holders. Big, bright festive throws and cushions were everywhere and the room was beautifully decorated with garlands of baubles and flowers entwined with fairy lights. There was a big tree with gold baubles and ribbons sparkling next to a log burner, which was roaring away. The room smelt of gingerbread and cinnamon, and Evergreen wondered briefly if it was created with some kind of incense. Then she spotted the gingerbread men which had obviously been artfully decorated by the two girls Heath had mentioned before. She picked one up and bit off its head just as Heath walked through the door.

'This place is spectacular, the children are absolutely going to love this,' Evergreen said, looking around in wonder. 'You've created something incredible here.'

'Thank you. Star and Tierra were at the very heart of our design when we were building it, we wanted something for them,' Heath said. 'But also we wanted it to be a comfortable home too so we can rent it out as a treehouse for guests to stay in after Christmas is over. So you'll find everything you need if you did choose to stay here, a working kitchen over there, and through here is the bedroom.'

She followed him into another room to see a gigantic bed covered in a bright red Nordic blanket.

'Come and see how comfy it is,' Heath said, sitting down on the bed and giving it a little bounce.

'I'm sure it's great,' Evergreen said, watching him from the door.

'Come on, just lie down on it for a minute.'

She rolled her eyes but there was something about this man that just made her smile. His happiness was infectious and she found herself wanting to bask in it. She lay down and had to forcibly suppress a groan of pleasure. It was like lying on a giant marshmallow.

Heath lay down next to her although the bed was huge enough that they could both spread out their arms and legs and not touch each other. 'It's pretty good, eh?'

She rolled over to look at him and he rolled over to look at her and there was a moment when it just felt so right to be lying there next to him as if they had known each other for years not just half an hour.

And she didn't like that.

'You know what's weird,' Evergreen said.

'What's that?'

'You lying here next to me like we really are husband and wife.'

Heath shot up. 'God, sorry, that's really inappropriate.'

'It's fine,' Evergreen said, feeling guilty for making him feel bad. It hadn't felt weird at all. There was an ease between them that she hadn't experienced before and that's what was scaring her. She didn't want a relationship or complications. That involved trusting someone and that inevitably meant getting hurt and she didn't want that. She needed to keep him at arm's length.

'I am sorry,' Heath said. 'I don't want to do anything that would make you uncomfortable. I wasn't trying it on with you, I was just…'

'Selling the merits of the bed. It's fine. Please don't worry. And you're right, the bed *is* super soft.'

She sat up, giving it another bounce to satisfy him.

He smiled cautiously. 'There's something about you that makes me feel so… comfortable.'

She swallowed because honesty deserved honesty. 'I feel the same but…'

His face cleared in understanding. 'But you don't do relationships.'

'Exactly.'

He stared at her for a moment and nodded. He turned

to open the nearby door. 'And through here there's the ensuite,' Heath said, clearly changing the subject. She stood up and moved to have a look at a massive walk-in shower that Thunder could easily fit in and a large freestanding bath. 'There's also a toilet off the lounge for any little guests and their families to use so they're not coming into your bedroom to use yours, if you were staying here.'

'That's thoughtful.'

'Only the best for Mrs Christmas. I want to make sure I stay on the nice list.'

She grinned. 'No coal for you. And these are a lovely touch,' she waved the half-eaten gingerbread man in the air.

'I'll pass on the compliments to my daughter.'

'How old is Star?'

'She's eight, so I don't know how many more years I'll have of her believing in this kind of thing. If it was up to me I'd make the magic last forever.'

'We'll make this one really special for her,' Evergreen said.

Heath smiled. 'Thank you. Although if you're handing out special treatment she would absolutely love a ride on your caravan at some point or just on the back of Thunder.'

'That can totally be arranged. Right, we need to have a dry run with your make-up before we start on Saturday. Do you want to do that now or tomorrow?'

Heath frowned. 'Are we not just going to use one of those tie-on beards and a cushion up my jacket?'

Evergreen let out a little gasp. 'You insult me. I will not be working with any Father Christmas with a beard held on by a piece of string. My make-up is a little bit more refined than that. Will your daughter be visiting Santa? Because if you don't want her to know it's you, we need to use the prosthetics too to hide you in plain sight.'

'Yes she will and my niece as well, she's just turned six.'

'That's fine, full disguises are totally my thing.'

'Why don't we do that tomorrow morning when we have a bit more time to play around with things?' Heath said. 'I have to help finalise the preparations for the Christmas market tomorrow afternoon but I could have a look now at doing some of the repairs in your caravan.'

'Are you sure you want to do it? You must have so much work to do round here and now your week is going to be curtailed by playing Santa you're not going to have a lot of time to yourself. I don't mind if you can't do it.'

'It's no problem, and I never back down from a promise. Come back with me and show me everything that needs looking at and then you might as well have a wander round before it gets dark, familiarise yourself with the place.'

She smiled at the thought of seeing more fairy tree-houses. She couldn't deny she was excited to see it all. 'That sounds like a plan.'

CHAPTER THREE

Looking at the list of things that needed repairing, Evergreen felt really bad. She'd deliberately left a lot of things off because the list was getting too long and she felt like she was taking the piss. But Heath had insisted he didn't mind and had practically pushed her out the door so she could explore her new surroundings. Following Heath's directions, she decided to pop in and see Meadow and Indigo, the events manager, on the reception first. She'd spoken to them both so much over the last few weeks, either through email or on the phone, it would be good to meet them.

She pushed open the door and saw there were two blonde women and a man sitting behind the desk. The man was on the phone. One of the women shot up out of her seat when she saw her.

'You must be Evergreen, Heath said you were on your way over. I'm Meadow and this is Indigo and Bear.'

The others waved.

Meadow came out from behind the desk and Evergreen

couldn't fail to notice the small baby bump. She gave Evergreen a big hug. 'It's so good to finally meet you, I feel like I know you, we've talked so much.'

Evergreen jolted a little at the overfamiliarity of a hug. It had been a long time since she'd been hugged by anyone. She tentatively moved her arms around her, she didn't want to be rude after all. She was surprised how good it felt.

'It's good to meet you too. And thank you for the job. I know I'm not the traditional Mrs Christmas you were expecting but I promise once I'm done with my make-up, you won't know the difference.'

'I'm sure you'll be fantastic.' Meadow stepped back.

Indigo moved forward to give her a hug too. 'I'm excited to see what you turn yourself and Heath into. If your credentials are anything to go by, it's going to be very impressive.'

Meadow giggled. 'How did he take the news that he was going to be Santa?'

Evergreen laughed. 'Not great. Why didn't you tell him?'

'Well it was more fun this way, plus he'd never have agreed to it if I'd asked him. But he always likes to help people out, so I knew he'd never say no to you. I'd have paid good money to see his face when he found out though.'

Evergreen rearranged her face into the best impression of Heath's shocked one and Meadow and Indigo laughed.

Bear finished his phone call and stood up to greet her. He was tall and exceptionally good-looking, just like his brother. He didn't hug her like the women had but instead offered out a large hand to shake.

'Hey, I'm Bear. It's good to have you here. We've never really pushed the boat out for Christmas before, other than decorating the treehouses, but this one wanted to pull out all the stops,' Bear gestured to Indigo. 'And I think it's going to be wonderful, with the visits to Santa being the cherry on the cake.'

'I hope so, we'll make sure the kids enjoy it,' Evergreen said. 'I was going to have a look round the place. Is there a map or a route I should take?'

'No map, I'm afraid,' Bear said. 'But if you go left out of here, you'll see the main path through the woods and then there are other paths off that that will take you to other treehouses. You can't go too far wrong, all the paths have lights along them, so if the lights come to an end then you need to turn round and come back. If you finish up at the lake then you've probably gone a bit too far. If you stay on the main path you'll come to where we are having our Christmas market. There are lots of wooden lodges at ground level among the trees and the traders are all coming tomorrow to set up their wares ready for the opening on Saturday. But it's still quite impressive to see now, everyone has worked very hard to get it ready. Felix, one of our grounds staff, is down there now making it all Christmassy and River is there too.'

'I'll go and have a look.'

'What are you doing for dinner tonight?' Meadow said. 'You'd be very welcome to join us all at my house.'

Evergreen hesitated. It had been a long time since she had been in a big social gathering but she suddenly found that the idea appealed. She had spent far too many nights alone in her little caravan and maybe she needed some company for a change.

'I'd really like that, thank you.'

'Heath will show you the way. We normally eat around six-ish but you can come around five.'

'Great, I'll see you later then.'

Evergreen was just about to leave when a lady, probably in her eighties, swept into the reception area looking undeniably glamorous with her long sheet of silvery hair, tight black velvet trousers and red satin blouse.

'You're early today Amelia,' Meadow said. 'I was just about to leave to pick the girls up from school.'

'I was passing, didn't seem any point in going home and coming back out again. Who owns that fabulous Clydesdale out in the paddock?'

Evergreen grinned. 'That would be me.'

'Amelia, this is Evergreen, she'll be helping us in Christmas Tree Cottage for the next week. Evergreen, this is Amelia, Bear's grandmother and great-grandmother to Star and Tierra.'

'Hi,' Evergreen said.

'Hello. Your horse is beautiful. I used to own one myself, many moons ago, when I lived in Australia. He had this beautiful pinto colouring but the patches weren't as solid. He was an absolute dream to ride, so gentle-tempered. He was called Spirit and I loved him so much. What's yours called?'

'Thunder,' Evergreen said.

'Do you ride him?'

'Sometimes, though generally I use him to pull my caravan. He's so loyal and steadfast. They're so empathic, aren't they. He always knows what I'm feeling and he just stands there and lets me hug him and pour out my heart to him.'

'Horses are such wonderful creatures,' Amelia said.

'I didn't know you used to ride, Amelia,' Indigo said.

'Oh, I was younger than you are now, it feels like a lifetime ago.'

'Would you like to ride Thunder?' Evergreen said.

Amelia's eyes lit up like all her Christmases had come at once. 'It's been a long time since I've ridden.'

'But you never forget, right?' Evergreen said. 'You don't have to take him far, just around the paddock a few times.'

'I would love that.'

Evergreen smiled. 'How about tomorrow?'

'I'll be here to look after the girls when they finish school for the year. I can bring them down to the paddock to meet him and maybe we can all have a go.'

'That's fine, I'm happy for them to ride him too. He's very gentle and he knows when he has children riding him that he has to be extra careful. I have a saddle, reins, bridle, everything you'd need to ride him, but I don't have any hats,' Evergreen said.

'The girls can wear their cycle helmets,' Meadow said. 'Especially if they are just going for a slow walk around the paddock.'

'I can lead Thunder or ride on the horse with them, but they'll be perfectly safe,' Evergreen said.

'We'll be there about three then,' Amelia said.

'The girls will love it, thank you,' Meadow said.

'Right, I'm going to explore before it gets dark,' Evergreen said. She gave them a wave and left the reception, heading into the woods. This was a different route she'd taken with Heath but as soon as she walked under the canopy of trees she spotted several treehouses, all bedecked in their Christmas splendour with fairy lights and festive garlands. They looked magical. The Brookfield family had created something incredible, she could imagine families being enchanted to stay here. Each one was completely different, some had turrets or multiple levels, some had round or triangular windows, and some even had small Christmas trees out on the decking. It looked wonderful.

She followed the path to what appeared to be a large clearing and there were all the wooden lodges for the Christmas market tucked into the bottom of the trees. They didn't look like traditional Swiss log cabins, more like little fairy dwellings, the roofs made from twigs and leaves, although the insides were probably far more waterproof. They had the same quirky charm as the treehouses, with wonky roofs that looked like they had been stuck on and irregular-shaped windows. Some had glittery white roofs and she glanced around to see a man spraying the tops of some of the other houses with a sparkling white paint from a machine that looked like a jet washer. There was another man nearby hammering something into one of the lodges. She wandered over to say hello to them.

The man with the white paint spotted her first and turned off his machine. He had a friendly open face with a big smile.

'Hello, can I help you?'

He also had an accent and, if she had to guess, she'd say he was Danish.

'No, I'm fine. I'm just exploring. I'm Evergreen Winters, I'll be working here until Christmas Eve as Mrs Christmas.'

'Oh hello, I'm Felix. We've been waiting for you to arrive. Although you're a lot younger than I expected.'

She laughed. 'My day job is stage make-up, I'll be a lot older than this when the children come.'

'Oh brilliant, I can't wait to see it. I'm sure you've already been told, but there's an onsite restaurant here and all the staff eat for free. Alex, our chef, cooks the most amazing food and she'll cater for any dietary requirements too. Most of the staff are wearing green t-shirts or hoodies so if you see us in there, feel free to come and join us, rather than eating alone. We're a friendly bunch.'

'Thank you, yes Heath did mention the restaurant too. I'll be sure to look out for you. So have you worked here long?'

'From the very beginning. It's been a treehouse resort for around eight years now and it grows bigger every year. I love working here. The team is great, everyone helps everyone else out. We all have our jobs but we help everyone else with their work too.'

'How wonderful to be part of a community like that. My work is freelance so I don't have any colleagues or a team that I'm part of and I think I miss out by not having that camaraderie. It would be lovely to be part of a collaboration to create something so beautiful and to know you always have good people around you that you can rely on. And this place, it feels like something magical to be a part of.'

'It is. But you know, they are always looking for people to work here – the bigger they get, the more there is to do.

And they plan to expand even more next year. I'm not sure there will be much call for stage make-up but there are always jobs that need doing. Lindsay does shifts everywhere, a bit of cleaning, a bit on reception, just wherever is needed. I'm sure they would be happy to take you on if you wanted a job here more permanently.'

The thought of staying in one place scared Evergreen but there was a part of her that loved the idea of working somewhere like this, being a member of a team, even though it felt unattainable. She'd always hoped she'd have her own family one day too, but that felt like an impossible dream as well.

Just then the other man came wandering over and it was clear straightaway that he must be Heath's other brother.

'You must be River.' Evergreen held out a hand and he grinned as he shook it.

'I am. Evergreen, right? How did Heath take to the news that he's going to be Santa?'

'He was pretty shocked. Were you all in on this?'

'It was Meadow's idea,' he smirked. 'But we all went along with it. Did I hear you were looking for a job?'

'Oh no, I have a job. Sure it would be nice to have something a bit more stable but that doesn't fit in with my chosen career. Doing make-up for TV and film takes me all over the country. Got to follow your dreams, right?' Evergreen said, knowing that by avoiding any kind of permanence in her life she was running away from her dreams, not following them.

'I'm a big believer in that,' River said. 'I met my wife, Indigo, at the beginning of the year and she made me realise dreams I never knew I had. Life has not always been kind to me and my brothers, and it's very easy to stop dreaming and hoping for anything better, but with Indigo and my two beautiful kids and this place, I feel like I have a future now, and it's one I'm very excited and happy about.'

Evergreen couldn't help smiling at his optimism.

'This place is good for the soul,' Felix said. 'I know it's a cliché but it's where dreams come true. I met my husband here six years ago. He was a guest, staying here with his nephews. I found multiple things that needed fixing or maintaining around his treehouse and we flirted with each other outrageously. Next weekend he came back without his nephews and, well, we didn't actually leave the treehouse that weekend. We've been head over heels in love with each other ever since. Many of our staff have come here when they were at a crossroads in their life and the answers have always been found among the trees.'

Evergreen smiled and River shook his head goodnaturedly.

'Well, I'm going to explore the place and see if I can find my own answers,' she said.

Felix nodded, seriously. 'I hope you do. Enjoy your walk. If you get back to the reception area around sunset you might see a herd of deer, they seem to congregate around there at this time of year.'

'Oh, I'll look out for them.'

She gave them a wave and walked on through the trees admiring all the treehouses and the way they glittered and sparkled with Christmas magic.

She thought about her own life and how ever since her stepmum died she had stagnated, never moving forward, never moving on. She had been so scared of trusting anyone and getting hurt again that she had built this fortress around her and no one was ever getting in. Maybe it was time for a change. Although she had no idea what that would look like and what she could do to change it. Maybe Felix was right and she could find her own path while she was here for the next few days.

She looked around and realised she had been walking for a while and there was no longer any sign of the tree-houses. She wasn't even following the main path any more, she'd just been making her way through the woods. She turned around in the hope she could see something or someone but she only had the trees for company.

Up ahead she could see the trees came to an end and a pinky light was streaming into the woods. She moved in that direction to see if she could get an idea where she was.

She stepped out of the woods onto the clifftops. The sun was making its last descent into the sea, leaving trails of plum and candyfloss across the sky. The days were shorter at this time of year and it would soon be dark but she had a while to enjoy this spectacular view. The horizon seemed to stretch on forever, the waves painted glorious shades of pink, purple and orangey gold. There was an icy wind blowing in off the cliffs and she wrapped her cloak tighter around her. The sea was choppy today and a little fishing boat was struggling against the waves as it made its journey home. She imagined the fisherman's wife and kids waiting for him when he got home, welcoming him back with a big hug.

Living on her own, she'd never had that. She didn't even have any friends she could meet up with. When she was working on a film or TV programme she'd sometimes see the same faces also working on the production and sometimes they'd go out for drinks in a big group after but she could hardly call them her friends. She didn't have any of their contact details, and even if she did, she would hardly call on them for a chat or if she needed help with anything, they didn't have that kind of relationship.

She thought more about what Felix had said about how everyone here at Wishing Wood having each other's backs, and she wondered what that would be like: to always have someone to rely on or someone to talk to.

The sun disappeared beneath the waves and, though the sky was still light right now, she knew she wouldn't have long before the night rolled in.

She looked up and down the coast to see if she could place where she was but there was no sign of life in either direction. She guessed if she kept walking back through the woods, she'd come to some treehouses eventually and she could probably find the main path from there, although there weren't even any lights in this part of the forest so she needed to be quick.

She turned back around and gasped because, standing at the edge of the woods, was a huge white stag, just looking at her. He was massive, with an impressive-looking mane around his neck. His antlers were a huge tangle of thorns that towered above his head. He was majestic and clearly completely unfazed by her.

His fur gleamed in the fading light and she wanted to step forward and stroke him but she had to remind herself that this was a wild animal and he probably wouldn't appreciate being touched.

She didn't dare move and the stag was clearly quite happy standing there too. Suddenly he turned and walked back into the wood a little way but then stopped and looked at her as if he wanted her to follow. She frowned in confusion and stepped forward towards the deer. The deer moved off a little way but again stopped as if waiting for her. She looked around at the sky behind her. Now the sun was gone it was getting dark way too quickly and, though the child in her would dearly love to follow this deer in the hope he might take her to some magical kingdom, she didn't have time for some wild goose chase now.

She walked into the woods and the gloomy darkness swallowed her. She had no chance of finding the route she had come now. The deer moved off slightly and again seemed to be waiting for her.

She remembered that Felix had said the herd of deer would gather around the reception at sunset. If this stag was part of that herd he might be on his way back to them. If she followed him, he might take her all the way back to reception. It was a long shot, the deer could be taking her anywhere or run away at any second, but, with no other option, she had no choice but to follow. The stag kept a good distance from her as they walked through the trees and he was no longer checking to see if she was following, he wasn't even looking at her any more, so the idea of him purposefully leading her anywhere was clearly a delusion. Evergreen had only been in these magical fairy woods for half a day and already she'd concocted some fantasy that the deer was trying to help her.

Lights started appearing through the trees and she saw several treehouses glowing in the darkness, fairy lights hanging from the roofs and intertwined with the branches of the trees. With the garlands and red ribbons wrapped around the staircases, it looked spectacular and so festive. She was fairly confident she could find her own way from here but the deer walked on slowly in front of her so she continued to follow anyway. If he was heading back towards the reception area, her little caravan would be nearby and Heath might still be working in it.

She came to a treehouse that was actually two separate treehouses joined by a rope bridge and she wondered if this was Heath's home. It fit his description exactly. She couldn't help smiling at its whimsical charm. What a wonderful, magical place to live, especially if you were a child.

Something must have startled the stag as he suddenly bolted through the trees, disappearing into the darkness. So much for leading her somewhere, although she supposed he had got her back to the treehouses safely, which was probably more than she could have managed on her own.

'Hey.'

She looked around and saw Heath walking towards her.

'You look like a beautiful fairy queen walking through the woods in that cloak.'

She laughed. 'Thank you. It's more elven than fairy cloak though.'

'I was going to say elf queen, but I wasn't sure you would take that as the compliment it was intended to be, especially with the pointy ears.'

'I'd definitely take it as a compliment. My stepmum bought this for me when I was sixteen. I'd read *Lord of the*

Rings for the first time and loved it and she made me sit down and watch the movies and they were just the best films I've ever seen. I'd watch them over and over again, every night I'd play them on my laptop before I went to bed. I thought they were amazing. Still do actually.'

'I love *Lord of the Rings* too, we should watch the movies while you are here, I haven't binged on them for ages. I keep wanting to introduce them to Star but I wonder if she's a little young – the ringwraiths are a little scary, as are the orcs.'

'They are a little, but I'm sure if you're sitting with her, she would be fine. Those films have some kick-ass women. I loved the characters of Galadriel and Arwen especially, and all the elves actually. I started writing these fan fiction stories where I was the elf queen, just silly little things, but my stepmum was so supportive of them, always asking for more of them to read. At Christmas she bought me this cloak to encourage me in my elf dreams.'

Evergreen smiled fondly, swallowing the huge lump in her throat. 'I loved it so much, I'd wear it everywhere. I was sixteen and desperate to be different rather than conform to what the other kids were wearing. And a couple of years later when my stepmum died, this became hugely sentimental for me. I couldn't throw it away when really I'd outgrown it and it's too beautiful to keep in a box under my bed. I've worn it ever since.'

Heath frowned. 'I'm sorry to hear about your stepmum.'

Evergreen chewed her lip. She never spoke about stuff like that, she wasn't sure why she'd felt compelled to tell Heath. She cleared her throat. 'Thank you. It was a long time ago.'

'Doesn't mean it hurts any less,' he said, staring at her as if he could see into the very depths of her soul.

She quickly looked away and changed the subject. 'Did you see the white stag?'

'Wait, you saw the white stag?'

She turned back to see Heath was looking at her incredulously and she pushed away the emotions surrounding her stepmum's death.

'I got a bit lost but luckily a white stag guided me back to here. He was beautiful. You must see him all the time.'

He shook his head. 'There are a few white deer around that are part of the red deer herd, and occasionally I see them, but I've only seen the stag once.'

'Oh wow, I feel very lucky then.'

'Not many people have seen him,' Heath said. 'There is a legend associated with him, if you believe in that kind of thing.'

'Sure, we all need something to believe in.'

'Well people say he is the guide for lost souls, that he'll appear when people need help finding their way and he'll guide you home or wherever you need to be.'

Evergreen pulled a face. 'I think that's a bit of a stretch to expect that from a deer.'

Except she had blindly followed the stag through the trees, hoping he would help get her back to the reception. Although that had partly been based on what Felix had said about the herd congregating at the reception at sunset. She'd ignore the other part of her that had some whimsical notion that the deer wanted her to follow him.

'Yeah, I'm a level-headed guy and I'm not sure I believe it either.'

'Did you have some life-changing moment when you saw the stag?' Evergreen said.

She waited for him to laugh it off but he didn't.

'I can't tell you what happened the day I saw the stag as that's too big a secret to share, and it's not even totally my secret, but I guess because of the stag I was in the right place at the right time and what happened next changed my life forever in the best possible way. And of course the rational part of my brain says it was merely a coincidence and that… *change* probably would have happened anyway, with or without the stag, but I'm not the first person to have a life-changing experience because of the stag.'

Evergreen smiled. It was a nice idea, but not one she could buy into. She looked at the two wisteria trees side by side, a treehouse in each one and a rope bridge between the two.

'Is this your home?'

'Yes it is. Or rather the one on the left is mine and the one on the right is Meadow and Bear's.'

'And Star just chooses which one she wants to sleep in or who she has dinner or breakfast with?'

'Yes, well we tend to have breakfast and dinner all together most days. Either just me and Meadow and Bear or the whole clan.'

'I love that. What a lucky little girl.'

Heath smiled at that. 'I wouldn't change it for the world, but I do wonder how any potential girlfriend will feel about slotting into that way of life. My weird family is a lot to take on. And most divorced men don't still see their ex-wives every morning and night. It feels like it might be a lot to put up with.'

'Heath, if Scarlet or any woman you end up with loves you, they will love all of you, your brilliant little girl, your ex-wife, your wonderfully weird family, and they won't *put up with it*, they will want to be a part of it, warts and all, because the life you lead here is who you are.'

Heath stared at her. 'I suppose you're right. But it feels optimistic to hope for that.'

'Not really, you just have to have high standards. The right woman for you is out there.' She looked up again at the twinkling lights of his home. 'And I guess the stag did guide me to where I'm supposed to be as Meadow invited me for dinner.'

Heath grinned. 'See, you're in the right place, right time.'

'I'm now expecting this dinner to be life-changing.'

'Well, Meadow is a good cook, but I'm not sure if her food could be considered life-changing.'

Evergreen laughed. 'Well, let's see.'

They moved towards the treehouse.

'I made a start on the list of jobs and found a few other things that needed fixing too so I did those,' Heath said. 'I should be done in a few days but, I have to say, you really do need a whole new roof. Some of those timbers are so wet and rotting, I'm surprised some parts of it haven't caved in completely.'

Evergreen groaned. She'd known it was bad but hadn't realised it was that bad.

'I can re-felt it, similar to what you'd do on a shed roof, but I'd just be covering over damaged wood. I can replace the whole roof for you but with a lot of my time being monopolised by playing Santa over the next few days and then Christmas, it would take me longer than you're here. It's certainly something I could do for you after Christmas if you were to hang around.'

'I was planning on leaving Christmas Eve.'

'Yeah, I figured you'd have some exciting plans for the big day.'

Evergreen thought about her non-existent plans for the big day. She hadn't celebrated Christmas properly for years. Sometimes she would put up a few extra lights in her little caravan, sometimes she would pitch up on the seafront and eat fish and chips on the beach. She tended to avoid any big celebrations. She supposed she could stay here. If other families were staying in the treehouses over Christmas it meant the restaurant would probably be open for her to get food. She could sit in her caravan, play her Christmas music and read her favourite book, maybe go for a walk on the beach. If she was out the way, she didn't think anyone would mind if she hung around a bit longer. But completely redoing the whole roof was a massive job and she couldn't ask Heath to do that.

'Replacing the roof feels like it would take up a lot of your time.'

'It would take me a few days, yes.'

'I can't let you do that, not for free.'

'It's not for free, you're going to owe me a big favour, remember. Anything I want.'

'Well, yes, that still stands but I have to give you more than that. Maybe I could work here for a few days after Christmas for free. Felix said there were always jobs that needed doing. I'm not very practical but I could clean or something.'

'We could totally take you up on that. Felix is right, there are always some jobs that need doing and at this time of year a lot of people like to take some time off to spend with their families so there will be holes in the rota to fill.'

'Well, I'll do anything you want me to for however long it takes to finish the roof.'

'Now that's a promise. What about your Christmas plans?'

She thought about her favourite book. 'They will still go ahead.'

But she couldn't hide the smile about spending Christmas somewhere as enchanting as this. It didn't matter that she would be alone, being here would make it magical.

CHAPTER FOUR

They climbed the steps and Heath opened the door to Meadow's house. Immediately Star spotted him and came running over to throw herself into his arms. 'Daddy! You're here, where have you been?'

He picked her up and hugged her tight. 'Hello munchkin,' he hoisted her onto his hip. 'This is my friend Evergreen, she's going to be helping us in the Christmas treehouse. Evergreen has the coolest job in the world. You know you got those scars on your face for Halloween? That's the kind of thing Evergreen does for her job, she makes people into monsters, aliens and other hideous creatures. Evergreen, do you have any photos of your finished clients?'

'I do actually.' Evergreen took her phone out of her bag. 'Some of these are really scary, Star. Can you handle it?'

Star nodded, her eyes filled with excitement. Heath put her down and Evergreen crouched to show her some of the photos, clearly completely at ease with chatting to his daughter. He smiled and left them to it. Meadow was busy dancing in the kitchen, laughing with Bear as he chopped some vegetables. Heath walked over to give Meadow a kiss on the cheek. Her little baby bump seemed to be getting bigger every single day.

'Hey, thanks for the stitch-up,' Heath said, stealing a slice of mushroom.

Meadow laughed. 'Well, it's not like you have other things to do right now. The weather is too rubbish to build the new treehouses River has planned. I thought you needed a project. Also Evergreen asked for someone with patience. Well, you're the most patient man I know.'

'I'd argue Bear has a lot more patience than me. He's so chilled-out he's practically horizontal.'

'Yes, but I'm on baby-growing duties,' Bear said, stroking Meadow's bump affectionately. 'If the baby wants ice cream at three in the morning, I have to get it, if the baby wants gherkins for breakfast I have to go out and get them. It's a full-time job.'

Meadow giggled.

'I'd forgotten about all the weird cravings you had when you were pregnant with Star. Yeah, that is a full-time job. Anyway, I met Evergreen outside, she said you'd invited her for dinner.'

'Yes, I didn't really like the idea of her eating alone in the restaurant on her first night here,' Meadow said. 'Thought it would give us all a chance to get to know her better, especially as you'll be working so closely with her over the next few days. I'll go and say hi.'

Meadow walked over and Heath watched as she gave Evergreen a hug. Hero, the dog, came wandering over to sniff the newcomer and Indigo quickly moved to make sure he didn't knock her over, but Evergreen was already stroking Hero, clearly giving him the best ear scratch he'd ever had in his life. Tierra came over to inspect Evergreen's cloak and Evergreen took it off and swept it round Tierra's shoulders. Tierra flounced around the room parading around in it, and Evergreen stood back up, chatting to Indigo, Meadow and Star easily. Heath couldn't help smiling; she'd obviously been talking to both Indigo and Meadow over the phone and via email about the Christmas event, but she fitted in as if she'd been here all her life.

River came over, his baby son, Alfie, snuggled against his chest in a papoose, fast asleep. 'Most of the snagging is done with the Christmas market, a few more little things will need doing tomorrow and the traders, when they arrive tomorrow to set up, will be told to make a list of anything that is wrong in their huts and we can hopefully fix it all tomorrow afternoon.'

'No problem. I'll be busy tomorrow morning. Evergreen wants to do a trial run for my make-up but after that I can help.'

River arched an eyebrow. 'I didn't know Santa wore lipstick and mascara.'

'More like wrinkles and prosthetics.'

'I look forward to seeing it,' River said.

'Star and Tierra have both been so excited about Father Christmas coming, I'm not sure how they're going to take the news that you're him,' Bear said, offering Heath a beer.

He opened it and took a swig. 'Star is at that age where she wants to still believe but she's so smart she's starting to realise how increasingly unlikely the magic of Father Christmas really is. I almost feel she's humouring

44

me and Meadow with our "write your letter to Santa" and "let's get the reindeer food in for Santa". I'm not sure how I'm going to explain to her that I'm him for the next week. Maybe I'll tell her I'm helping him out, or maybe Evergreen's make-up will be so good the girls won't recognise me anyway, so it might not come up. I can do quite a convincing Scottish accent for when they come in to see him, so perhaps that will be enough to convince them.'

'Because Santa is Scottish?' River deadpanned.

'They're eight and six and have lived their whole lives in South Wales, I don't think they've been exposed to that many different accents. As long as I sound different to how I normally sound, it might work. Besides, our resident elf is Scottish so that kind of fits if Santa is Scottish too.'

Bear grinned. 'Knowing Lindsay, she will absolutely give you hell if you even attempt a Scottish accent, unless it's spot on.'

Heath smiled. Lindsay McGhie had started work there a few months before doing bits of everything: a shift on reception, putting up a shelf, cleaning. It had started as a part-time occasional thing but had quickly turned into a full-time job. She was such a no-nonsense woman, blunt, subtle as a low-flying brick. He really liked her. Her husband, Bruce, who he'd met a few times, had such a dry sense of humour too. They were a great couple.

'Maybe she could give me some tips. Anyway, we'll try to keep what I'm doing a secret for now. If the girls realise who I am we'll cross that bridge when we come to it.'

Meadow laughed loudly at something Evergreen said and he realised as they both turned to look at him that it was clear he was the butt of the joke. He caught Evergreen's eyes and it made him smile; *she* made him smile.

'She seems nice,' Bear said.

'She is,' Heath said.

'She must be, you've barely taken your eyes off her since you've arrived here tonight,' River said.

'No, it's not like that. I find her intriguing. I just think there are many layers to Evergreen Winters. I want to know more about her.'

'That's a new one for you,' Bear said. 'Normally you meet a woman, buy her a drink and an hour later you're back at her place getting intimately acquainted rather than intellectually. Is this *getting to know her* a new thing you're trying? I have to say, you're probably going to have more luck finding the one if you take the time to get to know these women properly rather than just jumping into bed with them.'

'Thanks for that, oh wise one,' Heath said, dryly.

Although Bear had a point, he had deliberately avoided any kind of serious relationship for most of his life. In his mid to late teens, he'd chosen women he could have a good time with and nothing more. His parents leaving when he was little had taught him that relationships didn't endure, that love wasn't strong enough and that falling in love would only lead to pain. And while he didn't believe that any more, he'd still avoided anything serious ever since Star was born.

When she was young, it had been too complicated to bring another woman into his arrangement with Meadow. He loved Star more than anything in the world but even he had to admit that a crying baby, dirty nappies and sleepless nights was not conducive to starting a proper relationship with someone, so he'd always kept that side of his life separate his daughter. He kept things casual and fun and never the twain shall meet.

Even now she was older he didn't want to rock the boat. His life here with his family and his daughter was perfect and he was keen not to do anything to ruin that. It was only recently he had looked at his life and those of his happy, loved-up brothers and thought he might want a piece of that too, but he had no idea how to reconcile the two. How could he invite someone into this world with his family and expect things not to change? How could anyone fit in with his way of life? And he knew it was selfish of him to want someone to fit in with his life instead of fitting in with theirs but he couldn't begin to imagine moving out of Wishing Wood and moving in with some woman and not seeing his daughter every day, not coming home and being able to cuddle her, or sit down to breakfast and dinner with her. That was unthinkable.

'I'm just saying, being interested in someone on that level is not something to dismiss,' Bear said. 'If you connect with her beyond the physical attraction, that's got to be a good thing.'

'Have you taken a leaf out of Amelia's book, trying to fix me up with the first single woman that walks through that door. I've got my long-awaited hot date with Scarlet on Saturday night.'

'I don't know if you should pin all your hopes on that,' Bear said.

'Why not?'

'It's been a year since you shared that incredible weekend. I feel like if there was going to be a great love story, it would have happened by now.'

'Says the man who took over eight years to tell the woman you love how you feel for her,' Heath said. 'And now you're happily married to her.'

Bear nodded. 'Fair point. But how often do one-night stands really work out?'

River cleared his throat.

Heath laughed. 'Exactly, it worked out pretty damn well for River and Indigo.'

If Heath was honest, the thing with River and Indigo was making him cling onto the hope he could work things out with Scarlet. River and Indigo had a wonderful one-night stand where they had both fallen in love with each other. She'd got scared the next day that it wouldn't mean as much to him as it did to her and ran away, turning up here two months later purely to tell River she was pregnant with his child. She'd started working here and their connection was as strong as it had ever been. It was clear for anyone to see that they were completely head over heels in love with each other. Heath wanted what they had, that forever kind of love. What he and Scarlet shared that weekend was incredible. He didn't see why they couldn't build on that.

'I really hope it works out for you,' River said. 'You deserve to find someone who loves you. But I wouldn't necessarily only look for women who you think can give you the great love story. Sometimes just having a bit of fun with someone can lead to something spectacular.'

'Hopefully, after Saturday I won't need to look any more,' Heath said, but what Evergreen had said to him outside – about how the woman he ended up with would not only accept his complicated life but embrace it – had made a seed of doubt grow in his mind. Would Scarlet want this life with his family? She had run before when she'd found out he was married with a daughter, would she really want to be a part of this world, warts and all?

CHAPTER FIVE

Evergreen looked around the table with a smile as she finished off her mince pie and ice cream. It had been a long time since she had sat down to a big family dinner like this and, although this wasn't her family, it made her happy to be a part of it, even if it was only temporary.

She was sitting at the end of the table, Heath to her right, Tierra and Star to her left, Meadow and Bear to the left of them.

'I think I might ask Santa for a cloak for Christmas,' Tierra said, licking the ice cream off her spoon.

'I think you'd look very good in a cloak,' Evergreen said. 'What colour would you want?'

'A blue one,' Tierra said, decisively.

'I'd have a purple one,' Star said. 'What colour would you have, Daddy?'

'I'm not sure that I would like to wear a cloak,' Heath said.

'Do you not like Evergreen's cloak?' Tierra asked,

clearly shocked by the possibility that not everyone would wear a cloak.

'Oh very much, I think she looks amazing in it,' Heath said.

'She looks beautiful, doesn't she?' Tierra said.

'Yes she does.'

Evergreen suppressed a smirk.

Tierra's eyes flicked between the two of them. 'Heath has never come to dinner with a woman before. Are you Heath's girlfriend?'

Star's eyes widened. 'Are you?'

'No, no, no, I'm just staying here to help your parents with the Christmas plans,' Evergreen said.

'And technically I didn't bring her,' Heath said, clearly alarmed with how this conversation was going. 'Meadow invited her to dinner.'

Evergreen was surprised by how much that hurt; it hadn't occurred to her that Heath might not want her here.

'But of course I would have invited her if Meadow hadn't,' Heath hurriedly said, clearly realising how bad his denial had sounded.

'Would you like to be his girlfriend?' Tierra said, ignoring her uncle.

'He doesn't have one,' Star said. 'And he gives the best-ever hugs.'

'That's good to know,' Evergreen said. 'Hugs are definitely one of the things I look for when looking for a boyfriend.'

'There's nothing like being embarrassingly set up by my niece and daughter,' Heath said.

'Would you like to be Evergreen's boyfriend?' Tierra asked.

Evergreen couldn't help the smile spreading across her face as she sat back in her chair and watched Heath squirm uncomfortably.

'I think…' Heath said, slowly. 'That if I was looking for a girlfriend then Evergreen would be exactly the kind of person I would want. She's funny, easy to talk to, interesting—'

'And beautiful,' Tierra said.

Heath nodded. 'And incredibly beautiful. But I'm not really looking for a girlfriend right now.'

Evergreen frowned slightly. Clearly the hot date with the wonderful Scarlet on Saturday night was not something he'd told his daughter about. Although she could understand him not wanting to tell her until he was sure there was something to tell.

'But if you were looking, would you look at Evergreen?' Tierra said, bluntly.

'Of course I would,' Heath said.

Although that was only a throwaway comment to placate a six-year-old, it still made Evergreen's heart leap.

'You two, you're embarrassing our guest,' Meadow said to the girls.

'It's totally fine,' Evergreen said. 'But I am going to go. It's been a long day.'

'Thank you for coming tonight, it's been lovely chatting with you,' Meadow said.

'Thank you for having me.'

'It was our pleasure.'

Evergreen eyed the big bowl of fruit in the middle of the table. 'Is it OK if I take an apple for Thunder?'

'Oh please do.'

'I want to meet Thunder,' Star said.

'Me too,' Tierra said.

'Daddy said he was huge,' Star said.

'He is. Certainly one of the biggest horses I've ever seen. You are both welcome to come and say hello to him tomorrow and if you each bring an apple, maybe cut into slices, I think he will love you both.'

The girls smiled excitedly.

Evergreen stood up and to her surprise Heath stood up too. 'I'll walk you back.'

'That's not necessary.'

'I'd like to, I don't want you getting lost.'

Evergreen had to accept that with her sense of direction that was a very real possibility. She waved goodbye to everyone, pulled on her cloak and stepped outside. Heath fastened his coat as he followed her.

It was raining, not heavily but it looked like it had been, the ground was sodden, parts of the path squelching underfoot. Evergreen put her hood up and Heath did the same. They walked through the woods in companionable silence for a while, listening to the gentle pitter-patter of the rain hitting the leaves above them.

'I'm sorry about the girls trying to matchmake us,' Heath said as they walked down the steps together.

'The girls are wonderful, you have nothing to apologise for. Plus you said some very nice things, even if you were coerced into saying them.'

'I meant what I said.'

'That you'd consider me for a girlfriend if it wasn't for your hot date with Scarlet?'

'No, I… If it wasn't for Scarlet, I wouldn't really be looking for a girlfriend right now. If it happens with someone, great, but I'm not actively looking.'

Evergreen looked at him wondering if he was going to elaborate – but why should he? She certainly didn't want to go down the route of explaining why she had actively avoided a relationship for the last eight years.

'It's just… I worry about Star,' Heath said. 'At the beginning of this year I was still married to Meadow and now we're divorced, she's married to Bear and there's a baby on the way. Star absolutely loves Bear and she's totally accepted that he now lives with Meadow and is really excited about their baby, but I do wonder if once the baby arrives she might feel a little unsettled. I don't really want to introduce a new girlfriend for me into the mix too, unless it was someone incredible. I want her to have time to get used to this new life before I add someone else to our family. I want her to know without any doubt that a new husband and baby for Meadow and a new girlfriend for me will not change our love for her.'

Evergreen couldn't help smiling at that. He was such a thoughtful, considerate man and a wonderful father.

'This thing with Scarlet was very unexpected. I feel like I need to see if we have something beyond great sex and if I don't take this opportunity now then I'll always be wondering if she was the one that got away or… not the one at all.'

'I get that.'

'But if it wasn't for her and if my life was somewhat

normal and I was in the market for a girlfriend and if you weren't so anti-relationships, you would absolutely be the kind of woman I would be interested in. I meant every word I said back there, I wasn't coerced into anything. I'm attracted to you, I'm not going to lie about that, just as you've made no secret about the fact you're attracted to me. But as we've both drawn the lines between us, we can say those things comfortably without any weirdness as we both know nothing is going to happen. We can be friends who admire each other, simple as that.'

She smiled. 'OK.'

They walked on for a bit and she loved how easy it was between them. They came to the field where her caravan was sitting waiting for her.

'I'm just going to give Thunder his apple. Did you want to come in for a coffee?'

'Sure, OK.'

'I won't be a second.'

She let herself into the field and found Thunder standing in the shelter. It was good that Wishing Wood had this. Although her horse was used to grazing in the fields on very cold days, he was getting older now and he probably liked the warmth and protection of the shelter, especially on nights like this. She checked he had enough food and water and then handed him the apple. He took it gratefully and she leaned her head into the side of his face, stroking his nose as he ate. He whickered softly.

She came back out and smiled to see Heath waiting for her. She'd always liked being alone in her little caravan so she wasn't sure why she'd felt compelled to invite him in. But on some level she knew why: she was enjoying talking to him and she didn't want it to end just yet.

She climbed up into the caravan, opened the door and turned on the lights.

'Oh no,' she said, staring in horror at the ceiling. As Heath had predicted, the roof had partly given way under the weight of the rain and there was now a hole as big as a dinner plate letting in tons of water right on top of her bed.

Heath stepped up behind her and swore under his breath.

She quickly started dragging some of her bedding off the bed, hoping the mattress wasn't too soggy. If it wasn't she could cover the hole as best as she could for tonight and sleep in the small lounge area near the door.

'What are you doing?'

'Trying to move my bed so I don't have to sleep under a waterfall.'

Heath stared at her in shock. 'Evergreen, I'm calling in that favour.'

'What? Now?' She dumped the pillows on the floor and went back for the duvet.

'Yes, absolutely now. And you can't go back on it. You promised you would do anything I want. I've already made a start on the list of jobs and completed a fair few so you owe me big time.'

'And I'll do anything you ask, but right now—'

'I want you to stay in Christmas Tree Cottage until I can fix the roof for you.'

'What, no, I can't do that.' Evergreen dumped the

soaking wet duvet on the floor, only to see that the mattress was soaked too.

'You can because you promised me you'd do anything I asked. That's what I want.'

'But that favour doesn't benefit you, it benefits me.'

'No, it's completely selfish. If you don't stay there, I'm going to have to start repairing the roof tonight and I'm way too tired for that. Nor do I have time to fit it in over the next few days unless I work twenty-four hours a day and I'm not doing that either. I'd also have to worry about you for the whole time you're here in case you caught bloody pneumonia from the damp draughty caravan and then I won't get any sleep either. So this is totally for me.'

'But I don't want to be in the way.'

'The house was literally built for you. Get your things, you're moving into Christmas Tree Cottage and I'm not taking no for an answer.'

Evergreen sighed as she looked around. The water had got everywhere and the hole was so bad that there would be no patching it over tonight. Heath was right, there was no other option.

Tears smarted her eyes. 'My poor home.'

Heath put an arm around her, stroking her back, and she had an overwhelming urge to lean her head against his chest and have a good cry, but she didn't like being vulnerable like that with someone.

'It's OK, we'll fix it up for you, I promise,' he told her. 'Just not tonight.'

She nodded.

'Let us take as much of your stuff as we can carry

tonight so it doesn't get damp and ruined.' Heath grabbed a box and passed her a bag hanging near the door.

As it turned out, she didn't have a lot. Most of her clothes fitted in one bag, her toiletries in another. She put all her books in the box and that was it. It wasn't a lot to show for her life.

Even Heath was surprised when they walked out with their small load. 'Is there nothing else you need to take?'

She shook her head. After Thunder, her home was her most important possession and she was leaving that behind. It was probably going to be under six inches of water by the next day.

'I'll help you get these to the treehouse and then I'll come back and put something over the top of the hole to try to protect the caravan as much as I can.'

'Thank you, Heath, you're being very kind.'

He shrugged like it was no big deal but it obviously was.

They walked to Christmas Tree Cottage together. Heath let her in and they put her meagre belongings down in the lounge. He immediately went to the log burner and built her a fire. 'This will get the place cosy for you.'

She wandered around. This was a beautiful place and she got to sleep here for the next few nights. It was hardly a bad thing.

Heath stood back up and moved into the bedroom as she went into the kitchen to boil the kettle. He returned a few moments later and came over to her.

'I'm going to get off and try and put some tarpaulin over the hole.'

'I'll come and give you a hand.'

'No, honestly, it will take me a few minutes. Stay here and get warm. Enjoy the bed.'

She smiled, despite everything. Heath and that bloody bed.

He moved closer to her, his hands on her shoulders. 'Are you OK?' he asked, gently.

She nodded. 'I am. Thanks to you. Thank you for this, for everything you're doing for me. You've only known me for a few hours and you've already helped me more in those few hours than most of my family ever did.'

He frowned. 'I'm sorry your family never gave you that.'

She waved it away. 'It's fine but, honestly, I can't say thank you enough. You didn't sign up for any of this, being Santa, doing the repairs, looking after me,' she gestured to the log fire burning away merrily inside the burner and the ginormous, amazing bed. 'And now fixing a few things has turned into replacing a whole roof and you're just shrugging it off like it's no big deal and it is, it really is. I hate being a burden to anyone and I'll pay you back for this, for all of this somehow.'

He suddenly stepped forward and enveloped her in a hug and she didn't realise how much she needed it. While Meadow and Indigo's hugs had been welcoming, this was different. It made her feel safe and protected and she hadn't felt that for a very long time. She slid her arms around him, leaning her head against his chest.

'Everyone needs a little help sometimes and I'm happy to give it. I like helping people. It makes me feel good. See, it's all completely selfish.'

'Heath Brookfield, there is definitely nothing selfish about you.'

He stroked her hair and it was such a sweet, intimate gesture, it made goosebumps erupt across her body. This wasn't good. She wasn't here looking for a relationship or even a fling. She didn't want to get emotionally involved or attached to Heath. That would just lead to her getting hurt. But saying these things in her head didn't make her want to step out of his arms.

'It's no bother at all. Now get some rest. I'll see you tomorrow for my makeover.'

He stepped back, looking her in the eyes to make sure she was OK.

She nodded and waved him away. He closed the door behind him and she looked around. It felt almost wrong to be here instead of her home but, as she glanced across at the huge squashy bed, she knew that wrong would feel infinitely good. She quickly got changed into her pyjamas.

She suddenly realised the TV in the bedroom was on and the opening credits of *The Fellowship of the Ring*, the first *Lord of the Rings* movie, was paused, ready to play. She swallowed the lump in her throat at Heath's thoughtfulness.

She climbed into bed and pressed play. The bed really was like lying on big deep cloud and, even before Galadriel had explained how the ring of power had been forged and what happened to it, Evergreen was fast asleep.

CHAPTER SIX

Heath knocked on the door of Christmas Tree Cottage the next day. At least the rain had stopped in the early hours of the morning, and there had evidently been a frost overnight too, covering everything in a sparkly sprinkling of sugar.

He had already been to check on the caravan and the tarpaulin had stayed in place, protecting the inside of the caravan from any further damage, but it was going to be a big job to repair it.

There was no answer from Evergreen so he knocked again. After a few moments he opened the door and stepped inside. 'Evergreen?'

There was still no answer. He didn't want to walk in on her in the shower or getting dressed so he moved cautiously into the room. There wasn't a sound from inside and he wondered if she'd gone out, and then he saw her, fast asleep in the bed.

He smiled as he stepped closer. It was just coming up to half past eight, which he supposed was quite early for some people. He was always up early to have breakfast with Star or the rest of his family and get on with the jobs that needed doing that day.

Her hair was sprawled across the white pillow, its rainbow hues glowing in the early morning sunlight. She looked magical. He had a sudden overwhelming urge to climb into bed with her and hold her, but he couldn't do that.

He wandered off to the kitchen and made them both a coffee. He left hers on top of the drawers next to her bed and moved back into the lounge.

He saw the box of books he'd brought over from the night before and smiled when he spotted *The Hobbit* and *The Lord of the Rings* on the top. He shifted them to one side to inspect what other treasures she had. Someone's book collection was hugely personal and he hoped she wouldn't mind him looking, but then most of these books had been on a shelf which he would have seen had they had that coffee the night before.

He saw quite a collection of fantasy books in there, many of which he had read and loved. There were some more by Tolkien and some of his favourite Terry Pratchetts were in here too, as well as some paranormal romances. They weren't really his thing but he had enjoyed *Elvish*, which was in here. He spotted *Eragon* and picked it up, reading the blurb. Star had started taking an interest in his fantasy collection recently, after falling in love with Harry Potter and Percy Jackson, but none of his books were age appropriate. This book was aimed at young adults and involved a young boy and his friendship with a dragon. Maybe this would be suitable for her to get her teeth into the fantasy genre.

He sat down on the sofa and started reading.

He'd just got himself hooked on the first chapter when he heard a noise from the bedroom.

He heard Evergreen yawn softly

'Oh shit, I'm late,' she muttered.

'You're not late,' Heath called out. 'No need to panic.'

There was silence as she clearly digested that he was there. He heard movement and then she was standing in the doorway looking gorgeous and dishevelled in a pale blue satin pair of pyjamas covered in sparkly snowflakes.

'Except you're here, so clearly I am.'

'Not at all, I'm a very early bird.'

'Normally I am too but it's that bloody bed.'

He frowned. 'Was it not comfortable?'

'It was the best bed I've ever slept on in my entire life. I had the best night's sleep I've had in a very long time. When I leave here, we're going to need to find some way to shoehorn that mattress into my tiny caravan because I don't think I can ever go back to my old mattress now.'

He grinned. 'Well that can be arranged. I can just build a big extension on the back of your caravan.'

'Poor Thunder will be delighted. Look, just give me five minutes to have a quick shower and brush my teeth and I'll be right with you.'

'Take your time, I've just started reading this,' Heath held up his book.

'Oooh, that one's a good one. It's an easy one to read too, especially when a series like *The Wheel of Time*, which I loved, has a cast of thousands. Sometimes it's nice to give your brain a bit of a rest with a good young adult book which isn't so… epic.'

'I get that. I was wondering if this might be a good book for Star.'

'Oh I think she'd love it. I won't be long.'

He watched her hurry back off to the bedroom and a few moments later he heard her brushing her teeth. Shortly after he heard the shower door open and the shower start. He focussed on the book and not the fact that she was naked merely a few metres away from where he was sitting.

Not long after, he heard her come out the bathroom. At the movement in the bedroom doorway he glanced up then quickly looked away when he saw she was wrapped in a tiny bath towel.

'Sorry, I left all my clothes out here.'

He tried to read the same paragraph for the tenth time as she walked past him to grab her bag. He couldn't fail to notice her gorgeous legs. Jesus, what was wrong with him? Had it really been that long without a woman that Evergreen simply walking out in a towel turned him on? But it was OK to appreciate she was attractive, just like he could appreciate that Blake Lively or Beyoncé were beautiful women. It didn't mean anything. Nothing was going to happen between them.

She disappeared inside the bedroom and shut the door and he felt himself sigh with relief.

He shook his head. He was going to be in trouble with Evergreen Winters.

❄

Evergreen pulled her hair back into a ponytail and decided that when she went out into the lounge in a few moments to do Heath's make-up, she would be completely professional. It had unnerved her having him here in her space while she was getting dressed. Mainly because she didn't like what she felt when she was around him. She didn't like that it had felt completely normal having him sitting on the sofa reading a book while she got dressed, as if they had known each other for years. She didn't like that he made her heart race just by being here or that it had made her feel warm inside when she'd woken up and he was there. He was too nice and lovely and she didn't like that. She was here to do a job and nothing more.

She opened the door and walked out into the lounge. 'Right, let's make you into an old man.'

'Great, where do you want me?'

'Let's have you on one of the dining chairs, that way I won't get any make-up on the sofa.'

He got up and she grabbed her toolbox and the other things she needed.

She looked through her things and sighed. 'Crap, I haven't got my make-up cape to protect your clothes. It must still be in the caravan. I'll use a towel over your shoulders but it might be best if you take your top off so I don't stain your clothes.'

She moved back into the bathroom to grab the spare towel. This was fine, she had worked on a lot of topless men in the past because the alien or zombie make-up had to go all down their necks and sometimes on their bodies. This would be no different.

'You want me to strip off?' Heath said from behind her.

'Just your top, I don't want to get make-up on your clothes. Don't worry, I won't look. Oh, I could give you a fake six-pack for your date with Scarlet. I can make it look really convincing,' she turned around to look at him and felt her mouth fall open. 'Bloody hell, I can see you don't need any help in that department.'

He'd stripped off down to his jeans and was standing in her bedroom like a perfectly sculpted Adonis. God, he was so beautiful. It had been a long time since she'd been attracted to a man and she'd worked on a lot of handsome actors over the years. But there was something about Heath Brookfield that made her feel something she hadn't felt in, well forever.

He laughed. 'You have no filter, do you? You just say the first thing that goes through your head.'

She shook her head. 'Yeah sorry, I mean… umm. Please take a seat.'

He shook his head with a smile. 'It's actually really refreshing. I like it.'

He sat down and she stepped closer to look at him.

'I'm just going to touch your face for a moment, just so I can see how taut or stretchy your skin is.'

Heath nodded and she stepped closer. People's faces were like a blank canvas and it always gave her a little flurry of excitement when she was transforming someone new for the first time. She ran her thumb and fingers gently across his cheeks, round his mouth, under his eyes and his forehead and he watched her. She had done make-up for hundreds of people over the years but for some reason this felt a lot more intimate and she didn't know why. Maybe because he was studying her as intently as she was studying him. She was hyperaware of him, how his skin felt, what he smelt of, like the ocean on a summer's day, and how he was staring at her so intently.

'You have really good skin,' Evergreen said, trying to avoid his gaze. She touched round the sides of his eyes and smiled. 'You smile a lot.'

'Sorry about that.'

'You never need to apologise for smiling, we need a lot more of that in the world. Besides, your laughter lines are something I can definitely work with. So I'm going to add some prosthetics around the eyes to give you some slight old age sagginess and then I'm going to add a layer of latex around the rest of your eyes to get that lovely old man crinkly face texture, but the rest of the face is going to be covered with a beard and moustache so we don't need to spend ages wrinkling that. Your neck too will be covered with the beard. I'll give you a wig as well so you don't necessarily have to keep your Santa hat on all day.'

She grabbed a hairdryer, plugging it in next to Heath before going to her toolbox and taking out some foam eye bags. She peeled away the plastic covering and held them up against his eyes, then grabbed a pair of scissors and trimmed them so they fit. She picked up the bottle of Pros-Aide and started applying it to the back of the foam. 'This glue is really sticky, don't touch it, don't touch your face, don't touch your hair, don't touch anywhere.'

'Yes ma'am,' Heath said and she laughed.

She carefully applied it under his eyes and then stuck the small foam eye bags underneath. She used the glue on a sponge to smooth the transition between the foam and his skin before dabbing on some powder to set it and to make sure it didn't stick to parts of his face that it shouldn't.

She picked up some liquid latex and a brush and turned back to him.

'Am I allowed to talk?'

'Yes, as I'm just doing your eyes for now, but try not to move your head around too much.' Evergreen stretched out the skin to the side of the eye and applied a thin layer of latex on it.

'So do you prefer the make-up side of things or the acting?' Heath asked.

'This definitely, I could do this all day long. Making someone look old with latex and beards and wigs is easy. But I love the horror side of make-up or anything gory I can get my teeth into. Injuries like scars or zombie make-up is right up my street. I've done several demons, aliens and monsters over the years and I love it. I went to stage school to train to be an actor as I always thought that's what I wanted to do but I found the behind-the-scenes stuff much more fun. I've always been into art, painting with texture, but making up someone's arm like it's been sliced open, adding the torn and lacerated skin for the texture, that ticks all those creative boxes for me. It really is an art form and I love it.'

'Star was talking about you so much this morning, she is so excited about what you do. We went to the Harry Potter Experience a few months ago and she absolutely loved the make-up side of the films, what they did to create the trolls and goblins, the Robbie Coltrane head they made for Hagrid, she was fascinated by it. At Halloween one of the local fancy dress shops was offering scar make-up and she came out with this massive gash across her face, she couldn't stop looking at it in the mirror. She loves gory stuff like that. Whenever I take her to theme parks or fairs, the haunted houses or ghost trains are the first thing she wants to visit.'

'Oh, I can make her up to look hideously terrifying.'

'She would love you for that, far more than if you offered her a ride in your caravan.'

Evergreen smiled. It was clear Star was everything to him. 'Right, let me get the hairdryer on this.'

Still holding the skin taut, she switched the hairdryer on. 'Try not to blink. Look up as that will help.' She started drying the latex until it was a lot clearer, added some powder and then repeated the process all over again. 'We probably need at least two layers of latex, maybe four or five, and each layer needs to be dry before I add the next layer. So your whole makeover is going to take an hour or two. We're going to get to know each other a whole lot better by Christmas. Either that or you'll be sick of the sight of me and be putting your headphones in so you don't have to listen to me waffle on. Which is actually what a lot of clients do, headphones in and go to sleep. I don't mind. I can just get on with my art that way. So if you come here in the morning and just want to go back to sleep rather than chat to me, I won't be offended.'

'Evergreen, you are fast becoming one of the most interesting people I've ever met. I'm more than happy to talk to you.'

She stepped back a little to look at him. The sound of her full name on his lips made her heart leap a little. No one called her Evergreen, it was always Ever, and she'd told him that. And what he'd just said was one of the nicest things anyone had said to her. No one ever took the time to get to know her. She was there to do a job and she did it very well, they didn't need any more than that from her.

Heath studied her. 'And I mean that platonically. I've got this thing with Scarlet and you don't do relationships, so I'm not flirting with you when I say that. But as your friend, I'd very much like to learn more about you.'

She smiled. Friendship. She could handle that. If she put Heath Brookfield firmly in the friend box then she didn't need to worry about how he made her feel. They were friends. They didn't need to complicate things.

She nodded. 'I'd like that too.'

CHAPTER SEVEN

'OK, now for the beard and wig,' Evergreen said and Heath watched her as she reverentially pulled a full beard out of a box and laid it down on the table next to him, followed by a long flowing silvery-grey wig.

'I'm going to look like Gandalf by the time you've finished with me.'

'Well, I'm sure Santa Claus is probably part wizard too, especially if he can deliver all the presents in one night.'

'True.'

The latex had taken quite a while and his face felt dry and tight where the latex had dried, especially round the eyes. Then Evergreen had spent an inordinate amount of time adding various colours to his skin to add tones and highlights, to make the skin look pale and sunken in some parts.

It should have felt strange having her lean over him, touching his face when they'd only just met, but somehow it didn't. He felt completely at ease with her and he hadn't felt so comfortable with a woman for a long time. She smelt amazing, like the sweet, spiced fruit you get in mince pies, and being so close to her he could see the tiny freckles on her cheeks and nose, the flecks of gold in her greeny-grey eyes.

She started brushing the glue around his jaw and chin, which felt weird and didn't smell that good. She picked up the beard and very gently pressed it onto his face, tapping it to make it stay in place. It was such a lovely sensation. Then she picked up the big moustache with curly points on the ends and placed that on, her eyebrows crinkling as she focussed on the task. He had never had anyone study his face so intently and for so long before, although he knew she wasn't really looking at his face, but more the space that needed to be worked on. She was taking it all very seriously. Lastly, she added the bushy eyebrows, patting those gently on too.

'OK, now the wig and we're done.' She picked up the long grey wig and swept it rather grandly over his head. Pulling it firmly over the forehead, she dabbed another blob of glue at the front to secure it. She grabbed a damp cloth and pressed it round his face, sealing the beard, hair and moustache to his skin, and then stepped back to survey her work.

'You look great,' Evergreen said. 'Old but friendly. Which is what we want.'

Heath stood up and moved into the bedroom so he could have a look in the mirror. His reflection was completely unrecognisable. He stepped closer, studying the wrinkles around the eyes, the beard which actually looked like it was part of his face not just stuck on. It was really effective.

'This is incredible, I wouldn't even recognise myself,' Heath said, turning to find Evergreen leaning on the doorway watching him. 'You have an amazing talent.'

'Thank you. But this is quite the juxtaposition,' she gestured to his face and then his chest. 'Sexy old wizard.'

He laughed.

She looked at her watch. 'OK, so that took just under two hours but we'd need to get you into costume too. So if you want to start at nine in the morning for our breakfast with Santa appointments, you're going to have to come to me around half-six.'

'Good lord, that's early.'

'I know, and if it's any consolation I'll be up at half-five to do mine before you come and, like I said, you can always go to sleep while I do it.'

'Not a chance. I can always help you with yours as well if you need it and you tell me what to do.'

'I might take you up on it. It's always good to have two pairs of hands. OK, let me get this stuff off you. I'm going to use acetone to remove the glue from the back of the hair and beard – it stinks so try not to breathe it in.'

He sat back down and watched her work to remove the beard, washing down the plastic layer at the back to clean all the glue from the beard before putting it back in its box. She very carefully repeated the process with the moustache, eyebrows and the wig and then very gently peeled off the bags under his eyes, before giving his face one last rub over with a wipe.

'If you want to wash your face off with soap and water now, then I'll put some cream on it.'

He walked into the bathroom and rinsed his face,

smiling to himself at what Meadow had signed him up for. Although it would be a pain to sit there for two hours each day having the make-up applied, he was actually really enjoying himself and he knew that part of that was because he was getting to know Evergreen.

He came back out, drying his face on a towel, and sat back down in the chair.

'This is just a really thick moisturiser, your face might be a bit dry with all the glue and make-up so this will help to keep it in its normal beautiful state.'

He smiled as she gently massaged the cream into his skin, spending a lot of time around his eyes; it felt wonderful.

'You're all set. So what's the plan for the next week?'

Heath pulled out the schedule Meadow had given him. 'So tomorrow and Sunday we'll have breakfast at nine with a small group of children and their families. Then we have a break until one where we'll see individual children for a few hours in the afternoon and then another short break before our bedtime story with Santa sessions. Next week it will just be the bedtime story sessions early evening although there are a few groups that have booked to come during the day. Breakfast on Christmas Eve will be the last session.'

Evergreen nodded. 'OK, sounds good. And I still owe you something for all the jobs you're doing and for this,' she gestured to the treehouse. 'I'm not letting you get away with putting me up here as payment for your work.'

He grinned because he knew she would still feel like she owed him. 'I'll think of something big but if you want to help we need to finalise the preparations for the Christmas market this afternoon. They open to customers tomorrow so all the traders will be there setting up today. There'll be a list of snags that me and River will need to fix but we're putting up a few more Christmas decorations and lights so you can help with that.'

'I'd be happy to.'

He watched as she pulled on her boots and her cloak and he couldn't help smiling; there was something just so damned endearing about her.

They stepped outside and started walking through the trees towards the Christmas market.

'Is Star looking forward to Christmas?' Evergreen said.

'She is,' Heath said slowly. 'But I'd love to maintain all our big Christmassy traditions. We call it our Christmas Hullabaloo, where we do all these activities in the lead-up to Christmas, like making and decorating cookies. We have a big Christmas movie marathon and a sleepover in the lounge all together under the Christmas tree lights, and there's a few other things we organise as well. I reckon there's a part of her that secretly wants all that too, but she's growing up so fast. I worry she thinks some of it is silly and too young for her. Before I know it, she'll be this overdramatic teenager who thinks Christmas is naff. With all the changes we've been through this year, I'd really like to make this one special for her but I feel like she'd just prefer to spend her time playing on the Xbox.'

'I'm sure if you carry on with your traditions, she'll take part and secretly love it. I look back on the stuff we used to do as kids and I do miss it. I was that teenager who didn't want to take part in the silly stuff but I did secretly love our traditions.'

'Are you big on Christmas?' Heath asked.

'Not really. Not any more. Suki, my stepmum, always was. We never had much money but there were always presents and decorations and games. On Christmas Day, she always used to hide the gold chocolate coins around the house and the garden. It was always a big competition who could find the most. It didn't matter who won because we'd always put all the coins in the middle of the table like a big treasure haul and shared them out anyway, but it was finding them that was the most fun. Me and my sister Cally were always so competitive with each other. I almost always won. I think that was my favourite Christmas memory, trying to find those coins and Suki's face as we all got so into it, even when we were older. After she died and I was alone, Christmas just didn't seem so important any more. I was never in the mood for a big celebration, it just reminded me too much of Suki.'

'But by the sounds of it she loved Christmas and always tried to make it special for you. I think she'd love it if you continued to enjoy Christmas, not shy away from it. What are your plans for this Christmas?'

She was silent for a moment. 'Well, I was going to read my favourite book.'

He stopped dead. 'You're going to be alone?'

'It's not a big deal, I'm always alone.'

'What about your family?'

'I don't see them any more.'

He couldn't even begin to imagine what that was like. Although his parents had left when he was young, his brothers had always been there and now his family had expanded to include Meadow, Indigo, Star, Tierra, Alfie and a big crazy dog too. He loved seeing his family every day, working alongside them, having breakfast or dinner with them. They were a team and he couldn't imagine being in a team of one and how isolating that would be.

'What about your friends?'

'I move around too much to have many of them.'

'Evergreen, that's one of the saddest things I've ever heard.'

'Oh thanks very much.'

'No, I don't mean sad as in lame, I mean the thought of you spending Christmas alone makes me really sad.'

'I don't need your pity,' she said defensively.

'It's not pity Evergreen, I just…' he trailed off because he supposed it was. 'Will you spend Christmas with me and my family this year?'

'Oh hell no,' Evergreen said. 'As lovely as I'm sure that will be because you all seem wonderful people, I don't want to gatecrash anyone's celebrations. I'd hate to be in the way.'

'You couldn't possibly be in the way. It's not like our Christmases are a quiet, intimate affair, there'll be all of us, all the kids, my grandmother Amelia will be there, Indigo's sister Violet is coming up on Boxing Day. I think River has a friend coming over Christmas Eve night. One extra person won't make any difference to our crazy menagerie.'

'You've just told me how you want to make Christmas special for your daughter, how can it be special when you have some random stranger turn up in the middle of it all?'

'You're not a stranger, you're a friend and Star adores you, you're very good with her. My family will be more than happy to make room for you at our table.'

She shook her head. 'I don't want anyone to be lumbered with me, especially not at Christmas. I'm happier on my own and I'm sure you guys will be a lot happier without having to put up with me.'

Heath frowned. He didn't like that she thought she would be a burden. He'd practically had to force her to stay in Christmas Tree Cottage the night before, even when water was pouring through the roof of her home, but she'd said then that she didn't want to be in anyone's way. There was something deeper going on here, some other reason for wanting to be alone. But he couldn't bear the thought of sitting down to his turkey lunch on Christmas Day with his big, wonderfully noisy family and Evergreen sitting in her cold caravan or at Christmas Tree Cottage all alone with only a book for company.

They walked on in silence for a while and an idea started to form in his mind.

'Evergreen, I know what I want from you as payment for all the jobs I'm doing for you.'

'You can't make me spend Christmas Day with you as a favour to you. That's ridiculous.'

'If you want to spend Christmas Day alone, I'm not going to push you to change your mind, but I want you to spend our Christmas Hullabaloo with us. Make and decorate Christmas cookies, watch Christmas movies, join our sleepover. If we have snow as predicted, we'll make snowmen together, roast marshmallows around the fire, the full shebang.'

Evergreen sighed like it was a big hardship for her. 'What can you possibly gain from me being there for all those family activities?'

'Because Star will want to do it if you're doing it. You're the cool new novelty. She couldn't stop talking about you this morning at breakfast. If she sees you taking part in all of that, and you're so cool, then the Christmas Hullabaloo will suddenly become cool too.'

Evergreen clearly thought about it for the longest time and Heath almost laughed. She was giving this as much thought as someone being asked to donate a kidney.

'OK, I can do that.'

'Are you sure?'

'It's fine. It's just a few cookies and a snowman, it's no big deal.'

'And you might find yourself secretly enjoying it.'

She smiled. 'Don't count on it.'

CHAPTER EIGHT

Evergreen watched the buzz of everyone getting ready for the Christmas market with a smile. The traders were busy unloading all of their wares into the huts and presumably laying them out, but it was the numerous members of staff wearing green t-shirts or hoodies that caught her attention. One was holding a ladder for another while the person at the top put up more Christmas lights, others were carrying boxes between the huts, some were dressing the trunks of nearby trees with garlands or ribbons, it was a real team effort. Everyone was helping everyone else out and they all seemed really happy about it. What a lovely place to work.

As a freelancer, working on TV and films, everyone had their job: the sound guys were in charge of sound, the lighting team were in charge of lighting, she was in charge of make-up, and though everything came together to create a finished TV programme or film, there wasn't this team spirit where everyone was doing all jobs, not just focussing on their own area of expertise.

She walked over to Meadow with Heath.

'What needs doing?' Heath asked.

'Can you go and see River? I'm sure he will have a snagging list a mile long you can help with,' Meadow said.

'Sure.' He turned to Evergreen, placing his hand briefly on her back which made her body erupt in goosebumps. 'I'll catch you later.'

She watched him walk away and then turned back to Meadow. 'What can I do to help?'

'You can hang these wreaths that Greta made on the doors of each of the huts. There's a hammer and some long nails in this box. If you hammer the nails half in, then the wreaths should hang on them.'

'I can do that.' Evergreen hoisted a box of wreaths onto her hip. 'I'll come back for the others once I've done these.'

'Thank you. Will you come to dinner again tonight so we can thank you properly?'

'Oh there's no need, I'm doing this to say thanks to all of you for letting me stay in Christmas Tree Cottage and especially to Heath who has been helping me with my caravan.'

'Well, come to dinner tonight and you can thank us properly.'

Evergreen laughed. 'OK, I will, thanks.'

She walked off carrying the box of wreaths. It felt good to be involved. She hadn't been part of something like this for a long time.

She reached the first hut and could see the trader inside laying out candles on the low tables, all different colours and shapes. Christmas music was playing and there was a scent of gingerbread in the air.

'Hello, I'm just going to close your door for a moment so I can hang a wreath on the door.'

'Oh sure, thank you,' the woman said, coming out to look at the wreaths. 'Oh wow, these are beautiful.'

Evergreen looked inside the box and saw how each one was completely different, some with gold-painted ivy and ribbons, others with holly leaves, berries and red baubles. They looked spectacular.

'Can I choose which one I want?'

'Oh, of course,' Evergreen said, hoping the other traders wouldn't get upset that she'd got first dibs.

The lady rooted through the box for a moment and extracted one with spectacular satin turquoise ribbons mixed with peacock feathers and various greenery. 'This one is wonderful.'

Evergreen pulled out the hammer and nail and set about banging it into the door, hoping the door was strong enough to take it. The woman took great care to hang the wreath on the door and stepped back to admire the effect. 'I love it, thank you.'

Evergreen smiled at it. It was a small contribution but it was something.

She moved on to the next hut and saw a woman in a green t-shirt struggling with some lights that had snagged on a branch.

'Oh let me help,' Evergreen said, putting her box of wreaths down. The tree was one with twisty branches and low-hanging boughs so she was able to climb up onto the lower part very easily and unsnag the lights. 'Where do you want it?'

'Could you wrap it round the branch above that?' the woman said.

Evergreen did as asked and the woman passed her another section of the lights to wrap around a slightly higher section.

'That's perfect, thanks,' the woman said as Evergreen climbed down. 'I'm Greta by the way.'

'Evergreen.'

'What a great name.'

'Thank you. Oh, you're the one responsible for these beautiful wreaths,' Evergreen said.

'That would be me. They're pretty easy to do and I love doing them.'

'Well, the owner of the last hut was delighted with her peacock one. And did you make the one on the door of Christmas Tree Cottage, with the red and white candy canes?'

'Yes I did.'

'I love it. You should sell these at the market, people would pay good money for something like this.'

'River, Meadow and Indigo have all suggested it but I figured they were just being nice. I'm not sure they would be good enough.'

'They're definitely good enough. They're so unique and bold. People will love them. And I don't do nice, I just say it as it is.'

A slow smile spread across Greta's face. 'Maybe they'll let me have a trestle table somewhere.'

'It'll be worth an ask.'

'I will, thanks. Are you working in Christmas Tree Cottage?' Greta asked.

'Yes, I'm Mrs Christmas.'

'How wonderful. I've heard the children around the wood talking about seeing you and Father Christmas, they're all very excited.'

'That's nice, I'm looking forward to doing it.'

And for the first time since she'd agreed to do it, Evergreen really was. She was contributing to something bigger here, it wasn't just a job any more, she was going to be a key part in making some children's Christmases very special.

'I like her,' River said.

Heath tore his eyes away from watching Evergreen laugh and chat with Lucien, one of their housekeepers, to find that River was watching her too.

Heath focussed his attention on the piece of wood he was sanding ready for a small shelf for one of the traders.

'You know, me, Indigo and Meadow have been on at Greta for weeks to sell her wreaths and she has refused, saying they're not good enough. Five minutes talking to Evergreen and she's come to Meadow to ask if she can have a table to sell them.'

Heath smiled at that but he refused to be baited.

'And she just gets involved here, helping everyone. I like that,' River went on.

'I think she feels like she owes us, because of the work I'm doing on her caravan, but I can't deny how much she's enjoying herself.'

River was silent for a moment. 'Are you planning on doing anything about this little crush you have on her?'

Heath opened his mouth to protest but shut it again. 'I have my date with Scarlet tomorrow.'

'Why are you clinging to that? You had great sex. If you had anything more than that, I feel like you would have connected before now.'

Heath was beginning to wonder that himself. What did he and Scarlet really have to build on other than a weekend of amazing sex?

'Do you not think it's worth finding out?' Heath said.

'It depends what you're looking for. If all you want is some more great sex then go for it, I'm sure she will tick that box for you. But in conversations we've had in the last few months, I get the impression you want something more than that now.'

'I do but…'

'You're worried about Star.'

'She's gone through so many changes in the last year,' Heath said.

'You know, Tierra was my everything, just like Star is for you. I wanted to be the best dad to Tierra that I could be and I didn't want anything to get in the way of that. I didn't have a relationship with anyone for five years because she was my priority. But being with Indigo hasn't changed that. Having Alfie hasn't changed that either. My priorities have grown but there is room in my life and my heart to love more than just my daughter. It doesn't mean I love her any less. And Tierra absolutely adores Indigo, she just fits here with us, it's like she's always been here and I know my life is infinitely better because of her.'

River handed him another piece of wood.

'You will find that person for you. The one that completes you, the one that was missing all along and maybe it's Scarlet and maybe it's Evergreen or maybe it's someone you haven't even met yet, but don't be afraid of it or how it can change your life. When you find it, it'll be the best thing that ever happened to you. Star knows she is loved, and not just by you and Meadow, but by Bear, me, Indigo, Tierra and Amelia. She will be absolutely fine because you'll make sure she is. You will make sure that, no matter what happens, she will always know she is loved and treasured by you. And let's face it. You're never going to end up with someone that hates children. The right person for you will love Star as much as you do.'

Heath nodded. 'You're right, about all of it. I have been avoiding relationships out of fear of change but that change doesn't have to be a bad thing.'

'The right person definitely won't be.'

Heath finished sanding the wood and passed it to River. He thought about Scarlet and tried to picture her sitting down to dinner with his crazy family or spending time chatting to Star. It was such a jarring juxtaposition that he couldn't even begin to imagine it. One of Star's favourite books when she was younger was *The Tiger Who Came to Tea*. Even that was more realistic than Scarlet fitting in with his family. He glanced over at Evergreen, who was now helping one of the traders hang some Christmas bunting outside the hut. He tried to imagine Scarlet helping Greta hang some Christmas lights or assisting Felix by carrying a box of decorations. He wasn't sure he could. But Evergreen fitted here. And as River said, maybe his person was Evergreen, or maybe it was someone else entirely, but the more he thought about it, he was pretty damned sure it wasn't going to be Scarlet.

He shook his head because didn't Scarlet deserve a chance? They had connected on a more intimate level than he ever had with anyone. Wasn't it worth finding out if they had something deeper? He'd so badly wanted a second chance with her. For six months or more he'd hoped he would get one before he'd finally given up. And now it was going to happen, he was throwing it away before it had even started. He'd thought she was wonderful but meeting Evergreen had made him doubt all of that. But if he didn't go on this date, would he always be wondering what could have been?

He couldn't pin his hopes on Evergreen. She had given him no sign at all that she would be interested in a relationship beyond her attraction to him. He had no idea whether they had any kind of future together at all. He knew he had to spend some time getting to know her properly to see if she fitted with him as well as she fitted here.

But in the meantime, it wouldn't hurt to go on this date with Scarlet, even if it was to draw a line under it once and for all.

CHAPTER NINE

Evergreen stepped inside the caravan and looked around. It didn't look as wet as she had feared. Heath had fitted the tarpaulin over the top of the hole and that had stopped any more water coming in. The mattress and bedding were still soaking but if she brought them into her Christmas Tree Cottage they would dry out quicker. She could see that Heath had made good progress with some of her little jobs before the rain had ruined it all.

She heard a noise behind her to see Heath had stepped inside.

'Hey,' he said, softly. 'It probably looks a lot worse than it is. Once we get the new roof on, a lot of this will dry out.'

She smiled slightly at his attempt at cheering her up. 'It's OK. I mean, this is the worst it's been so far, I've never had a gaping hole before, but it's not the first time I've had water damage from leaks and I'm sure it won't be the last. This caravan was never meant to be lived in long-term. It was made for show to take part in parades or to be rented out for special events. I think I've pushed it to its limits.'

'I hate the thought of you living like this, waiting for the next leak or the next thing to go wrong,' Heath said.

She shrugged. 'It is what it is. I don't really have a lot of choice and it's not like I can stay in Christmas Tree Cottage for the rest of my life. Come on, I'm sure the girls are itching to take Thunder for a ride.'

'I think Amelia is more excited about it than they are,' Heath said.

Evergreen opened the cupboard underneath the bed, which had thankfully remained protected from the water. She grabbed Thunder's saddle and passed it to Heath before picking up the rest of the gear and they went back outside.

The girls were standing on the outside of the paddock feeding Thunder apples and carrots over the fence. His ears were pricked forwards and he looked so content. She smiled; he'd always had an affection for children.

Amelia was stroking him too with a huge smile on her face, while Meadow and Indigo were also watching.

'So have you girls finished school for the holidays now?' Evergreen asked.

'Yes we don't go back for two and a bit weeks,' Star said.

'And what are you most looking forward to in the next two weeks?' Evergreen teased, knowing what the answer would be.

'Christmas Day,' Tierra said, practically bouncing up and down on the fence. 'It's seven days today.'

'Oh so it is. Right, I'll go and get Thunder ready.'

Evergreen walked into the field, stroked the horse's neck and then put his saddle and bridle on, adjusting the stirrups so they were short enough for the girls.

'Who wants to go first?'

'Me!' Tierra said, excitedly.

'Tierra, sometimes it's nicer to let other people go first. Amelia or Star might want to go first,' Indigo tried.

'I don't mind,' Star said and Meadow gave her shoulders a squeeze.

Amelia gestured for Tierra to go first.

'See, they don't want to go first,' Tierra said.

'But it's always nice to ask first,' Indigo said.

Evergreen suppressed a smile. 'OK, Tierra, looks like you're up first. Do you want me to ride with you?'

Indigo nodded but Tierra shook her head. 'I can do it on my own.'

'Well why don't I lift you up there and if you think it's a bit too high, I can ride with you and make sure you don't fall off?'

Tierra nodded and Evergreen lifted her onto the back of Thunder. She looked so tiny, dwarfed by this giant horse. Tierra gazed down at the ground with wide eyes. 'I think I'd like you to ride with me,' she said in a small voice.

'No problem,' Evergreen said, pulling herself up into the saddle behind Tierra. She held the reins with her arms either side of Tierra to ensure she didn't fall off. Although she knew she didn't need to worry too much, Thunder was a very gentle walker and somehow he knew he was carrying a precious load because, when she clicked him on, he was much slower and gentler than normal.

Tierra let out a shriek of delight when they started moving and Evergreen held her a little bit tighter so she would feel secure. Tierra didn't stop giggling all the way round, and her laughter was completely infectious.

'What do you think?' Evergreen asked when they got halfway round the paddock.

'It's funny,' Tierra said.

She rode Thunder once round the paddock and came back to where everyone was standing. Indigo was filming it with her phone, presumably to show River later.

'Well done Tierra,' Amelia cheered and everyone else joined in.

Evergreen slid off and then lifted Tierra down. 'Did you enjoy it?'

'Yes, but it was very high,' Tierra said and then climbed back through the fence to rejoin Indigo.

Evergreen smiled. Clearly horse riding was not totally Tierra's thing, at least not yet.

'Thank you,' Indigo said to Evergreen. 'That seemed very gentle.'

'He's a nice walker,' Evergreen said. 'Star, do you want to go next?'

Star climbed through the fence eagerly. 'Can I try riding by myself?'

Evergreen checked with Meadow and Heath, who both nodded. 'I'll lead you round then to start with and if you feel happy you can do it by yourself.'

She lifted Star into the saddle and adjusted the stirrups for her. She showed her how to hold the reins then took Thunder's bridle and started walking round the field, checking on Star the whole time.

'Would you like a go on your own now?' Evergreen asked, when they got halfway round the field. 'I'll walk with you but you'll be in control.'

Star nodded, excitedly.

Evergreen let go of Thunder's bridle and walked by his head. He was quite happy to continue plodding by her side and, when they reached the corner, the horse followed her in the new direction.

'I'm doing it,' Star said, excitedly.

'Yes you are, and he's a big horse to control, you're doing great,' Evergreen said, even though Thunder was simply following her.

They came to a stop where everyone was waiting and Star quickly scrabbled down. 'That was fantastic, thank you Evergreen, thank you Thunder.'

She climbed back through the fence and Heath gave her a hug. 'You were brilliant out there, a complete natural.'

Star couldn't help the grin from spreading all over her face.

Evergreen turned to Amelia. 'Looks like you're up.'

To her surprise, Amelia climbed through the fence too, sliding under the bar easily. She was wearing leggings today with a blue tweed jacket and black knee-high boots. She looked like she'd just walked off the pages of *Horse and Hound* or *Country Living*.

Amelia approached Thunder's nose, giving it a gentle stroke while Evergreen adjusted the stirrups. Within moments, Amelia had hoisted herself up into the saddle with ease. She looked right at home up there. She spent a few moments pulling the stirrups into the right position and getting comfortable and Evergreen wondered if she was nervous to be riding again after all this time. She was just about to offer to lead Thunder round the field for her when Amelia suddenly clicked Thunder on and they started walking. Within seconds they were trotting and, as they reached the top of the paddock and turned back, they broke into a canter.

Evergreen couldn't help smiling. Both Amelia and Thunder looked in their element. She never rode Thunder like this, she'd take him out for a walk sometimes, but she never cantered him or even trotted him. She never wanted to push him too much when he had been pulling the caravan for large parts of the week. But he looked like he was having the time of his life. And so did Amelia.

Everyone cheered behind Evergreen, clearly as surprised by this as she was.

Amelia effortlessly turned Thunder and cantered up and back down the field one more time before pulling the horse to a stop in front of them.

'Amelia, you looked magnificent,' Meadow said.

'That was the best thing I've done for a very long time,' Amelia said, then turned to Evergreen. 'Thank you for letting me have that.'

'It was my pleasure. Feel free to ride him anytime you want while I'm here, it was clear he loved it too.'

'I may take you up on that. Right, come on girls, I'm sure Evergreen is very busy and we need to let Thunder have a little rest. Why don't you help me paint some pine cones?'

The girls cheered and took Amelia's hands, dragging her off into the woods.

'Thank you for doing that,' Indigo said.

'Yes thank you, I can see that horse riding lessons might feature in Star's future,' Meadow said.

'Well at least if she does go horse riding, the horses will be considerably smaller than Thunder,' Evergreen said.

'That's true. Anyway, we better get back, we'll see you later for dinner.'

Indigo and Meadow walked off towards reception, leaving Evergreen alone with Heath.

'I don't think I've ever seen Amelia smile as much as she did when she was riding Thunder,' Heath said.

'She did love it, but then so did Thunder.'

He climbed through the fence. 'The girls loved it too. You have a way of making people smile.'

Evergreen didn't know what to do with that compliment so she tried to deflect it. 'Do you want a go too?'

Heath's eyes widened as he took in Thunder's huge frame. 'I've only ridden a horse once in my life and I fell off so it wasn't the hugely positive experience that Amelia clearly had.'

'You know, if you fall off the horse, you have to get straight back on,' Evergreen said.

He grinned. 'OK, I'll have a go if you ride with me.'

'I can do that.'

She swung herself back into the saddle, adjusted the stirrups again and then held out a hand to help Heath up. He hoisted himself up so he was sitting behind her and then there was the awkwardness of where to put his hands. She had never ridden a horse with a man before, especially not one she was insanely attracted to.

'You'll need to hold onto something, so we can move together, otherwise we'll be bouncing off each other,' Evergreen said.

There was a pause from Heath before he put his hands on her waist. Clearly neither of them had thought this through when he suggested it. The heat of his hands burned into her skin and it suddenly felt very intimate for him to be holding her in this way.

'Is this OK?' Heath asked.

'Yes that's fine,' Evergreen said, although her heart was now racing.

She encouraged Thunder to move forward and, as he started walking, Heath instinctively wrapped his hands around her stomach, holding her tighter.

'You won't fall,' Evergreen said.

'I know I won't, because I have you to protect me.'

She smiled at that but she couldn't ignore how wonderful it felt to have his hard, strong body pressed up against hers.

The walk around the field went by way too quickly for her liking but equally she was almost relieved that it was over. She didn't want anything to happen between her and Heath. She was quite happy being single without any complications of a relationship. She had to protect her heart and someone like Heath could shatter it.

'There you go, a nice safe walk,' Evergreen said.

Heath was silent for a moment before he cleared his throat. But when he spoke his voice was rough. 'I enjoyed that, thank you.'

It was clear he'd enjoyed it as much as she did.

He swung his leg over and slid down and she climbed down too so she was standing in front of him. He stared at her and she couldn't drag her eyes off him either. She was desperate for him to kiss her but fearful that he would.

Eventually she forced herself to take a step back, noticing Bear watching them from the reception doorway.

'I… erm… should probably take care of Thunder.'

Heath nodded. 'I have some things to take care of before dinner. I'll see you later.'

He took a step backwards, his eyes still on hers a moment longer before he spun and climbed back through the fence.

She watched him go for a moment before turning round to remove the saddle and bridle from Thunder, but when she glanced round Heath was watching her over his shoulder as he walked away.

CHAPTER TEN

Dinner with the Brookfields had been noisy and chaotic and utterly wonderful. Amelia had joined them too and the girls had sat up the other end of the table with her, where whatever she had been talking about had made them laugh a lot.

But that left Evergreen and Heath up the opposite end of the table and while they weren't alone it sometimes felt like they were, she was so hyperaware of his proximity.

'I hear you're going to be joining us for our Christmas Hullabaloo,' Meadow said, licking the ice cream off her spoon. It was her second helping but, as she reminded everyone, she was eating for two.

Evergreen cringed. She hadn't thought how everyone else would feel about her gatecrashing their family celebrations.

'I don't have to,' she said. 'It was just an idea. If you have a problem with it I…' She stalled when Heath put a hand on her arm.

'No one has a problem with it,' he said, firmly.

'Oh god no, it's totally fine,' Meadow said. 'If you're brave enough to want to endure it, we would love you to be a part of it. We like to make a big fuss of Christmas for the girls so we have all these silly events lined up. It's chaos and fun but the more the merrier.'

Evergreen smiled in relief. She hated the thought that she would be in the way. But Meadow was so genuinely warm and welcoming that Evergreen knew she didn't have a problem with it. 'Thank you, I'm looking forward to it.'

And actually she was. Since Heath had coerced her into agreeing, she had been looking forward to it. It had been a long time since she had been part of any family Christmas celebrations and she had missed it.

'I should go, I have to get up really early tomorrow to help with the Christmas preparations,' Evergreen said, being careful not to mention what she was doing to help in front of the girls.

'We'll be coming to breakfast with Father Christmas tomorrow,' Meadow said, encompassing the girls with a nod of the head. 'So we might see you there.'

'Oh, well, I won't be there,' Evergreen said, carefully. 'I just have to get everything ready before.'

Meadow smiled. 'Well, we'll probably see you at some point tomorrow.'

'Definitely. Thank you so much for letting me join you tonight.'

Heath stood up. 'I'll walk you back.'

She caught the slight exchange of glances between Meadow and Bear at this offer.

'I'm fine, stay here with your family.'

'It's OK, don't want you getting lost again,' Heath said.

'You might not be able to rely on the white stag to get you home next time.'

'You saw the white stag?' Bear said, sitting up in his seat.

'Yes, it was on the clifftops at the top of the woods,' Evergreen said.

'I've lived here most of my life and I've never seen him,' Bear said. 'But I know others have.'

'I haven't seen him either,' Meadow said. 'But there is supposed to be a legend attached to him for those lucky enough to see him.'

'Heath already told me,' Evergreen said. 'I'm not sure I believe it.'

'You'll see,' Heath said.

Evergreen smiled and rolled her eyes and then waved goodbye to everyone else.

They stepped outside and she fastened her cloak under her chin and then wrapped it tighter around her.

Outside the treehouses were lit up in all their Christmas splendour, some with multicoloured fairy lights twinkling in the darkness, some with lights of white or gold, some had garlands with red baubles, some with blue. It looked spectacular.

'I love looking at the Christmas lights,' Evergreen said. 'That was one of my favourite memories when I was a child, being driven round all the different houses to see how they had been decorated for the festive season. We always put a few lights up but some houses would really go to town with full-size reindeer or a full-size sleigh with Santa sitting in it. Seeing how all these treehouses are decorated differently reminds me of that.'

'We didn't want a uniform approach to the decorations.

Each treehouse is different so the decorations had to be different too,' Heath said.

'It works really well.'

They walked on in silence for a bit.

'Listen, you don't need to worry about not being welcome at the Hullabaloo,' Heath suddenly said. 'If it makes you feel uncomfortable then obviously I don't want you to suffer through anything you don't want to do, but they all love you so you'd be very welcome to join us.'

She looked at him. 'They all love me?'

'Well River likes the way you muck in and help everyone and that you talked Greta into selling her wreaths. The girls think you are cool and fun. Meadow and Indigo love how brilliant you are with the girls and you've definitely won Amelia over by letting her ride Thunder.'

She smiled at that.

'So you've met my crazy family, tell me about yours. You said you have a big one,' Heath said.

'Oh Heath, you and your brothers all seem lovely, I bet you had a very normal, happy upbringing. My life is very messy.'

Heath was silent for a moment and she remembered he'd told her he had terrible parents. Maybe his childhood hadn't been happy at all.

'If you don't want to talk about it, that's fine,' Heath said. 'But would it help if I told you more about my also very messy and not at all normal life first?'

She looked at him. 'Sorry, I shouldn't have assumed everything was rosy. You don't have to talk about it either if you don't want to.'

'It's OK, I don't mind talking about it. I find it quite

cathartic actually, realising how far I've come. My parents decided they didn't want to be parents any more when we were tiny children. River was eight, I was six and Bear was three. They just packed their bags and left. They divorced for a while but got back together years later and lived a life without us.'

She had an overwhelming desire to hold his hand while he told her his crappy life story. She knew what it was like to be abandoned by her parents. Before she could talk herself out of it, she reached out and took his hand and he entwined his fingers with hers as if it was the most natural thing in the world. 'I'm so sorry, that must have been so tough.'

'I'm not going to lie, it was. And it was something that took us a long time to get over. We were raised by a multitude of cousins, aunts and uncles and other distant relatives that would come for a few weeks of childcare and babysitting in return for free food and a place near the sea. I don't think any of them really wanted to be there.'

She knew what that felt like too, to be in the way, unwanted, unloved. She gave his hand a squeeze.

'When my parents died in a car accident years later, the authorities decided we needed something more official,' Heath said. 'My uncle Michael, my dad's twin brother, took us on here when it was no more than a camping site. I think he was quite happy to have us around, he built us a lodge for us to live in, he'd feed us, buy clothes for us, was always quite supportive of what we were doing at school and would take the time to listen and talk to us, but there was never any real love or affection there. Not because he didn't love us, but I think because he didn't know how to show it. He and my dad were given up for adoption by my grandmother Amelia. She was only fourteen when she fell pregnant and her parents forced her to give them up. She hoped they were going to a better life but by all accounts their childhood was pretty shitty. So because of that they were both crap at being parents themselves, well my dad more than Michael. My uncle didn't do a bad job of raising us, he just wasn't particularly affectionate. He died when I was fifteen and Amelia came over from Australia to look after us for a year until River was old enough to take care of us. So yeah, it hasn't always been a bed of roses.'

'God Heath, I'm so sorry. You all seem such lovely, normal people.'

'Well, thanks. Once Tierra and Star were born I think we all decided that we couldn't let our past impact on our future like our parents did. We knew we had to do a better job. We are a product of our pasts, of course we are, but we used that experience to make sure we were better people, that Star and Tierra never ever felt unloved or in the way, like we did.'

She nodded. 'That's a great attitude.'

'So… want to tell me yours?'

They'd reached Christmas Tree Cottage by then. 'It's a long one. Want to hear it over a mug of hot chocolate?'

He smiled. 'Absolutely.'

They climbed the steps and he lit the fire for her before following her into the kitchen as she set about making two hot chocolates.

'I was an only child so it was just the three of us in the beginning. My parents argued constantly, I remember that. One day, when I was around four, Dad came home and told Mum he was leaving her for another woman, Suki. Mum decided she wasn't to be outdone and practically moved some random guy in a week after he left. The divorce went through quite quickly and Mum and Blake got married straight after. He had no interest in having me around and therefore my mum didn't either.'

She heard her voice break as she spoke. She had never talked about this with anyone but retelling it now the pain of not being wanted by her own mum still hurt. She put the milk in the microwave to heat up and focussed on that so she wouldn't have to see Heath's face.

'I went to live with my dad's mum for a little while, but she lived in a tiny one-bedroom cottage so there really wasn't room for me. She was also quite frail, not really suited for looking after a hyperactive four-year-old, as much as she tried. So I went to live with my dad and Suki. I didn't like her at first, she was the reason my mum and dad split up, but Suki was always utterly lovely. She was hard not to like. She had a daughter, Celeste, a year older than me, who didn't want me around but we grew to tolerate each other. She also had a two-year-old daughter called Cally, who was my dad's, so evidently the affair had been going on for some time. I absolutely adored Cally. I'd always wanted a brother and sister and here was this chubby cute two-year-old half-sister, who I never knew existed. She was always toddling after me, big toothy grin, giggling at everything. I loved her. And for a while it was nice to be part of a normal family.'

She poured the hot milk into the mugs and mixed it in with the hot chocolate.

'Then when Cally was three and I was five or six, my

dad disappeared, just didn't come home one night. The shitbag that he was, he didn't even have the decency to tell Suki before he left. She was worried sick. He phoned her a few days later to tell her he had fallen in love with some woman from Canada and was starting a new life with her over there. I never saw him again but I heard from his mum that he has had three other wives over the years and five more children, none of which I've ever met. But he had never married Suki so I knew that, with my dad out the picture, there was no reason for Suki to let me stay with her any more. But in her mind there was never any question of kicking me out. She became a mum to me and I loved her with everything I had.'

Evergreen swallowed down the pain because now they were getting to the really hard part.

'She met a man, Rob, who she married and went on to have three more children with. Me and Rob never really got on, but he tolerated me for the sake of Suki who he absolutely adored. And there were now six children living in the house so he always had his hands full with his own kids and Cally, too busy to worry about me and Celeste. I loved being part of a big family though, having brothers and sisters to play and talk with.'

Evergreen carried the two mugs into the lounge and placed them on the wooden coffee table in front of the sofa before sitting, curling her legs up to her chest as she stared at the flames dancing inside the log burner. Heath sat down next to her as he watched her, listening carefully.

'Suki was always very supportive of my dreams and I was set to go off to university to study drama and stage production. We were in the car one day, we'd just gone shopping for all the things I'd need to move into student accommodation a few weeks later. It was just me and her, I was driving as I'd just passed my test the week before and wanted to get experience behind the wheel and… and a lorry ploughed into the side of us and… she didn't make it.'

'Jesus Christ, Evergreen, I'm so sorry,' Heath said, immediately pulling her into a hug.

She blinked in surprise at the gesture. Heath's hugs were so protective and safe and it had been a long time since she'd been held like this. In fact, the last person to hug her like this was Suki and that brought tears to her eyes. She quickly wiped them away, she hadn't cried over Suki for years, she'd buried her feelings deep so they couldn't escape. She closed her eyes for a moment and relaxed into the hug, leaning her head against his chest. It was ridiculous to need something she hadn't even known she wanted a few moments before. They were silent for a while, there was no need for any words. Although the story wasn't quite finished and, now she'd opened this huge can of worms, she felt the need to tell the rest. She stayed where she was though, wrapped in his arms.

'There was barely a scratch on me. I cut my head here,' she pointed at her temple. 'I had terrible whiplash, but I was absolutely fine, at least physically. It was a big, complicated mess after the accident. Rob blamed me entirely. In fact they all did. I blamed myself too, despite knowing it wasn't my fault, I've always been such a careful driver. But I've always felt I could have done more to stop it. Rob told me it should have been me that died and if I hadn't insisted on driving, I would have been in the passenger seat and it would have been me that was killed that day. He never forgave me for that. Anyway, Rob kicked me out pretty much as soon as I got home from the hospital that night, he didn't want anything to do with me, none of my brothers and sisters did. That's what he said. I mean, the three youngest kids, Noah, Oliver and Lucy were ten, seven and six so they didn't really understand why Mummy wasn't coming home, other than what Rob told them, but I expected more from Celeste and Cally. Celeste was nineteen, she would have known it wasn't my fault. And me and Cally had always been so close growing up. She was sixteen when Suki died. I lost my entire family overnight.'

She chewed her lip as she relived that pain of nobody wanting her and everyone hating her.

'The investigation and court case, many months later, found the lorry driver guilty. He had failed to stop at a red light and tore through when my green light had been on for some time. The police and the CPS found him guilty of causing death by careless driving and he went to prison for two years. I was there at the hearing, as were Rob and Celeste, and I thought after, once they'd heard all the details and the driver had been found guilty, that they would change their mind, apologise, take me back, but they wouldn't even look at me. I haven't seen any of them since.'

'Evergreen, this is the saddest story I've ever heard.'

She looked up at him and smiled sadly. 'Yeah, sorry about that.'

He studied her, sweeping a hair gently from her face. 'You have nothing to apologise for.'

She only wished her family felt the same.

'I sent birthday and Christmas cards to the other children for a while, especially to Cally, but I never heard from her or the others. Maybe they still hated me like Rob and Celeste. I don't even know if they got them or whether Rob just destroyed them. Cally would be twenty-five now and I think about her often. Is she married, does she have children of her own, did she end up working in a zoo which was always her dream? I know the whole family moved house about a year or so after Suki died but I have no idea where they went, so I couldn't contact them even if I wanted to.'

'What happened then, where did you go once you were kicked out?' Heath asked.

'I had nowhere to go. My dad's mum had died a few months before and left me a little bit of money, so I stayed in a B&B for a few weeks until university started and then I moved into student accommodation as planned. I should have deferred the course, I was an emotional wreck, but a tiny part of me knew that Suki wanted me to do the course, she wouldn't have wanted me to miss out, so I did it for her. I was an absolute mess. That's why I ended up throwing myself into the behind-the-scenes stuff, the make-up and special effects, because I couldn't possibly stand up in front of people and perform. For everyone else in student accommodation I was the angry angsty girl who cried a lot. As you can imagine, I didn't make a lot of friends. Over the holidays, all the other students would go home to their families but I didn't have anyone to go home to. Once university was over I didn't feel like I could settle down, live in one place, I wanted to keep moving. Besides, working in the make-up industry, most jobs are freelance and, without a steady income, landlords or mortgage companies are just not interested. So I used the rest of the money my gran left me to buy Thunder and the caravan and it's just been me and him ever since.'

Heath was watching her, his eyes filled with concern.

She let out a little laugh. 'I bet you wish you'd never asked now.'

'No, I'm glad I got to know more about you, and you felt you could share it with me. I am so sorry you went through that. None of it was your fault and I think you're an incredible woman to have survived all that and still be lovely and normal.'

She smiled that he was using her own words against her.

He stroked her hair from her face again. 'I hate that you've been alone all these years.'

She stared at him and he stared right back, not taking his eyes from her face. She felt like he got her more than anyone else ever had. If anyone understood shitty childhoods it was him. His eyes scanned down to her lips and she suddenly had an overwhelming desire to kiss him.

She sat up and grabbed her hot chocolate, focussing on the creamy foam on the top. 'I prefer it that way.'

He picked up his own drink and they sat in silence for a while, although it was not quite as companionable as it had been before.

He finished his hot chocolate and put it down. 'I should go. I want to read with Star before she goes to bed. What time do you want me tomorrow morning?'

'I'll be up around five thirty to do myself before you come, so come round anytime after that. I'll make some chocolate and cinnamon French toast we can snack on while we're getting ready.'

He smiled. 'I'll definitely be here for that.'

He stood up and she followed him to the door. He opened it, letting in a cold gust of wind, and she snagged his arm.

'Thank you. For listening and being there.'

'Anytime. I'm glad you're here, Evergreen Winters.'

She stared at him, swallowing the lump in her throat. 'I am too. And thank you for the hug, I really needed that.'

He smiled then bent his head and kissed her on the cheek, just briefly but it was enough to burn her skin with his touch. Long after he had gone and she'd got changed into her pyjamas and was lying in bed, she could still feel his lips on her face.

CHAPTER ELEVEN

Heath walked through the wood the next morning admiring the sparkly frost that blanketed every surface like glitter. The sun wouldn't rise for hours yet but the Christmas lights on the other trees and treehouses twinkled in the darkness, and the lanterns that lit up the pathways sent puddles of gold across the crunchy white ground.

He thought about what Evergreen had told him the night before and his heart hurt just thinking about it. She had been broken by her past, he could see that. They had both been let down by their parents but Evergreen seemed to have taken a battering all her life, first her dad leaving, then her mum kicking her out, then her dad leaving a second time, then Rob, her sort of stepdad of ten or more years, saying he wished she had died instead of Suki. That was a disgusting thing to say to anyone, let alone an eighteen-year-old. The emotional trauma of being in the accident in which Suki had died was bad enough but to then come home from the hospital and be kicked out of her family home was just horrible. It was no wonder she preferred to travel, never putting down roots anywhere, because she couldn't trust in anyone not to betray her again.

He sighed, he wanted to help her but he didn't know how. After his parents had left when he was six, he had grown up feeling unloved and unwanted. The difference between where he was now and where Evergreen was, emotionally, was that he had something worth fighting for, first with Star and then with the Wishing Wood treehouse resort. He also had Bear, River and Meadow, while Evergreen had no one. He could have quite easily gone down a different path. When Star was born, he immediately knew he had to let go of the bitterness of the past and give his daughter a better life than the one he'd had. There was nothing in Evergreen's life that was making her want to let go of the past and fight for her future. And even if she did have something, the damage was so severe he wasn't sure she ever could.

He climbed the steps to Christmas Tree Cottage and knocked on the door. He heard shuffling inside and then took a step back as a wizened old woman answered the door.

Had Evergreen's friend Daisy turned up after all? Did that mean that Evergreen would be leaving? He couldn't help the feeling of disappointment that slammed into his stomach at the thought.

'Come in,' the old woman wheezed, beckoning him in like an evil witch. And then he caught the glint of amusement in her eyes.

'Shit, Evergreen, you really had me going then for a second, this looks amazing.'

Evergreen laughed, standing up straight from her hunched position. 'I thought you'd see right through it.'

'In my defence, I was fast asleep fifteen minutes ago.'

'Well, you can go back to sleep if you want, I only need your face, not your charming banter.'

'Well too bad for you, you've got both.'

She smiled. 'I think I'm going to enjoy making you over every day.'

'I'm going to enjoy it too.'

He sat down in the chair and she started work, first with the prosthetic eye bags as she'd done before.

'So how does it work with your job and Thunder? Do you get a make-up gig and spend two weeks getting there with Thunder taking you through the tiny back roads, and then park him outside the film studios for the day, while you nip in to turn someone into a zombie or something?'

Evergreen laughed as she worked on his face. 'Generally I'll get at least a few weeks' notice and I'll travel slowly up to the film location, taking lots of rest and only going relatively short distances each day. I stay at campsites on a farm so there is somewhere I can put Thunder while I travel to the set. I'm friendly with several different farmers and stable owners around the country and because he's a Clydesdale, which are becoming increasingly rare, he's always a bit of a novelty when I turn up with him so they're happy to have him. I tend to get a lot of work in the same areas because the make-up work I do will be for films or big TV productions so generally those are filmed in and around studios. Cardiff has some great film studios and

I've worked on a lot of *Doctor Who* programmes there and several other shows and films. London has a load of studios too, Shepperton, Leavesden, Elstree and Pinewood and many others, so most of my time is travelling back and forth between Cardiff and London. Sometimes I'll get offered gigs in Scotland but, as you've quite rightly pointed out, it takes me a long time to get up there. If it's only a one- or two-day job, say in London or Manchester or Edinburgh, I tend to leave Thunder on a farm near Cardiff and get the train to the set as it's not worth taking him all that way. I'll only take him if it's a few weeks' work.'

'If you get a lot of work around Cardiff, do you not ever think about getting your own place around there?' Heath asked as she started applying the latex.

She was silent for a moment and he wasn't sure if it was the question or a tricky bit of make-up. 'I love my little caravan, I love sitting in my chair with the fire flickering in the log burner with a mug of hot chocolate as I look out on the sea or the countryside. I love cooking my dinner on my tiny stove and waking up somewhere different. I love that the space is mine and mine alone. I very rarely have other people in there, it's my own little haven.'

'You don't ever have boyfriends in there?'

She shook her head. 'There have been a few men over the years but I've never brought them back to my caravan. It would feel weird to have someone else in my space. Well, for more than a coffee.'

He nodded. 'I can totally understand that. I've been with a few women but I've never slept with them in my tree-house. I think part of that is not wanting to bring anyone into my world with Star, I like keeping it separate. But I think I feel the same as you, that the treehouse is my home, my space, and it would take someone really special to want to bring them there.'

'I like that you understand. I had one guy I was sort of seeing who was quite insistent that we had sex in my caravan, mainly because he loved the idea of making it rock, like in some kind of saucy *Carry On* film.'

He laughed.

'Needless to say we never got that far in our relationship to make anywhere rock, least of all my caravan. But I do have to ask, you're seeing Scarlet tomorrow, how do you think she would react if you told her you didn't want her in your house?'

'Not well, but if it was someone I was serious about then it wouldn't feel wrong or weird making love to them in my bed, waking up and having them there in my home, it would just feel right. I've never had a serious relationship in my life so I've never found that someone I'd be happy sharing my space with.'

'Apart from Meadow.'

'Meadow was different. I've known her all my life. We never had any kind of real romantic relationship, not even in the beginning, so I can't count her as a serious relationship, but she was and still is my best friend so we fitted together really well in those early days after Star was born. We built the treehouse for the three of us, so it was always ours, rather than mine. My treehouse was built a few years later when we decided to live separately but still together. But I feel like you've sidestepped my question about getting your own place one day.'

'I wouldn't say sidestepped,' Evergreen said, flashing

him a smile which made him believe she'd deliberately steered the conversation away.

'I can see how living in a caravan could be fun, freeing, but does where you live make you happy or do you want something more?'

She flicked on the hairdryer to dry the layer of latex around his eyes and he knew she was playing for time. She switched it off and started powdering around his eye.

'Staying here for the last two nights was wonderful, having my own bathroom, my own proper kitchen, I haven't had that since… well since I was living with Suki and Rob. And I never had my own space even then, living in a house with two adults and five other children. And as you've already seen, the caravan comes with multiple problems which I don't have the skill or money to fix. Living in a caravan never feels totally safe either, some people are very against the travelling community so sometimes I get a bit of abuse. Others see me as a novelty and I get it, there's not many of us that do what I do. People knock on my door and want palm readings or tarot cards and I don't do any of that. And then there's the risk of being a woman spending the night alone in some deserted areas, sometimes you find yourself sleeping with one eye open, so to speak.'

Heath frowned, he hated the thought of her getting abuse or harassed or that she didn't always feel safe where she slept.

'Oi, no frowning, I have to stretch your skin to apply the latex, frowning makes it really difficult. You don't need to worry about me. I used to do judo when I was younger, I think I could take care of myself to a certain extent if anyone ever did try anything.'

Heath smiled. 'Of that I have no doubt.'

'But for the last two nights I've slept better than I have for a long time, I felt… safe. I woke up this morning and it was silent. I wandered around with my mug of coffee and just enjoyed all this space. I do sometimes think it would be wonderful to have my own place but…' she trailed off.

'Is it money?'

'Well, that's part of it, being able to afford a regular rent or mortgage and all the other household bills. Some months I do great, some months not so much. But I suppose mostly it's a fear of putting down roots. I've had three homes in my life, one with my mum and dad, one with my grandmother, one with Suki, and they were all taken away from me. No one can take my caravan away, it feels safer to put my trust in that than a landlord who can kick me out whenever he wants. Having a real home means settling down and putting my trust in people too, neighbours, friends, maybe even boyfriends, and I don't know if I'm ready for all that.'

His heart ached for her. 'You've been let down so spectacularly over the years and I totally get trying to protect yourself from getting hurt again.'

She moved back to look at him. 'You've had it as bad as me.'

'You had it a lot worse than me and I always had my brothers who had my back, we were in it together, you had no one, you still have no one. But I do wonder if a real home might give you the stability you need to move on from your crappy past.'

She didn't say anything for the longest time and he wondered if she was thinking about what he'd said.

She shrugged. 'Well, as nice as that sounds, I don't think a free house is going to fall from the sky like Dorothy's house in *The Wizard of Oz*. I'd need money for that and, unless I give up what I love for some boring nine-to-five job, I can't see I'd ever have enough money to get my own place. Plus who would hire me? I have no references and I have five years of making people into zombies and monsters under my belt, those are hardly transferable skills for, say, working in a bank.'

He nodded to concede this. 'True but—' he stalled as she held his mouth shut so she could apply some latex around his top lip and the bottom of his cheek.

'Heath, I love being a make-up artist, it's my passion, I never want to lose that. And I can see you want to fix me, patch me up and send me out into the world as a new woman, but some things can't be mended. There is no bandage or medicine that can fix this mess, though I do appreciate you trying. Now I need you to keep your mouth still for a while so no talking.'

He sat back in his chair and let her do her work. She was right that he wanted to help her. That's what he did. He'd always helped people whenever he could. But even though this was going to be a lot harder than he'd thought, he wasn't going to give up that easily.

CHAPTER TWELVE

Evergreen picked a few stray strands of fake hair off Heath's Father Christmas jacket as he fastened up the buttons, inspecting his make-up for any flaws as she did. She was rather pleased with how it had turned out. He was wearing a small fake fat belly strapped around his waist but it did nothing to disguise his huge muscular frame, though there wasn't a lot she could do about that. She pulled the hat on very carefully and straightened the wig and fluffed out his beard.

Suddenly there was a knock on the door and Evergreen turned round to see Indigo leaning on the door frame, her eyes flicking between them in delight as if she had walked in on something romantic, when nothing could be further from the truth.

'Sorry to interrupt,' Indigo said, a big grin on her face. 'The families will be here soon so Lindsay will be bringing them up at nine. I just wanted to go over a few things with you. We'd like you to know the children by name and a few things about them so the magic of Santa seems more real.

Obviously Star will be here with Meadow and Bear, and me and River will be bringing Tierra for breakfast. There are two other families coming too. The Nicholls have two children, this is Persia and Atlanta,' she continued, showing them photos of two little girls on her tablet. 'Persia is five and Atlanta is six. Atlanta had her birthday on Monday, they went ice skating and then to see a pantomime after. They have a pet dog called Princess Fluffybum and two goldfish called Ant and Dec. Persia loves painting, Atlanta loves climbing trees. The Collins family have a little boy called Chase, he is also five years old. He is obsessed with Lego and Star Wars. They have a house bunny called Darth and a cat called Vader.'

'OK, got it,' Evergreen said, trying to commit all of that to memory.

Heath nodded, biting his lips nervously. 'OK. I'll try my best but you do realise I'm not a professional Santa?'

'You're going to be amazing,' Evergreen said.

'The kids are not looking for professional, they just want to see a big jolly man in a red suit,' Indigo said. 'As for the rest, I'm sure you can improvise. Alex will be here shortly with all the breakfast things,' she went on. 'The plan is that you will greet the families and then we will all have breakfast together. You can chat to the different children throughout breakfast and at the end you can encourage them to write a Christmas wish and hang it on the Christmas tree and give them one of these presents.' Indigo indicated the big sack of presents she had brought with her. 'We've technically only got an hour but you can run over a little. You'll have a few hours off after breakfast before the afternoon sessions start. They'll be much less informal as people aren't booking but coming on an ad hoc basis.'

Heath nodded. 'OK, now listen, I'm going to have to put on some kind of accent or different voice so Tierra and Star don't recognise me. I need you to tell Bear and River not to laugh, and that goes for you and Meadow too.'

Indigo grinned. 'I'll do my best.' There was a noise outside and she looked down the steps. 'Oh Alex is here, it looks like she's brought enough to feed an army, let alone seventeen people.'

Heath grinned. 'She always does, let me go and give her a hand.'

They all went downstairs and started humping boxes and bags back up into the cottage.

'There's croissants, pains au chocolat, fruit, pancakes, waffles. Maybe we can put some of these things in the oven to keep them warm until the kids arrive,' Alex said, unloading some of her wares onto the long dining table.

'That's no problem, let me put the oven on,' Heath said.

Alex did a little double-take. 'Oh my god, Heath is that you?'

Evergreen felt enormously proud that someone Heath knew didn't recognise him.

'Yeah hi,' Heath said. 'And this is Evergreen, our Mrs Christmas. She looks decidedly more beautiful in real life too.'

Evergreen smiled and shook Alex's hand. 'Hi.'

'You both look amazing, I didn't even realise it was make-up, I just thought you were genuinely two elderly people.'

'Evergreen did the make-up,' Heath said, proudly, as he

flicked the oven on and came back to collect some of the things that needed to be kept warm. 'She does the make-up for lots of film and TV programmes. She's so super talented, you should see some of the photos of the make-up she's done before, she's even worked on *Doctor Who*.'

Evergreen found herself grateful that the large amount of make-up she was wearing hid her blushes. No one had ever sung her praises before, she wasn't quite sure how to handle the compliment.

'Well, it looks incredible. Right, I better get back to the restaurant. Just those three trays there need to go in the oven, the rest can be unpacked and put on the table.'

Alex gave them a wave and left.

'I better go so I can bring Tierra up with the other families. And by the way, Amelia is coming too. Good luck,' Indigo said with a smirk before following Alex out and leaving them alone.

'Why would we need good luck with Amelia?' Evergreen said.

'Because she saw us leave together last night and now has it in her head that something is going on between us. If she gets any sniff at all of anything between us, or even the potential of something happening, she will be all over you like a hot rash.'

'In a good way or a bad way?'

'There is nothing good about a hot rash.'

Evergreen laughed. 'I meant, will she try to stop it or encourage it?'

'Oh encourage it for sure. She's been desperate to see all three of us happily married off for as long as I can remember. Bear and River got married in the autumn so now all of her attention is on me. She has tried to set me up with multiple women in the last few months: granddaughters of friends, the receptionist at our local doctor's, even random strangers. I'm pretty sure she'll be pushing us together, quite forcibly.'

'I'm sure I can handle a little old lady.'

'She's a force to be reckoned with. And don't let her catch you calling her that.'

Evergreen smiled, wondering how bad it could really be.

They spent a few moments unpacking the food and putting some of it in the oven.

'Thank you for the, erm… nice things you said about me,' Evergreen said, awkwardly.

Heath shrugged. 'It's true. I've seen the photos, you have an extraordinary talent.'

'Well, thanks.'

'So how do you want to play this? Touching or not?'

She frowned in confusion. 'What do you mean?'

'Well, you're supposed to be my wife, should we hold hands, shall I put my arm around you? If you prefer I didn't then of course I won't, but I wonder if we should to make it more realistic. Or do you think the kids won't care about that, they'll just be interested in the presents and the food?'

'Oh I see. I don't think the kids will care about us portraying a realistic couple, but if the occasion calls for it, we can absolutely hold hands or hug. It's probably not appropriate to have a kiss with tongues or have hot sex on the dining room table though.'

Heath grinned. 'I'll try to rein it in.'

Just then there was a knock on the door. Evergreen

turned round to see a woman with wild red curly hair dressed as an elf, complete with red and white stripy socks and green shoes with bells on the ends of curly points. Even the oversized pointy green hat had a bell on too.

Heath let out a laugh.

'Don't start with me, Heath Brookfield,' the woman said in a soft Scottish accent. 'I look utterly ridiculous and I jingle every time I move.' She did a few steps to prove it, jingling as she walked.

'You look amazing,' Heath said. 'Lindsay, this is Evergreen, our Mrs Christmas for the next six days and make-up artist extraordinaire. Evergreen, this is Lindsay McGhie, our resident elf, receptionist, kitchen assistant, cleaner.'

'General dogsbody,' Lindsay said. 'Jack of all trades, master of none.'

'Nice to meet you,' Evergreen said. 'And I think you look great, plus the kids will love it.'

Lindsay grunted her disapproval. 'Well, I'm only doing it for them. No one mentioned making a tit of myself when I started work here.'

'Part and parcel, I'm afraid,' Heath said.

Lindsay rolled her eyes. 'You guys look great, very festive, and the make-up is brilliant.'

'Thank you,' Evergreen said.

'Are you ready, shall I bring the little urchins up?'

'Yes,' Heath said. 'I'm going to have to put a voice on so Star and Tierra don't recognise me. Don't laugh, OK?'

Lindsay gave a mischievous grin. 'I'm not going to make any promises there.'

'I was going to try a Scottish accent.'

Her eyes widened in horror. 'If you even attempt a Scottish accent, you can guarantee me taking the piss.'

Heath laughed. 'Fair enough.'

'I'll go and get them.' Lindsay turned and jingled her way out of the cottage.

'Just go deep, Santa always has a deep jolly voice in the films I've seen,' Evergreen said. 'Practise some ho, ho, hos.'

Heath cleared his throat and put on a rich, deep voice. 'Ho, ho, ho!'

'Perfect, and again.'

'Ho, ho, ho.'

'That's great, now all you have to do is maintain that deep voice for the next hour.'

'Crap.'

'Yeah, good luck with it.'

Suddenly there was the thunder of little feet as two girls burst into the cottage, followed quickly by two out-of-breath parents.

'Ho, ho, ho,' Heath said. 'Hello Persia, hello Atlanta, welcome to my home.'

Evergreen couldn't help smirking as he knelt down to meet them and Persia threw her arms around him and gave him a big hug, then Atlanta joined the group hug too.

Heath wrapped them both in his arms and then stood back up, taking their hands and leading them to the table. 'And Atlanta, I need to say happy birthday for last week too. Did you have fun at the pantomime?'

Evergreen watched as the girls stared at him in wonder.

'How did you know that?' Persia said.

'Ah, I know lots of things.'

'The pantomime was fun, wasn't it girls?' said their mum.

'It was, they threw out sweets from the stage and I caught one,' Atlanta said.

Evergreen smiled that after weeks of rehearsing, stage-building and getting beautiful costumes made, the high-light of the panto for Atlanta was that she caught a ten-pence sweet when it was thrown from the stage.

'Did Princess Fluffybum come with you to the panto?' Evergreen asked.

Persia giggled. 'No, silly, they don't allow dogs at the theatre.'

'What about Ant and Dec?' Heath asked.

Atlanta laughed. 'They don't allow fish either.'

'Oh that's a shame, I'm sure Princess Fluffybum and Ant and Dec would have enjoyed the panto,' he said. 'Why don't you all take a seat here and help yourself to any food while we go and greet the next guests, and then we'll all have breakfast together.'

The family sat down and Heath went over to the door to meet Chase and his family. Evergreen crossed to the oven and brought out the plates and trays of pancakes and waffles and carried them over to the table. 'These plates are hot so be careful,' she said.

She glanced over at the door to see that Chase was bubbling over with so much excitement he looked ready to explode. She smiled at how something as simple as meeting Father Christmas could be so utterly magical for the children.

Heath was patiently listening as Chase talked to him about seeing a fox in the woods the night before, as evidently Chase's family were staying in one of the tree-houses for the weekend.

Heath took Chase's hand and walked him to the table while he talked to him about *Star Wars*. It was just a pleasure to watch someone so completely at ease with children and with being so on display.

The door opened again, with Tierra and Star holding hands with Lindsay at the front and River, Indigo, Bear and Meadow bringing up the rear. Behind them was Amelia.

'Hello, welcome to our home,' Evergreen said and then regretted saying that. As they lived here they would know that Father Christmas and Mrs Christmas didn't stay here permanently. Although Tierra didn't seem to notice.

'Hello,' Tierra said, shaking her hand firmly.

'Hello Tierra.'

The little girl's eyes widened. 'How do you know my name?'

'We know lots of things,' Evergreen said, mysteriously. 'I know you live in a treehouse, I know you are one of the sheep in the school nativity and also that you love making crafty things,' she added, listing some of the things she had learned the night before at dinner.

Tierra's face lit up in wonder just as Heath walked over.

'Ho, ho, ho,' Heath said, really hamming it up. 'This must be Tierra and Star.'

Evergreen watched Star carefully. Heath's make-up was good, she knew that, but was it good enough to convince his own daughter?

Star shook Heath's hand, studying him closely.

'How's that beautiful dog of yours, Star?' Heath asked. 'I

hope you'll tell Hero not to bite me when I come into your house on Christmas Eve.'

'He doesn't bite,' Star said. 'He's a big softy. If you stroke him under his chin he loves that.'

'I'll remember that,' Heath said. 'And Tierra, how's that gorgeous baby brother of yours?'

As they moved further into the room, Evergreen noticed River was carrying Alfie in a car seat, and he was still fast asleep just as he had been the night before.

'He just sleeps all the time,' Tierra said, grumpily. 'I thought we could play together but Daddy says we have to wait until he's a tiny bit older.'

'Yeah, babies are a bit boring,' Heath agreed. 'But he'll be running around soon enough. Shall we go and have breakfast?'

He took the girls' hands and led them over to the table. Star couldn't take her eyes off Heath, and Evergreen suspected she totally knew who Father Christmas really was.

Evergreen watched Amelia remove her purple velvet coat and hang it up and then fluff out her hair as she glanced over at Father Christmas.

'You guys look great,' Meadow said quietly to Evergreen as they walked past to take their places at the table.

'Thank you,' Evergreen said.

'How long is he going to be able to keep that fake voice going though?' River said.

'I don't know, hopefully the whole hour,' Evergreen said.

'He sounds like he's channelling Barry White,' Bear muttered.

Evergreen snorted.

'Do you think the girls will notice?' Indigo said.

'I don't think Tierra has noticed anything yet but Star definitely suspects something,' Evergreen said.

'She's so smart, nothing gets past her,' Bear said.

They all went to their seats and Evergreen smiled. They were such a close-knit family and she felt a pang that she didn't have anything like that.

Amelia moved forward to greet Evergreen.

'And is there anything you want for Christmas?' Evergreen asked.

'I wouldn't mind a hottie like that under my Christmas tree,' Amelia said, eyeing Heath.

Evergreen snorted so loudly everyone in the room turned to look at her. She quickly turned it into a cough. Clearly no one had told Amelia that Heath would be playing Santa today.

Heath gave a 'Ho, ho, ho' and everyone turned their attention back to him.

'I really don't think you would,' Evergreen said, quietly.

Amelia stared at her in confusion.

Evergreen leaned closer to whisper in Amelia's ear. 'That hottie is your grandson.'

Amelia looked horrified. 'Ewww, oh god, no.' She gave a shudder for good measure. 'Why did no one warn me? I didn't realise it was make-up. God, I'll never hear the last of it if they find out.'

'Your secret is safe with me,' Evergreen said.

Amelia studied her more closely. 'Evergreen?'

Evergreen nodded.

'I saw you two getting cosy last night and, when Heath

walked you home, he was a very long time. Is there something going on between you two?'

She smiled. 'No there isn't. We just had hot chocolate and chatted about how we are going to handle today.'

'Are you single?' Amelia asked, clearly not to be deterred.

'Single but absolutely not looking for love.'

'Hmm,' Amelia said, disapprovingly. 'We'll see about that.'

With that, she swept off to sit with her family and Evergreen couldn't help thinking that woman was going to be trouble.

CHAPTER THIRTEEN

'Time to say goodbye to Father Christmas,' Lindsay said, after the breakfast was finished and all the children had received a small gift and left a wish on the Christmas tree. Evergreen smiled. She was obviously sticking to the hour time limit religiously.

The parents all gathered their children and after some high fives and waves they left, the Brookfield family being the last to depart.

Heath let out a sigh of relief as the door closed. 'I think we pulled that off and at least I won't have to do that stupid voice again for any of the other children. Do you think Tierra and Star suspected anything?'

'I don't think Tierra did, I'm not sure Star was a hundred percent convinced.'

Just then the door burst open again and Star came running back in. She went straight up to Heath and gave him a big hug. 'I love you Daddy.'

Heath smiled and knelt down to return the hug, holding his daughter tight. 'I love you too munchkin, so so much.'

Star pulled back and grinned at Evergreen. 'Great make-up. See you later, Dad.'

She ran out just as Meadow stepped back in. 'Just had word that there's a small leak in the roof of Oak Tree Cottage, can you give River a hand fixing it?'

'Oh crap,' Heath said. 'I'll be there in five minutes.' Meadow left and he turned to Evergreen. 'Can you help me out of this stuff?'

'I can get you out the costume and the facial hair, but the rest will need to stay. It will take too long to put it back on before this afternoon.'

'That's fine. I just don't want to damage the clothes or the hair.'

He moved into her bedroom and started stripping off. She tried really hard not to stare at him but he had the most incredible body.

He pulled on his jeans and jumper, which hugged the muscles in his legs and arms perfectly.

'Come and sit down here when you're ready and I'll get the hair off you,' Evergreen said, hovering in the lounge.

He sat down and she set about very carefully removing the wig and facial hair, cleaning them and putting them back in their boxes or bags. 'OK, you're free to go.'

He moved to the door, pulling on his coat, and she followed him. He stepped outside. 'Don't work too hard.'

He laughed.

'I mean it, try not to do anything that will make you sweat or half your face might fall off.'

'That won't be a good look for the children.'

'No, quite,' Evergreen said.

He set off at a run and then quickly changed it to a fast

walk and she laughed. She noticed Meadow was still hanging around on the decking watching her.

'Why don't you come and join us for a coffee,' Meadow said. 'And then we'll make you both an early lunch before you have to get back. Star wants to try her hand at making chocolate gingerbread men so you can be the guinea pig. And she already knows you're Mrs Christmas so you can come over in your make-up.'

'Sounds good to me,' Evergreen said. 'I'll just get changed.'

Her fake hair was already tied back in a bun so it was out the way but she certainly didn't want the clothes to get wet or muddy. She quickly changed into one of her dresses and joined Meadow back out on the decking.

They walked down the steps together.

'Heath said you live in the caravan you arrived in, that must be cool.'

'It can be a lot of fun, it can also be draughty and damp, but it's home.'

'And is there a Mr Winters who lives with you? I could imagine that would get a bit cramped.'

Evergreen smirked. Was this Meadow's way of finding out if she was single rather than brazenly coming out with it like Amelia had?

'There is no Mr Winters,' Evergreen said, obtusely not giving anything else away.

'A Mrs Winters?'

'No.' Evergreen decided to put her out of her misery. 'No boyfriend either. I don't really hang around long enough to have relationships. I don't have designs on your ex-husband if that's why you're asking.'

'Well, I don't have a problem if you do. He needs someone smart and brilliant like you to keep him on his toes.'

Evergreen smiled. 'Thanks for that but he's kind of seeing someone, isn't he?'

'Oh I don't think Scarlet is going to give him his happy ever after. They had a great weekend of… instant attraction, I don't think it was anything more than that.'

'He seems to think it was.'

'I don't think Heath has ever been in love, he's never even had a serious relationship.'

'Apart from with you.'

'We were never in a relationship and we definitely weren't in love. I don't think he's ever experienced falling in love. He was nineteen when we got married so he never really had a chance to meet someone, build a relationship with them, fall in love. I was pushing him to date other women and he did but it was always casual flings because he never wanted any woman to interfere with his life with Star. He and Scarlet had this incredible weekend and he was gutted when she ran away because he wanted to get to know her more but, beyond their bedroom antics, I don't think they really talked about anything. I don't really think they have a lot to build on and I think in his heart he knows that too. River and Indigo had this wonderful one-night stand and she turned up two months later, pregnant with his child, and they really did fall head over heels in love with each other. I think Heath is looking at them and thinking he wants what they have and that maybe Scarlet is the one to give it to him.'

'But you don't.'

'I don't know. If this is his big love story I'll be delighted, but my gut says it isn't.'

'Well, even if it isn't, I don't think I'll be his big love story either. Being in a relationship requires trust and I'm not good with that.'

'I'm not going to say any more about this. I know what it's like to be on the receiving end of people interfering with my relationship. But if there is one man in this world that you can trust, it's Heath Brookfield.'

Evergreen followed Meadow up the steps to Wisteria Cottage. Heath seemed like a decent guy but it would take a hell of a lot more than a recommendation from his ex-wife for Evergreen to hand over her heart.

Heath walked back towards Wisteria Cottage with River after fixing the leak. He'd been thinking a lot about Evergreen and her living situation. What she'd said the day before when they'd been standing in her caravan looking at all the damage had stuck in his mind.

'It's not like I can stay in Christmas Tree Cottage for the rest of my life.'

And this morning, while she'd been doing his make-up, she'd talked about all the downsides of living in the caravan and how much she was enjoying staying in the cottage. He'd known then that he had to do something.

They walked into Wisteria Tree Cottage to find Bear making cakes in the kitchen with Tierra, and Indigo and Meadow sitting chatting on the sofa. Hero, their dog, wandered over to greet him, wagging his tail. Heath stroked his head.

'Hey, did you fix the roof OK?' Indigo asked.

'Yes no problem.' He looked around. 'Where's Star?'

'She's playing on the Xbox with Evergreen.' Meadow gestured with her head to his house.

'Oh, we better go and rescue Evergreen in a minute, Star will force her to play that racing game for hours.'

'I've been over twice, Evergreen seems to be having a great time.'

Heath smiled, although he was sure Evergreen was only being polite to his daughter.

'Listen, as we're all here, I wanted to ask you all a favour,' he said.

Bear moved further into the lounge and River sat down next to Indigo, stroking Alfie's head and kissing his wife.

'Whatever it is, it's a yes,' River said, simply.

Heath smiled and looked around at his family and they were all nodding. 'You don't know what it is yet.'

'It doesn't matter,' River said. 'Do you need money? Most of the profits are tied up in the company account but that's not a problem.'

'It's not money.'

'Are you OK?' Meadow said.

'Yes I'm fine.' Heath sat down.

'Look, whatever you need, we'll do it,' Bear said.

'OK, I'd like you to not rent out Christmas Tree Cottage next year.'

River shrugged. 'Done.'

Bear nodded. 'Fine by me.'

'I've not even told you why yet,' Heath said.

'You wouldn't ask if it wasn't important,' Meadow said.

'We haven't got any bookings for it yet, as we were thinking we might adapt it slightly so it wasn't so Christmassy,' Indigo said. 'It's not even on the system as somewhere guests can stay so in terms of bookings that's not a problem at all.'

Heath let out a sigh of relief. That had been a lot easier than he'd thought.

Bear glanced back to the kitchen and hurried over to help Tierra spoon the cake mixture into the cake cases.

'Is this to do with our Christmassy guest?' River said, gesturing towards Heath's house.

'Yes. The caravan she arrived in is her home. She's had a crappy life and was let down spectacularly by her family, just like we were, but she has no one and I just feel like she needs some stability, somewhere to call home. Also her caravan is unliveable. I can do some repairs but I guarantee a hundred more things will go wrong with it the week after.'

'Are you hoping that if she stays here, then something might happen between you?' Indigo said.

Heath shook his head. 'No, this is nothing like that. I just want to help her.'

'You've always wanted to fix people's problems,' Meadow said.

'I've always felt that if you can help someone you should. That treehouse was never in our long-term plan or part of the expansion for next year, it was something we did on the spur of the moment so why not do something good with it. She said that the last two nights she slept better than she had for a long time because she didn't feel so vulnerable camping out at the side of the road on her own. I want her to feel safe. Everyone should have that.'

Meadow smiled. 'You were always one for big gestures of generosity.'

Heath knew what she was talking about. He glanced over to his treehouse where Star was playing.

'That wasn't an act of generosity. As lovely as it would be to claim that as an act of altruism and heroism, it was probably more for me than it was for you. And it was the best thing I ever did, so hopefully this will turn out to be something good too,' Heath said.

'I'm sure it will,' Indigo smiled as if she knew something he didn't.

'Right, I better go and rescue Evergreen,' Heath said. 'Thanks guys.'

He walked back out the door and across the rope bridge, letting himself into his own treehouse. He stopped and watched his daughter and Evergreen playing together. Star loved a particular racing video game in which the other racers did everything in their power to stop their competitors, including throwing bombs at them, leaking oil underneath the cars so the other vehicles would skid, and other dastardly things to ensure they would win. Star was brilliant at it. To his surprise Evergreen was laughing so much she was literally crying as Star lobbed everything in her arsenal at Evergreen's car. No sooner had her vehicle escaped from a storm cloud or a swamp of crocodiles, Star would throw something else at her. But despite losing spectacularly Evergreen was clearly really enjoying herself.

The race finished with Star as the clear winner and

Evergreen was still laughing at being so completely thrashed.

'It looks like you could do with some help,' Heath said, sitting down next to Evergreen.

'Your daughter is an evil ninja.'

Star laughed triumphantly.

'Well, how about we work as a team to bring her down?' Heath picked up the spare remote.

Star giggled as she added Heath to the game. 'I'd like to see you try.'

CHAPTER FOURTEEN

Evergreen smirked as Lindsay escorted the last family out after the afternoon sessions, jingling with every step she took.

'I'll be back at six for the bedtime story sessions,' Lindsay said, giving them a wave, making her costume jingle even more.

She disappeared and Evergreen let out a snort of laughter. 'Did you guys buy the most obnoxious outfit for her deliberately, knowing she would hate it?'

Heath grinned in a way that said they absolutely did. 'That's an outrageous and scandalous thing to say.'

Evergreen smiled, shaking her head. 'Right, we have three hours to kill before the next session.'

'I wanted to talk to you about something actually,' Heath said, flopping down onto the sofa.

'Do you want me to take your beard and hair off for a bit?'

'You could do actually, if it's not too much hassle putting it back on.'

'It's no bother.' Evergreen set to work, gently removing his facial hair. 'What did you want to talk to me about?'

'Well, I thought about what you said this morning, about how sometimes you don't feel safe sleeping alone and—'

'Heath, I told you, you don't need to worry about me, I can take care of myself.'

'Anyway,' Heath pressed on. 'If you wanted, you could stay here.'

'Here at Wishing Wood?' She removed the beard and the hair and placed them back in their boxes.

'I meant here, in Christmas Tree Cottage.'

She stepped back to look at him. 'What?'

'It's yours, if you want it.'

She folded her arms across her chest, sceptically. 'You're giving me a house?'

'Yes, if you wanted it.'

'A completely free house?'

'Yes.'

'And what would you expect from me in return?'

'Nothing, this is not a conditional offer, this is just me giving you a helping hand.'

'I don't need charity,' Evergreen snapped. 'I may not be able to commit to a monthly mortgage or rent but that doesn't mean I'm broke. I do just fine with my job, I never go hungry and neither does Thunder. I can buy new clothes whenever I want, gas for the oven, logs for the log burner. I may not lead a glamorous life but I'm happy.'

'Are you?'

Evergreen felt her defences shooting up. 'You know nothing about me.'

'I know quite a lot about you. I know your family are assholes, just like mine were, and you were let down spectacularly by them, multiple times. I know that you've been on the run ever since and are too afraid to put down roots in case you get hurt again.'

She took another step back, hating him a little bit right then, hating herself for spilling all her secrets.

'You can have a home here.'

'No I can't.' She moved back to him, swiftly removing his eyebrows and moustache. 'I'm going for a walk, I'll see you back here just before six.'

She quickly walked out the house, her mind and her heart whirling with a myriad of emotions.

He was offering her a house. A home of her own. Her heart filled with hope before she quickly pushed it back down again. No, she couldn't accept. That was a ridiculous idea from a man who clearly lived in a stupid rose-tinted world. That wasn't how the real world worked. He'd obviously been living in this stupid fairytale wood so long, he thought of himself as some crazy fairy godmother granting wishes. But what happened after midnight when the magic vanished? Would her home be torn from her again?

She moved to the clifftops overlooking the grey sea, which was swirling and angry today to reflect her mood. The wind roared over the cliffs and tugged at her clothes. It was freezing and she hadn't even had a chance to grab her cloak.

Suddenly something warm was wrapped around her and she looked up to see Heath draping her cloak around her shoulders.

'Come and find me when you've calmed down and you're ready to talk.'

He walked off, sticking his hands in his pockets.

Stupid, infuriating, wonderful man.

When Evergreen knocked on Heath's door a while later, she could see he was lying on the sofa, reading a book. He glanced up, smiled when he saw her and stood up to let her in.

'Hey,' Heath said, stepping back as she walked inside.

'Hi.'

'Can I get you a drink?'

'No, I just came to apologise.'

He shook his head. 'There's no need.'

'Yes there is. What you offered me was the kindest, most wonderful thing that anyone has ever done for me and I yelled at you and then stormed out. I'm sorry for being so ungrateful. What I should have said is thank you, that's really generous.'

He smiled. 'Is that a yes?'

She shook her head. 'No, sorry, it isn't. It was a lovely offer, but I can't accept.'

He chewed his lip as he studied her. 'Want to tell me why?'

'For many, many reasons. Because I can't be indebted to you. I'd have to pay some kind of rent and I couldn't afford what that place is worth, because you'd be losing money every single day I was living there and I'd feel awful about that.'

'You can work here. On days where you don't have any TV or film jobs, you could do a shift on reception or in the restaurant, or you could offer face painting to the children during the holidays or weekends.'

She smiled at the thought of doing something so simple and enjoyable as that and how lovely it would be to be part of a team. But then she shook her head.

'I can't stay here, Heath. If I did, I'd get attached: to you, to your brilliant daughter and your wonderful family, to the sea views and the kooky fairytale treehouses, to your fabulous staff. Slowly but surely I would fall in love with it all.'

'You make that sound like a bad thing,' Heath said.

'It is, of course it is. Because what happens when it ends?'

'Why does it have to end?'

'Because it always does. Fairytales don't exist. And inevitably I will have my heart broken yet again and I've worked very very hard to protect it for the last few years. When Suki died, I lost my mum, my family and my home and that was utterly devastating.' Evergreen swallowed, blinking back the tears. 'And I can't go through that again.'

Heath stepped forward and wrapped her in a huge hug. She hesitated and then slid her arms around him. God, he felt solid, dependable. A big part of her yearned to trust him. She really, really bloody liked this man and that scared her a little too. When he held her close to his hard body like this, she had feelings she'd not had in a very very long time, maybe ever.

'Christmas Tree Cottage is yours for the rest of your life, you have my word on that,' Heath said.

'You can't promise that. What if you and your family decide to sell the place a few years down the line, what if—'

'That isn't going to happen.'

'OK, what if at some point in the future me and you…' she trailed off.

He leaned back slightly to look at her, his arms still tight around her, a big smile forming on his face. 'Me and you…?'

'OK, what if me and you have this big whirlwind affair where we have sex in every treehouse in the resort and after a few months you grow bored of me or decide you hate me? You won't want me here then.'

'Firstly, that whirlwind affair sounds like a lot of fun, but *if* it ends I'm not so petty as to kick you out of your home because of it. And there are very very few people I actually hate. I don't hate or even dislike any of the women I've slept with or dated. We've all parted on very good terms. So I can categorically promise you that no matter what does or doesn't happen between us, it won't impact on your home.'

She looked up at him. 'You have an answer for everything, don't you?'

'Yes, because I am most wise.'

She grinned. 'The answer is still no.'

'How about the answer is, "I'll think about it"?'

She stared at him. 'Why do you want to help me so much?'

'Why the hell not?'

She smiled and shook her head. 'You're impossible.'

'Impossible to say no to.'

'No.'

He watched her, as if waiting for her to say something, and for some reason she heard herself say, 'I'll think about it.'

He grinned. 'Good answer. Now about this passionate whirlwind affair…'

'I never said passionate.'

'You intimated. And I embellished.' He swept a hair from her face, the affection he had for her clear in his eyes.

She swallowed. 'There will be no whirlwind affair. Besides, you have your hot date tonight.'

And that reminder was enough to make her step back out of his arms.

He sighed. 'I know, but the more time I spend with you, the more I'm thinking of cancelling.'

She frowned. 'Why does spending time with me make you want to cancel your date? You said you weren't interested in a relationship, we both did.'

He stared at her as he thought how to answer that and for a moment all the amusement went from his eyes. He stepped closer. 'Because I want to get to know you more than any woman I've ever met. Because with every woman I've ever been with, it's always been about sex. Even with Scarlet. This…' he pointed between the two of them '…feels different.'

'It's called friendship. Maybe it's not something you're familiar with.'

'Maybe that's it. But there is a huge part of me that would rather spend tonight talking with you, getting to know you more, than see Scarlet again. Maybe I've moved on from her. Maybe we never really had something in the first place. But it says something about my feelings for her when I'd rather spend time with you, even if that time is purely friendship.'

She felt a need to push him away. Or run away. She needed to put some distance between them.

'You have to go on this date, you said yourself you'll always be wondering if she was the one that got away. And you absolutely can't cancel for me. I am not going to be the big love story that you're looking for. I won't be here long enough for that.'

'Unless you stayed.'

'You're infuriating.'

He laughed.

'Look, I think friendship is important in any relationship,' Evergreen went on. 'So don't go tonight with the intention of having sex with her, as amazing as it was the first time you met. Get to know her properly, ask her questions like you do with me. Be friends and see what happens.'

Heath nodded. 'I think you are most wise too.'

She sighed. She wasn't wise, because if she was she wouldn't seriously be considering Heath's invitation to stay.

CHAPTER FIFTEEN

Evergreen watched as Heath read from *The Gruffalo's Child*, the pyjama-clad children sitting around him in absolute awe as he put on all the voices for the different animals. When she'd first seen Heath she wondered how he was going to be in the Father Christmas role and whether she would need to carry him, but he was a complete natural with the children, hamming up his role, reading the stories with a perfect cadence and rhythm, the children hanging off his every word. Watching him be so kind and gentle with them, she knew she had fallen a little bit in love with Heath Brookfield. He was quite simply the most wonderful man she'd ever met.

She still couldn't get over his offer of a home. No one had ever been so kind and generous to her before. He was so lovely, she just wanted to hug him. OK, if she was honest with herself, she had an overwhelming desire to do a hell of a lot more than that. She couldn't remember the last time she had felt this way about a man. She had spent so long running from having any kind of connection with anyone that she hadn't been attracted to any man and a relationship had certainly not been on her radar.

Heath finished the story and she handed him the final book. There were three families and they had been allowed to choose one bedtime story each to be read by Santa and then he was going to finish with the poem *'Twas the Night Before Christmas.* He took the book from her, his fingers grazing hers, and a spark ignited between them. The smile he gave her melted her heart.

What was with this man and why did he affect her so much?

But this reaction to him made her conviction to leave even stronger. She couldn't stay and fall head over heels in love with him because what would happen when it ended? Despite his promises, she knew she couldn't remain here when they broke up and then she would lose her home and have her heart broken all over again. Everyone she had ever loved had abandoned her or rejected her. And although Suki dying wasn't a rejection, it had ended with the same result, Evergreen had lost someone she loved, and then Rob had kicked her out of her home too, and she just wasn't brave enough to go through that again. It was better to keep Heath at arm's length and leave, as planned, just after Christmas. That way she'd never get hurt.

'You're looking at him like someone looking at the last slice of chocolate cake,' Lindsay muttered in Evergreen's ear.

Evergreen blushed and smiled. 'I was enjoying the story.'

'Oh sure,' Lindsay said, clearly not convinced.

'He had a broad face, and a little round belly, that shook

when he laughed, like a bowl full of jelly,' Heath read, shaking his belly when he got to that part, making all the kids laugh.

'He certainly has a way with the children,' Lindsay admitted. 'It even makes my ovaries ache to watch him. And I suppose he isn't bad to look at.'

'He's definitely easy on the eye,' Evergreen said, knowing that was a massive understatement.

They both stood watching him as he finished the poem. *'But I heard him exclaim as he drove out of sight, Happy Christmas to all, and to all a goodnight.'*

Heath closed the book and the children gave a little clap.

'They seem to like him too,' Lindsay said.

There was a flurry of activity then as they gave the children their presents and there were goodbyes and hugs all round, before Lindsay led them out, giving Evergreen meaningful head nods in Heath's direction and not so subtle winks, obviously thinking something wonderful was going to happen between them the second they were alone.

'Let me get you out of your make-up,' Evergreen said, gesturing for Heath to sit down.

Heath did as instructed. 'That was fun.'

'You looked like you were loving it,' Evergreen said, carefully removing his beard and hair and then the prosthetics.

'I did. I like nothing more than to make a child smile. They are simple creatures, very easy to please, you put on a silly voice, make them laugh and they're putty in your hands. Women are much more complicated beasts.'

149

'I don't know. I think for many women they just want to be loved.'

He studied her. 'But not you.'

She wrapped up the prosthetics. 'I think I've spent a lifetime wanting to be loved, not really believing I deserve that, and the last eight or nine years too scared to go after it.'

She wiped the residual make-up off with a baby wipe.

'There, all done.'

He stood up and placed his hands on her shoulders. 'You do deserve to be loved.'

She stared at him, swallowing a lump of emotion in her throat, her heart racing in her chest.

His eyes cast down to her lips. 'Do you want me to cancel this date tonight?'

She hesitated, probably too long. 'No, why would you think I want that?'

'Because you're looking at me like you'd like to kiss me.'

She cleared her throat and stepped back. 'I think you're seeing what you want to see.'

'What would you say if I told you I want to kiss you too?'

Panic and joy battled in her chest, but fear won out. 'I'd say you should probably go, you don't want to keep Scarlet waiting.'

He stared at her and then nodded. 'I'll see you tomorrow.'

She stepped back. 'Yes, go. Have fun.'

He hesitated as if he wanted to say something, then gave her a quick kiss on the cheek and walked out.

Evergreen threw her book down and looked around the room in frustration. She had read the same page three times over and none of it was going in. All she could think about was Heath going on his date with a woman he'd had the best sex of his life with. She was insanely jealous and she didn't know why. She didn't want a relationship with Heath, or anyone, come to that. But she couldn't stop picturing him kissing this other woman, when what she really wanted was for him to kiss her.

She looked at her watch. It was just gone eight. He'd probably be at the restaurant by now or, even worse, in Scarlet's bed.

Why had she pushed him to go on this date if she felt like this? She sighed. She knew why, because she couldn't give him what he was looking for.

Suddenly there was a knock on the door of Christmas Tree Cottage and she lifted her head to see Heath standing there, looking very smart in a white shirt. He must be on his way out.

She hurried to answer the door, backing away to let him in. 'Hey, aren't you supposed to be at the restaurant by now?'

He stepped into the room and shut the door. Tiny flakes of snow clung to his hair and his eyelashes and she resisted the urge to sweep them away. He stamped his feet to get rid of the snow on his boots and then turned to look at her.

'I cancelled.'

She felt a swirl of emotions hit her in the stomach: relief, guilt, joy, confusion.

'But why?'

'Because I wanted to be with you.'

'Heath, I told you, that isn't going to happen—'

He stepped closer and the words dried in her throat. 'It doesn't matter. It makes no difference whether you leave here after Christmas and we haven't even shared a kiss. I didn't cancel with the hope that I could pick up with you instead. I cancelled because if I'd gone on that date, all I would have been able to think about was you, about how I wanted to be with you, talk with you. I'd be thinking about what it feels like to hold you in my arms and what it would feel like to kiss you and make love to you. And I know you don't want that but if I was with her thinking of you, that would make me a complete dick and I'm not that kind of man. No woman deserves that. I know my past with women has always been casual, nothing serious, but when I'm with a woman, I'm with her, one hundred percent. So I had to cancel. It wouldn't have been fair to Scarlet otherwise.'

Evergreen stared at him in shock. He wanted to kiss her and make love to her. He had cancelled his date with Scarlet because he had feelings for her. Her heart soared.

'But... aren't you disappointed? You had your hopes pinned on a happy ending with her, marriage, kids. You wanted to settle down with her.'

'I do want that but not necessarily with her. I think, if I'm honest, I moved on from her a long time ago. I guess I was curious to see her again to find out whether we still had that chemistry and whether we had anything there to build on. But when I thought about her, I just couldn't imagine her fitting into my life here. I remember that weekend we met so vividly and I remember her saying she never wanted children. That's when I told her about Star and Meadow and she blew up. I thought maybe she would come to accept Star in her life but after talking to you I realise I don't want anyone to *accept* her, I want them to love her.'

'She's a brilliant little girl. Any woman would be lucky to have her in their life. You and Star come as a package deal, along with your family and this enchanting place. But that package isn't something to accept or endure, it's something wonderful.'

Heath smiled. 'That's very nice of you to say.'

'It's true. And I think what we are attracted to changes with what our end goal is. A year ago, your end goal was sex, and there's nothing wrong with that but she ticked that box for you. Now you want something more, so you have higher standards. You need someone who is going to tick every single box for you.'

He nodded and shivered. She quickly took his hand and pulled him closer to the log burner. He held his hands out over the heat.

'But you need to aim higher than me,' Evergreen said. 'I'm not going to tick those boxes for you either.'

'Look, if you're not interested in a relationship with me, then I respect that. But something tells me you want this too.'

Evergreen instinctively shook her head but he had been honest with her so she could be honest with him. 'I do but I can't. I've never had a serious relationship in my life.'

'Never?'

'I went out with a guy for two months when I was

sixteen. That's been my longest relationship. The other men I've been with, I don't think I could class any of them as a relationship. They were fun, a nice way to pass the time. I've never wanted anything more. I built a wall around me and I never want to let anyone in.'

'Because you're scared.'

'I'm scared of trusting anyone.'

'I think when something scares us, we have to push the bubble just a little every day until the scary things becomes the norm. If you're scared of heights, you might push yourself to go up a twenty-foot ladder. On the first day you'd just go up to the first rung and that feels OK, so the next day you might go up to the second rung. And each day you push yourself that little bit further, that little bit higher, because you know at the top of the ladder the views are amazing.'

'But what if I fall?'

'I promise to catch you.'

She looked away, shaking her head.

'You know, the easiest way to find out if you can trust someone is to trust them,' Heath said. 'We could take things really slow, see how it goes.'

'I'm leaving just after Christmas.'

'Or you could stay for a little bit longer. What's the worst that could happen?'

'That I fall in love with you and you don't feel the same.'

'Love is a risk, for both of us. I could fall in love with you and you leave. But we can spend our life running from our past, or we can try and heal ourselves from the pain of it. Move forward and don't look back.'

She looked at him. 'You had a shitty childhood but you

seem to have grown up to be relatively normal. What's your secret?'

He grinned. 'I'll ignore the relatively normal comment. Can I trust you with a secret?'

'Of course.'

'It's a big one. The rest of my family know but Star doesn't and it needs to stay that way.'

She frowned in confusion but nodded.

He took her hand and led her to the sofa. 'I've been where you are now. When I was a child I felt unlovable – my parents didn't want me so I was clearly not worth anything. When I was in my late teens the only escape I had from these thoughts was drinking until I passed out or sleeping with a lot of women because at least I was something to them, even if it was only for one night. I had no job – this place didn't exist back then – and I had no desire to get one. I had nothing worth living for. Most mornings I didn't even want to get out of bed. I was only nineteen and I'd given up on life. I felt so worthless that one day I stood on top of the cliffs overlooking Pear Tree Beach and wondered if I threw myself over, would anyone miss me, would anyone care?'

'Christ Heath, you must never think like that.'

'I don't. It wasn't like I really considered doing it, more like would anyone care if I did. Would anyone notice if I wasn't here any more. And that's when I saw the white stag.'

She frowned, wondering where this story was going.

'I'd heard the legend that he was supposed to guide you to where you're supposed to be and, although I've always been level-headed enough not to believe in fairytales, I followed him. I'll never know why. I came back to the woods and found Meadow sobbing because she was pregnant and her parents had kicked her out. She was only seventeen.'

'Oh god, poor Meadow.'

He nodded. 'She had no job, no home and...' he paused. 'And the father of the baby didn't want anything to do with her.'

Evergreen froze. 'You're not Star's dad?'

'Biologically, I'm not her father, but that doesn't mean I'm not her dad. I love her with everything I have, she is my entire world. When Meadow was standing there crying in front of me, it was like a light switch went on in my head. Meadow and her baby was the thing worth living for. I could be the baby's dad, raise her as if she was my own. I offered to marry Meadow and look after them both and she said yes. My daughter was this wonderful gift, I suddenly had a purpose, something to get out of bed for. There has not been a single day since then that I regretted that decision.'

She stared at him, her heart filling with absolute love for this magnificent man. If there was someone she could finally trust with her heart, it was Heath Brookfield.

'Heath, you're a wonderful man.'

'Wait, you're looking at me like I'm some kind of hero. I didn't save them, they saved me. And I didn't tell you that so you would fall in love with me. I told you that because I know what it feels like to think you're not worth loving. But I had something to fight for and I thought by giving you this house you would finally have the stability and security of having your own home and you could open

156

yourself up to friendships with the people that work here and maybe eventually you could open yourself up to love, too. Not necessarily with me. We can't undo the pain of the past, but we are in control of our future. We can take steps to escape that pain, to move forward, to do the things that will bring us happiness, not run away from it. Sometimes we have to be a little bit brave.'

She stared at him. 'Taking on the responsibility of someone else's child *is* a brave and brilliant thing, don't dismiss the magnitude of that decision. And at nineteen too. I was a mess at nineteen and not just emotionally because I was grieving Suki, but I definitely didn't have the maturity to be a mum. I've seen the way you are with Star and you are an amazing dad to her, don't ever doubt that.' She took his hand and smiled when he entwined his fingers with hers. She took a deep breath. 'I think if you can be brave enough to turn your whole life upside down, then maybe I can be brave too.'

A slow smile spread across his face. 'What are you saying?'

'I'm saying that you're right, I have been running from any emotional connection all my life, afraid of having friends or boyfriends for fear of losing them and reliving that pain all over again. But there's something about you that draws me like a magnet. I haven't been able to stop thinking about you since I arrived here. And I want to be brave and take a chance with you.'

He grinned.

'Don't get excited. We can date with no pressure for anything more than that. We'll take things slow and we'll see what happens. But you've got to promise me you're not going to fall in love with me before the end of the year. If I decide to leave, I want a clean conscience. If we try it and it doesn't work, I can walk away, guilt-free.'

He smiled. 'I'm a big boy, you don't need to worry about me. So we're really doing this?'

She paused. 'I guess we are.'

'Does that mean I can kiss you?'

She let out a nervous giggle and then nodded. God, she'd wanted to kiss him ever since she'd arrived here.

He cupped her face, staring into her eyes, seemingly drinking her in. He stroked her cheeks with his thumbs and then his lips grazed the corner of her mouth in the softest of whispers before feathering his mouth across her cheeks, adoring her, teasing her with what was to come. She couldn't help smiling. He kissed her on the forehead, locking eyes with her again.

'If we're taking things slow, do you want me to stop there?'

'Hell no.'

He grinned and this time he kissed her on the mouth and she instantly melted into him. His kiss was perfect, gentle but confident, and it lit a fire inside her. The kiss was filled with so much desire, she suddenly wanted so much more despite having insisted they take things slow. There was so much passion and need from both of them and he was only kissing her. She stroked the hair at the back of his head and he moaned against her lips, wrapping his arms around her and taking her with him as he leaned back against the sofa. Christ, if he started undressing her now, started making love to her, there was no way in hell she was going to stop him. She had never ever thought about sex or wanted it so much during a first kiss. He stroked her face gently as he kissed her and it filled her heart.

She was in trouble here. They could take it as slow as humanly possible but she knew she could easily fall in love with Heath Brookfield.

CHAPTER SIXTEEN

Heath knocked on the door of Christmas Tree Cottage the next morning. Snow had fallen overnight covering everything with a thick crystal blanket, making it look magical. When Star woke up she would be over the moon, they so rarely got snow here on the coast. With only five days to Christmas it was the perfect way to start their Christmas Hullabaloo.

The night before hadn't turned out as he'd expected at all. A few days before he'd been so looking forward to his date with Scarlet but everything had changed when he'd met Evergreen Winters. And despite Evergreen pushing him away, encouraging him to go on the date with Scarlet, he'd known he couldn't, not when he wanted to kiss someone else. What had surprised him was that he hadn't felt disappointed the date hadn't happened, nor had he been upset that Scarlet hadn't been that bothered about him cancelling either. He was excited about what might happen between him and Evergreen, especially after their tentative agreement the night before.

They'd spent a long time kissing and it filled his heart with hope. And though there was a part of him that was keen to take it further, just like he had with all the other women he'd had one-night stands with in the past, Evergreen was different and he wanted to take his time to get this thing between them right.

She opened the door, already in full make-up, and he grinned, stepping forward to kiss her.

To his disappointment she put a hand on his chest to stop him. Surely she hadn't changed her mind already?

'Don't mess up my make-up, it takes me ages to get these wrinkles right.'

He grinned. 'I promise to be very gentle.'

He bent his head and kissed her on the lips and she smiled against his mouth as she kissed him back.

She stepped aside to let him in and he stamped the snow off his boots before stripping off his coat and sitting down ready to be made over again.

'I was thinking, as it's snowed, we should make the most of it this afternoon. I'm sure Star would love to build a snowman and have a snowball fight. It'll be part of the Christmas Hullabaloo today, if you still want to join us.'

She was silent for a while as she worked on his face, as if trying to decide whether to do it or not.

Eventually she answered. 'OK.'

He laughed. 'It sounds like you've just agreed to have your teeth pulled with a pair of rusty pliers.'

Evergreen laughed.

'Let me ask you this, if I'd asked you to make a snowman with me and Star this afternoon and we weren't dating, would you be happy to do it or would you still have reservations?'

Evergreen nodded. 'You're right, I'm being an idiot. I would totally have been up for it. Now my mind is working overtime with stupid thoughts like, building a snowman with you and your daughter sounds very coupley and romantic and I'm not sure I'm ready for that. But in reality, it's just building a snowman. What's the big deal?'

His heart hurt for her. 'It is a big deal because you've never dated or had any romantic relationships because you've been so afraid of getting hurt. I get it. But we did agree to take things slow and building a snowman together feels like a very tiny step.'

She grinned. 'I think I can cope with it.'

He watched her as she carried on applying his make-up. He really was going to have to take things slow with her. Or just gently push her out of her comfort zone.

He just hoped he wouldn't push her too far.

Heath flopped down on the sofa after their morning session and Evergreen immediately moved to take off his beard and hair, carefully storing the facial hair back in its boxes.

'What are your plans for the next few hours?' Heath said, letting out a yawn which made Evergreen yawn too.

'I think I'm going to take a nap,' she said. 'These early mornings are killing me.'

'Great idea,' Heath said, standing up and stripping out

of his Santa jacket and the white t-shirt underneath, removing his fake belly too.

He lay down on the sofa, his legs stretching out the full length of the furniture.

'You're sleeping here?'

'Yes, makes sense. Then I don't have to commute back to my house and back here again later.'

'It's, like, a two-minute walk from here.'

'That's too far.'

She sighed. That put paid to her plan to have a kip on the sofa.

'I guess I'll have the bed then.'

'Or you could join me here,' Heath said, opening his arms.

She eyed him sceptically.

'It's just a hug and a nap, it's nothing to be scared of,' he said.

Looking at Heath Brookfield, she knew she had every reason to be scared of him. She had guarded her heart for as far back as she could remember and the more time she spent with him, the more she could feel her carefully constructed wall starting to crumble.

Heath was watching her, waiting for her to come up with an excuse, waiting for her to run away.

She would show him. As he said, it was just a cuddle and a nap, it didn't mean anything.

She carefully climbed on top of him and snuggled down against the back of the sofa. She smiled when Heath moved both arms around her and she rested her cheek on his chest. Her heart was thundering, her breathing accelerated like she'd just run a marathon. This felt somehow more intimate than the kissing they'd shared the night before. She wanted to get up and sleep in the bedroom instead.

Almost as if he could read her thoughts, Heath slid his arms up her back and started stroking her hair. Any protests or thoughts of moving faded away. She closed her eyes, enjoying the bliss of the moment, and within minutes she had drifted off to sleep.

Evergreen woke up and smiled when she realised she was cuddled up to Heath, he was so warm and solid. She felt safe here wrapped in his arms. She had obviously shifted a little in her sleep though, as she found herself staring at his belly button.

He stirred and, sensing she was awake, he stroked her hair. She smiled, wanting the world to pause right there for a second before the doubt and fear crept in.

'Crap, we've overslept,' Heath said. 'Lindsay will be here in a minute with the first cohort of children for our afternoon sessions.'

Her heart leapt and she looked at her watch to see he was right. She immediately attempted to sit up but found she couldn't move. She tried again; her body could move just fine but her head felt really heavy. She tried once more and felt the pull on her cheek.

'Oh my god, Heath, I'm stuck to you.'

'What?'

'It must be the glue from the prosthetics or the latex. I'm stuck to your skin,' Evergreen said in alarm. As she gave her head a big tug, she felt the skin on her cheek stretch. 'Ow!'

'Yes, stop tugging, that feels like it's ripping my skin too.'

'OK, it's OK, I just need to put some stuff on it to loosen the glue. We need to get my toolbox from that cupboard by the door.'

She manoeuvred her legs off the sofa, her cheek still stuck to his belly. Very slowly, Heath swung his legs off the sofa too and, with a great deal of difficulty, he stood up, with Evergreen bent at the waist. She held onto his hips to steady herself as she started walking and shuffling backwards to get them to the cupboard. Heath tried to stay close, holding onto her head, but with every step back she made, her skin stretched painfully. This was ridiculous.

They made it to the cupboard and, with a bit of awkward manoeuvring, they got the toolbox out of the cupboard. Evergreen's back was starting to ache so she knelt down on the floor so she could access the toolbox more easily.

Just then Lindsay walked in, her bells on her shoes jingling to announce her arrival.

'Are you guys ready—' Lindsay started and then immediately covered her eyes. 'Oh my god, I'm so sorry. Christ, there's a time and a place for that kind of thing and when I have twenty children waiting outside to see Santa, now is definitely not the time.'

Evergreen looked up at Heath in confusion and Heath burst out laughing.

'Lindsay, we're stuck together, we're not doing anything dirty,' Heath said, between his laughs.

Evergreen suddenly realised what Lindsay thought they were doing. With her kneeling down in front of Heath and her face in such close proximity to his crotch, it was easy to jump to that conclusion.

Evergreen snorted with laughter. 'I promise, this is completely innocent, my prosthetic glue has stuck to his skin.'

Lindsay peered through her fingers and then, letting out a little sigh of relief, she moved forward to help them. 'I don't think I want to know what you were doing to get stuck like this in the first place, but what can I do?'

'Can you grab the baby lotion?'

'Oh god, now I do feel like I'm part of some kind of orgy,' Lindsay said.

'That's baby oil, not lotion,' Heath said.

'And how many orgies have you taken part in, Heath Brookfield?' Lindsay said, rooting around in the toolbox to find the baby lotion.

'Oh, one or two?' Heath said, giving Evergreen a wink.

Evergreen couldn't help but smile and roll her eyes. Lindsay passed her the bottle and some cotton wool pads. Evergreen tipped some out onto the pad and started working on her face to loosen the prosthetic but it was really hard when she was smushed against Heath's belly. Finally she managed to prise the eye bags off her skin, releasing her, although the prosthetic was still hanging off Heath's stomach like some kind of weird growth.

'OK, we're going to need some time to do a repair job,' Evergreen said to Lindsay. 'Can you stall for a few minutes and we'll come and get you when we're ready?'

'Stall? There are twenty rabid children out there

desperate to see Santa. If I don't let them in soon, I may have a revolt on my hands.'

'Why don't you do a song and a dance?' Heath suggested, amusement glinting in his eyes.

'I did not sign up for this job to sing and dance,' Lindsay huffed. 'But I'll think of something.'

She jingled her way out of the treehouse.

Evergreen started attacking the weird piece of flesh now attached to Heath's stomach, very aware how close she was to other parts of his body.

'I knew having a nap with you was going to be trouble,' she muttered. 'Although even in my wildest dreams, I never imagined this.'

Outside, at the top of the stairs, they heard Lindsay launch into 'Jingle Bells', which was very appropriate considering her outfit.

'What did you imagine?' Heath asked.

'I don't know, that maybe we'd share a kiss after and I wouldn't be kneeling before you with a face like a Picasso painting gone wrong.'

He smiled and, as she finally peeled away the eye bag from Heath's stomach, he bent down, cupped her face and kissed her.

God, kissing Heath was like nothing else. He was so sweet, so gentle, but there was an undercurrent there, a promise of things to come. Her stomach clenched with desire at that thought.

He pulled back slightly and then kissed her on the forehead. 'I was hoping for that too but, as Lindsay said, now is not the time or the place.'

She heard Lindsay finish 'Jingle Bells' and launch into 'We Wish You a Merry Christmas'.

She swallowed. 'No, it isn't.'

He held out a hand and helped her up.

'Come on, quick, let's get you sorted and you can go and greet the children while I do something with my face. You're the main attraction after all. No one cares about me.'

'Well that simply isn't true. I care about you,' Heath said.

Evergreen smiled. 'I meant the kids, they're here to see you. Come on, sit down and I'll put your beard and wig back on before poor Lindsay finishes her repertoire.'

She quickly refastened his wig and facial hair before passing him his belly, shirt and red jacket, which he pulled on.

He stood up, tugging on his hat.

'You look great, go and be fabulous. I'll come out and join you as soon as I can.'

Heath nodded and stepped outside onto the decking, next to Lindsay. 'Ho, ho, ho,' he said to his adoring fans beneath him who all let out a big cheer at his arrival.

Evergreen grabbed her toolbox, scurried into the bedroom and shut the door. She touched her lips and smiled. Getting involved with Heath Brookfield was definitely going to be trouble.

CHAPTER SEVENTEEN

The snowman-making turned out not to be the big romantic coupley thing that Evergreen had envisaged. Star had organised a big competition and, when Evergreen and Heath arrived after their afternoon session with the kids, Bear, Meadow, River, Indigo and Tierra were already limbering up as if about to participate in an Olympic event. Amelia was standing there with a clipboard, looking like she was taking the whole thing very seriously.

'I've split us all into three teams,' Star said. 'Evergreen, you can be with me and Daddy. Amelia will be the judge and she will give points for different things.'

Amelia consulted her clipboard. 'There will be points for the tallest snowman and the most inventive.'

'What's inventive?' Tierra asked.

'It means something different or unexpected,' Bear said. 'Instead of doing a snowman, you might do a snow dog or a snow unicorn.'

'I want to do a unicorn,' Tierra said, excitedly.

'Thanks for that wonderful suggestion,' River said to Bear.

'You will have exactly ten minutes to complete your snowmen. Does anybody have any questions?' Amelia said, clearly loving her role as judge.

'Can we make snowwomen?' Tierra asked and then giggled. 'With big boobs.'

'You can make any snow person or animal you want,' Star said. 'You can make a monster with twenty heads if you want to.'

'I want to make a monster with twenty heads,' Tierra announced cheerfully.

'That might be a little ambitious,' River said. 'Especially as we've only got ten minutes.'

'What counts as inventive?' Evergreen asked.

'Something that has never been seen before,' Star said, with a big mysterious voice.

'That clears that up,' Heath said.

'Enough questions,' Star said. 'On your marks, get set, go.'

There was a sudden flurry of activity as snowballs were made and rolled across the ground and Star came running over to join Heath and Evergreen.

'What are we going to make?' Star said as she started making a big snowball with her hands.

'You mean after your big speech of making something that has never been seen before you don't have any ideas?' Heath said, helping her to roll it along the ground. 'I thought there would be a plan.'

'I'm just the brains behind the competition, I can't do

everything. Evergreen is creative, I bet she has a ton of ideas,' Star said.

'No pressure then,' Evergreen said, as she started rolling up a big snowball too.

'I thought we could do a zombie or alien as that's your speciality,' Star said.

'Well, I normally do that sort of thing with make-up, but an alien should be fairly easy to achieve as that can be anything.'

'It has to be the tallest,' Star said.

'Right, one tall alien coming right up,' Heath said.

'We need a big base, so make two or three large balls for the body and then we need lots of smaller snowballs, small ones, big ones, medium-sized ones. Our alien can come from the planet of balls,' Evergreen said. She'd never been given totally free rein on a project before, she normally had a strict design to follow or at least a few sketches. She quite liked this freedom.

They worked together to get a big tall base and then frantically stuck as many snowballs to the outside of it as they possibly could.

Evergreen looked around to see that River, Indigo and Tierra were making what looked like a yeti or a bear. It seemed to have large feet and pointy claws, although it didn't have a face yet.

Bear and Meadow were going for a more traditional-looking snowman, with pebbles for buttons. Meadow even had a carrot sticking out of her coat pocket, which she was obviously going to use later, but on second glance their creation did appear to have two heads. It was also exceptionally tall, way taller than theirs.

'We're not going to win the tallest, but we can still win the most inventive,' Evergreen said. 'Keep going with those snowballs and I'll try to make something from its face.'

She grabbed a stick and started poking at the face area to try to carve out some features. However, working with snow and ice was not a medium she was used to and more of the face broke off than yielded to her will, but she was able to create three bulging eyes out of the snowballs they were making, and some saggy face jowls too.

'You have two minutes left,' Amelia announced as she walked around and jotted some notes down on her clipboard

'It needs big sharp teeth,' Star insisted, as she patted little snowballs into the alien's body. Heath was trying to shape some horns into its head, he'd achieved five of them so far.

Evergreen quickly carved out some teeth, making them all different shapes and sizes and sticking out at different angles. The effect was quite hideous.

'Ten seconds left,' Amelia said, consulting her stopwatch.

Evergreen smiled; when the Brookfields decided to compete with each other, they took it very seriously.

There was a last-minute flurry of activity as Amelia counted down. 'Three, two, one. Stop building.'

Everyone stopped, taking a moment to admire their handiwork before inspecting each other's.

River's yeti was actually really good, while Bear's two-headed snowman was odd. Though Evergreen could hardly judge when her team had made an alien of balls.

'Well, I award Bear and Meadow ten points for having

the tallest snow figure,' Amelia started and then turned her attention to the other two. 'I'm going to give ten points to Star's team for the most inventive and ten points to Tierra's team for the most original.'

'Wait, that means we all won,' Star protested.

'That sounds fair to me. Now, someone promised me some gingerbread cookies,' Amelia said, offering out her hand to the two girls who quickly forgot about their snowmen and dragged her back inside Meadow's treehouse. The others followed them, disappearing inside.

Heath slid his arms around Evergreen and gave her a sweet kiss. 'See, that wasn't too bad.'

She laughed. 'I enjoyed it. I love your family.'

Heath smiled and kissed her again and then stopped as he glanced over her shoulder. 'Oh, Meadow has just spotted us kissing.'

'Oh no, is she going to be weird about it?' Evergreen said.

'If you mean weird in the sense that she'll be all, "Oh my god, tell me everything, how did you two get together, this is so wonderful, I'm so happy for you," then yeah, she'll be totally weird about it.'

Evergreen turned round to look and, sure enough, Meadow had a big grin on her face as she disappeared through the door of her house.

'Just be grateful it wasn't Amelia that saw us together,' Heath said.

'Do you mind them knowing about us?'

He shook his head. 'Not at all. I only mind in the sense that they might all stick their oar in. The women will want to know all the details and my brothers might tease you,

"Oh Heath's looking tired today, have you been keeping him awake all night," that sort of thing. And if it goes wrong Amelia will wade in with her own skewed advice on how to fix it. We can mess this up perfectly well on our own and I don't want them to scare you off. My family are a lot to take.'

'Big families don't scare me. I know what it's like to have them all interfering, and actually it's nice that they care. I'm more scared of you than I am of them.'

He kissed her on the forehead. 'I totally get that.'

'What about Star, should we try to hide it from her for now?' Evergreen said.

Heath paused. 'I don't know. I guess so. When Meadow was dating, before she started seeing Bear, we agreed that we wouldn't tell Star until she was dating someone seriously so she wasn't bringing home a steady stream of men, not that Meadow would ever do that. But she was going out on these dates away from here, so Star would never meet any of them anyway. Star already knows you, she likes you. You're staying here so she's going to see us together every day anyway.'

Evergreen chewed her lip.

'Would you prefer that she doesn't know?' Heath asked.

'I don't know, maybe. I don't want to upset her if this thing between us comes to an end. You might get bored of me in a few days and then we have to tell her we've broken up just days after we've told her we're together. If I leave after Christmas just as she's getting used to the idea of us being together, that's not going to be good for her.'

'You care about her?'

'Of course I do.'

'That's very sweet. I'm happy to be discreet about it for now but if she asks I'm not going to lie to her.'

Evergreen nodded. 'I get that.'

'Right, I need to sort something out for a last-minute present for Star. Do you want to hang out with me while I do it? Or feel free to join Meadow and Indigo and the others for the Spanish Inquisition and some gingerbread cookies. Or you can do your own thing for a few hours.'

'As fun as the Spanish Inquisition sounds, I'll hang with you,' Evergreen said.

'We're also having a slumber party tonight as part of our Christmas Hullabaloo. We're going to watch some Christmas movies, have some popcorn and then we're all going to sleep in our sleeping bags around the Christmas tree. As you've survived the snowman competition, are you still prepared to go the whole hog and come to our slumber party too?'

She smiled. 'That sounds like a lot of fun.'

He slipped his hand into hers and they walked up the stairs and into his house.

'I've got some gingerbread latte sachets if you want one of those,' Heath said, throwing logs into the log burner and lighting a fire. 'Or I have white hot chocolate.'

'Oh the gingerbread latte sounds good.'

Heath set about making them.

'So what's the present you're doing for Star?'

'A few weeks ago, we went to a local zoo for Star's birthday. We had one of those behind-the-scenes guided tours.'

'Sounds fun.'

'Yeah, our guide let us feed cheetahs, groom a tapir, feed

ring-tailed lemurs and wallabies. Star was able to feed the giraffes, which she loved, and I wanted to choose one of the photos I took of her doing it and get it blown up. You can help me select the best one.'

Heath carried the mugs into the lounge area and placed them on the table before grabbing his laptop. Evergreen snuggled into his side as he fired it up and started flicking through the photos. There were ones of Star feeding the ring-tailed lemurs, brushing two tapirs, playing with an armadillo. Eventually they came to the photos of her feeding the giraffes. Heath started flicking through them.

'That one is cute,' Evergreen said.

'It is, I like that one,' Heath said. He flicked through to the next photo and stopped, frowning at it.

Evergreen looked at the photo. It wasn't a great one, one of the staff members was blocking half of Star from view and the staff member was facing away from the camera too.

'Where did you live when you were staying with Suki?'

Evergreen looked at him in confusion. Where had that topic of conversation suddenly come from?

'It was round here actually, near Tenby. We lived in the same house ever since I moved in with them. Suki had a gorgeous sea view from her house and she didn't want to lose that.'

Heath stared at the picture some more. 'So I suppose it's feasible that when they moved house they may have stayed round here.'

'I have no idea. Rob had a lot of family in the area so I guess he might have stayed local to them.'

Heath was silent for a while. 'OK, don't freak out.'

Her heart leapt. 'Well now I am freaking out. What is it?'

'The woman who did our tour of the zoo, this woman…' he pointed to the woman in the photo '…was called Cally.'

Evergreen's heart thundered against her chest, her blood roaring in her ears. She stared at the photo, desperate to see anything that might indicate it was her sister. But she couldn't see the woman's face at all. It could be anyone.

'It might not be your Cally, but it's quite an unusual name,' Heath said. 'In fact, I've never met anyone with that name before. And you said she'd always wanted to work in a zoo, which is a bit of a coincidence.'

Evergreen stared at him. 'Why didn't you say anything before?'

'I honestly didn't make the connection when you mentioned Cally before. It was only when I saw the picture of her that I remembered she was called Cally. She was with us for the whole day so the name kind of stuck. Is this good news or not?'

She turned her attention to the gingerbread latte, watching the steam swirl patterns in the air. 'I'm not sure. She never replied to any of my letters or cards.'

'She might not have got them.'

'But she could have tried to make contact with me.'

'You said yourself you had no idea how to reach them after they moved. Maybe she had no idea how to reach you either, you've spent the last eight years travelling around the country in a caravan, you don't even have an address.'

'What do I do, just turn up at her work? She might not want to see me,' Evergreen said.

'And she might be over the moon at seeing you again. Look, if you don't want to go and see her then don't. You were abandoned by your whole family, I don't know how you ever get over something like that. I certainly won't judge you if you decide to let sleeping dogs lie. But if you did want to go, I can come with you. You don't even have to speak to her, you could just see if it's her and then immediately come back home. Make a decision from there.'

She thought about it for a moment. She could do that. 'Tomorrow?'

'Yes absolutely,' Heath said.

Nerves and excitement bubbled in her chest. This time tomorrow she could be seeing her sister again for the first time in eight years. What would she say to her? Would she even recognise her?

She looked at Heath, who was watching her carefully. 'I'm glad you told me and I'll be very happy to have you there.'

'I'll always be there for you.'

'Bring Star if you want, at least we can have some fun seeing the animals before I make a twat of myself in front of my sister or run away and hide. If I'm brave enough to talk to her, you can take Star somewhere else or distract her with ice cream.'

'Are you sure?'

'Yes, please do, I could do with the distraction.'

'I'm sure she would love to come to the zoo with us. It's about an hour's drive from here, so we'll leave after break-

178

fast. We only have the bedtime story session tomorrow evening so we have all day.'

She nodded. 'It's a date.'

He paused. 'I think, for our first date, I could probably do better than that. How about the night after tomorrow, I take you somewhere special?'

She leaned up and kissed him, feeling warm that he wanted to make an effort for her. 'I'll look forward to it.'

She just had to get through tomorrow first.

CHAPTER EIGHTEEN

After choosing and ordering the photo of Star feeding the giraffes, they joined the others in Meadow's kitchen where they were busily decorating gingerbread cookies. Heath walked over to inspect Star's cookie, which was beautifully designed to look like a very intricate snowflake. He stole one of her white chocolate beads which made her let out a squawk of protest, and he kissed her on the head to mollify her.

'Are there any cookies left to decorate?' Heath said, putting an arm round Evergreen and moving her to his side next to the counter, a gesture not lost on Amelia, her face lighting up as if Christmas had come early.

'There are some over here,' Amelia said. 'Evergreen, why don't you come and pick some for you and Heath to decorate.'

Heath suppressed a smirk at her blatant tactics. 'I'll get them.'

He walked over to the other side of the kitchen and Amelia quickly scurried after him.

'You two are looking rather cosy,' Amelia hissed as she joined him near the freshly baked cookies.

Heath picked up a snowman-shaped cookie and a Christmas tree. 'We're friends, we work together, there's not really a lot more to say than that.'

Amelia was the last person he wanted to know about his tentative relationship with Evergreen, especially when it was so new and fragile. He had no idea whether she would stay beyond Christmas or whether this would only be something casual and fun for her, a fleeting moment of romance. So he wanted to protect it, not have her scared away by his nosy but well-meaning family. Although he didn't really want to hide it either. If he felt the urge to put his arm round Evergreen, or hold her hand or even kiss her, he wanted to be able to. He guessed there was a fine line but the less information he handed to Amelia the better.

'Come on, don't give me that. I've seen the way you two are looking at each other. Why not ask her on a date? What's the worst that could happen?'

'I don't think that's a good idea. We work together,' Heath tried to put her off.

'She's a very beautiful woman,' Amelia said.

Heath turned to look at her, laughing with Indigo. 'She is.'

'See, I knew it. You like her. Ask her out. You haven't been on a date with a woman in a very long time. I'll be dead by the time you finally settle down and get married. My only wish before I die is to see you happily married.' She gave a feeble cough as if she might die at any second when the reality was that his crazy old grandmother was as strong as an ox. 'Do you want me to go to my death bed miserable and unfulfilled? If you're not married by the time I die, I'll come back and haunt you every day, rattle my chains at you while you're in bed or trying to watch the TV.'

'Amelia—'

'I'll do it, if you won't,' Amelia said. 'Evergreen dear, can you come over here?'

'Amelia, can you just mind your own business, let me take care of my own life?' Heath said, exasperated.

Evergreen came over to join them.

Amelia clearly was not to be deterred. 'Evergreen, Heath would like to ask you out on a date.'

Evergreen stared at him with wide surprised eyes. 'You would? I had no idea you had feelings for me.'

Heath suppressed a smile. 'I'm very shy.'

Amelia let out a cough of disbelief.

'So you got your grandmother to ask me out on your behalf?' Evergreen wrinkled her nose a little. 'I'm afraid that a man who is too shy to declare his feelings is not the sort of man I would be attracted to. I like a man who is confident, who says what's in his heart. So I don't think we'd be a good match, I'm afraid.'

'Heath isn't shy. He was just building up to it, letting you settle in. He didn't want to ask you out on the first night you were here but I assured him that as you've been here a few days, now is the perfect time,' Amelia tried.

'Ah well, I'm afraid you've missed the boat,' Evergreen said. 'A very sexy, wonderful man has asked me out on a date the day after tomorrow. I'm very much looking forward to it. He didn't get his grandmother to ask me out, he came and banged on my door last night, told me he had feelings for me and that all he could think about was kissing me and making love to me. It was such a turn-on.'

Heath bit his lip to stop the laughter bubbling up inside him.

'He sounds nice,' Amelia said. 'But I do find that the men who ooze that much confidence are always trouble. If that doesn't work out would you go out with Heath?'

'I have a feeling this date will go very well. His kiss was like… magic. I haven't felt so much heat and fire in a kiss in a very long time. It was like he wanted to pin me to the nearest hard surface and make love to me and, believe me, I wanted that too. I've never wanted that after a first kiss before. I've even dug out my best lingerie just in case the date gets that far. But the man is really sweet and respect-ful, which is another big turn-on, so he might want to wait. But it's safe to say I'm completely smitten with him. Sorry Heath.' Evergreen gave him a consolatory pat and a sympa-thetic smile, took the cookies off him and walked back over to join the others.

He stared after her, his whole body on fire. She wanted him to make love to her already? He'd promised her he would take things slow between them but he couldn't deny he wanted that too.

He couldn't take his eyes off her.

'See, now look what you've done,' Amelia said. 'If you'd been brave enough to ask her out in the first place, none of this would have happened.'

Heath turned round to face her. 'I think you might have put the nail firmly in the coffin now and I can't say I blame her. No woman wants to date a man that needs his grandmother to ask her out for him. Even if this date with this other man ends badly, I don't think I stand a chance now.'

'I'll fix it,' Amelia said.

'No, it's fine. It sounds like she's well suited to this other man. I wouldn't want to get in the way of that. And it's for the best really. We work together, we don't want things to be weird between us. But I'm sure my soul mate is out there and one day I'll find her.'

'I'll be dead by then.'

'You can't hurry love, Amelia. Surely it's better for me to find the right person eventually than settle for the wrong person now?'

'It's true that you have to kiss a lot of frogs to find your prince, or in your case your queen, but you can have a lot of fun trying. You need to have some fun, Heath. If you hold out for the perfect person, she could pass you by.'

'I'll bear that in mind.'

He grabbed a few more cookies and went back over to join Evergreen.

They didn't speak at first as they set about decorating their cookies, Evergreen adding a red scarf to her snowman, Heath piping little yellow stars to his Christmas tree.

'Well, that was enlightening,' Heath muttered under his breath.

'Your conversation with your grandmother?' Evergreen said, quietly.

There was a lot of chatter and laughter around them so they were able to talk quietly without anyone overhearing. Star had gone down the other end of the table to help Tierra with her cookie-decorating.

'More your conversation with her,' Heath said. 'I didn't

realise you were looking forward to our date quite so much.'

He heard her breath hitch. 'I'm really looking forward to it but I do understand if you want to take things slowly.'

He focussed his attention on adding some tiny baubles to his cookie. 'I think I need to see that lingerie before I make my decision.'

Evergreen let out a laugh of outrage. 'So if I have nice lingerie you'll take me to bed, if it's a bit old and crap, you won't?'

'I have to be thorough in my decision making. There's a lot to consider.'

'Nice lingerie being part of that?'

'It's a factor.'

'There's a lot riding on this lingerie.'

'Look, if I don't like it, I can always take it off,' Heath said. The thought of doing that made his stomach twist with need.

'I think I better find my oldest, tattiest pair if that's the case, then maybe you'll take them off quicker.'

'I'm not sure it will make much difference. If you get to the point where you're showing me your underwear, it's going to come off, no matter how nice it is.'

'I'm looking forward to this date more and more.'

He cleared his throat. 'Me too.'

CHAPTER NINETEEN

Evergreen sat on the sofa next to Meadow waiting for Bear and Heath to bring the snacks through from the kitchen. She'd offered to help but Meadow had assured her the boys had everything in hand. Indigo was curled up on River's lap on the big armchair, she looked ready to go to sleep now, never mind watching a movie. Evergreen smiled at her; she knew how exhausting having a baby was. She'd seen Suki walk around like a zombie when Noah, Oliver and Lucy were born. Alfie was in a little basket fast asleep next to them, looking like butter wouldn't melt in his mouth and couldn't possibly be the cause of all the exhaustion.

Tierra and Star were lying together on an oversized beanbag chatting and giggling.

'Thank you for inviting me tonight,' Evergreen said to Meadow.

'Oh, my pleasure. It's lovely to have you here. You and Heath seem to be getting on well,' Meadow said.

There was no point denying it like she'd done with Amelia earlier, Meadow had already seen them kissing.

'I really like him, but we agreed to take things slow.'

Although they'd practically agreed to have sex on the first date, which kind of negated that rule.

'I've never seen him like this with a woman before. I think it's safe to say he really likes you too. And he told me he cancelled his date with Scarlet for you. I think that's a big deal. I figured he needed to see her again to get her out of his system but he just needed to find someone better.'

Evergreen blushed.

'Popcorn,' Bear said, handing a bowl to the girls, one to River and one to Evergreen before plopping down next to Meadow with the remaining bowl.

'I have chocolate,' Heath said, handing out dishes of what looked like Minstrels and chocolate buttons to everyone.

He sat down next to Evergreen and pulled the blanket over them both.

'What movie are we watching?' Evergreen asked.

'*Muppet Christmas Carol*,' Tierra cheered.

'We watch it every year,' Meadow said. 'Sometimes two or three times a year. The girls love it and, I have to admit, it never gets old.'

'It's crazy to think that film is thirty years old,' Bear said.

Evergreen swallowed a lump in her throat. 'My stepmum used to love that film too, we'd watch it together every Christmas. Even when I was a teenager and too old for that kind of thing, I still sat and watched it with her, huffing about how lame it was but secretly loving it. I haven't seen it for years.'

The opening credits started rolling with the familiar jaunty music and she was filled with such nostalgia and longing for a simpler happier time, surrounded by her family. She and Cally would cuddle up on the sofa together, sometimes plaiting each other's hair as they sang along to the songs. God she missed that so much.

Heath put his arm under the blanket and it filled her heart when he took her hand. She wasn't sure if he was offering her comfort or just wanted to be close to her, but she liked it either way.

She looked around the room at Heath's family. If things worked out between them, they would be hers too. A perfect, ready-made family of brothers, sisters, a niece, nephew and even a stepdaughter. It felt like it was too good to be true. She didn't deserve that.

She glanced up at Heath and he looked down at her with such adoration that she knew if anyone could make her believe that she did deserve that life it was Heath.

The movies had finished, the snacks had all been eaten and to Evergreen's surprise the girls were fast asleep in their sleeping bags under the twinkling lights of the Christmas tree. She'd assumed that with all the sugar they had been eating and general Christmas excitement that they'd be awake half the night but they'd both gone out pretty quickly after the last movie had finished.

Everyone else was asleep as well. Bear had insisted that

Meadow have the sofa and as she was pregnant no one had argued with it. They were both lying cuddled up together, looking very much in love. River and Indigo were still snuggled up on the oversized armchair, her head on his shoulder, his arms wrapped around her. Both couples were the epitome of real, everlasting love and she wondered if she would ever have that.

Maybe, reconciling with Cally tomorrow, if it happened, would help. She knew she was broken, she knew she had trust issues, but if she could regain some kind of relationship with her sister maybe it could be the first step in fixing herself and letting herself be open to a proper relationship with Heath.

She glanced over at him, lying next to her on the floor, and was surprised to see he was still awake, staring at the patterns the twinkling lights made across the ceiling.

'Hey,' she whispered.

He looked at her, a big smile filling his face. 'Hey, I thought you were asleep.'

'I was thinking about tomorrow and Cally and… you.'

'Oh? What about me?'

'How much I'd like to kiss you.'

'Well that's an easy fix.' He stroked her face and kissed her gently and she couldn't help smiling against his lips.

After a while he pulled back. 'Now as lovely as that was, want to tell me what's really keeping you awake?'

'I don't know, thinking about Cally, I guess, and what might happen, whether we have any hope of regaining what we had. I'm wondering whether having a relationship with her might help to fix this mess,' she gestured to herself.

He frowned slightly. 'There's only one thing that can fix your issues and that's you. You have to find that one thing that's worth fighting for, like I had with Star. When I became a dad to Star I was scared that I wouldn't be good enough. I didn't have a loving upbringing, mainly because my parents didn't have a great childhood either so they didn't know how to provide that for me. I worried that I might not be able to give that to Star either, what if it was cyclical? But I knew I had to make damned sure she had the best dad in the world, and that she was loved and she knew that. She was my one thing to give me that determination to succeed in becoming a better man. And maybe your thing is Cally or your home here at Wishing Wood or something else, but you have to make that decision to let go of the past and not let it impact on your future any more. And yes there will be blips, there will be times when you think you can't do it, and you'll get scared, but that one thing will drive you to keep moving forward.'

'I want that. I've always thought about marriage and kids and it always felt like that dream was very far away. But now I feel like it's time to go after that dream.'

'I think so too. Just don't go pinning all your hopes on Cally. It might not be her, for one, and even if it is, it's been eight years. I don't want you to be disappointed if it doesn't work out.'

'I will be disappointed if it doesn't work out, but I'm also not going to be any worse off than I am now so I'm trying to take a blasé attitude to it, although I can't promise there won't be tears.'

He smiled sadly. 'And my shoulder will be here for you to cry on if it does go wrong.'

She nodded. Having someone to lean on when things went wrong was going to take a lot of getting used to. She had been on her own for so long, doing everything by herself, she wasn't sure if she could share the load. But she wanted to try.

'What was keeping you awake?' she asked.

'I was thinking of that famous quote from Tennyson, "'Tis better to have loved and lost than never to have loved at all." And I think I would agree. Ideally love would last an eternity but it doesn't always work that way. But it's better to experience love in all its wondrous splendour even if that love is fleeting than to never experience it at all, don't you think?'

She frowned, not sure where he was going with this.

Just then Star marched past them as if on a mission. Heath watched her for a second as she moved to the door and then he was scrabbling out of his sleeping bag and on his feet a few moments later. He caught up with her as she tried to push open the locked door.

'Hey sweetheart, are you OK?' Heath asked, gently, taking her hand and crouching down.

'We're going to be late for school,' Star said and Evergreen couldn't help noticing her eyes were wide and vacant.

'It's OK honey, we've got a bit of time. Why don't you come back over here for a bit and then we can go to school in a little while.'

Star nodded and Heath stood up and gently led her over to where Evergreen was lying. 'Here, lie down there for a bit, honey,' he said.

Star immediately lay next to Evergreen and Heath

settled down too, curling himself around his daughter so she was sandwiched between the two of them. Evergreen stroked her hair and Heath kissed her on the forehead.

Star stared at the ceiling for a moment, then let out a little snuffle, closed her eyes and rolled towards Heath. He slid his arms around her and stroked her back as she drifted off to sleep.

'She's been sleepwalking quite a bit lately. Not sure why,' Heath explained. 'That's why we've taken to locking the door to try to stop her from getting out. We've been playing some relaxation music for her as she goes to sleep and that seems to have helped a bit, but obviously we didn't do that tonight. When she does it, I normally cuddle her for the rest of the night and she doesn't do it again.' He looked at her. 'Sorry.'

'You don't ever have to apologise for being there for your daughter. Also your relationship with her is a very attractive quality.'

He grinned. 'It is?'

'Heath Brookfield, you're the most wonderful man I've ever met.'

He smiled and leaned forward to kiss her briefly. 'Goodnight Evergreen.'

'Night.'

She watched him close his eyes and felt her heart open up a little bit more for him.

CHAPTER TWENTY

The zoo visit the next day was fun, well as fun as it could be when Evergreen was completely on edge the whole time. What if Cally was around the next corner they walked past? What if she was horrified to see her again after all this time, what if she was angry with her? She kept telling herself that it could be a completely different Cally, or that Cally might not even be working today, or even, in her crazy rose-tinted moments, that Cally would be over the moon to see her again. But these thoughts did nothing to quell the nerves and anxiousness.

Evergreen knew Suki's death wasn't her fault, she knew that in reality there was nothing she could have done to avoid the lorry that ploughed into them, but would Cally know that? What had Rob told her and the others about why she wasn't there any more? The hatred from Celeste after Suki's death was obvious, even at the court case months later. Would Cally feel the same?

They stopped by the wolves and Star eagerly leaned against the fence enclosure. 'These are my favourite animals. I love to watch them, their faces are so clever like they are always thinking or plotting. Cunning, that's what Dad calls them.'

'They do look cunning, that's a great word. They look so much like Hero. Maybe he is part wolf.'

Heath laughed. 'There's a funny story about that. Star, why don't you tell Evergreen how we met Hero.'

Star cleared her throat dramatically as if getting ready to tell the greatest story of all time. 'They called him The Wolf of Wishing Wood, lots of people had seen him in our woods and everyone thought it must be a wolf. Me and Bear set up webcams to catch foxes, badgers and other wildlife but the first night we set them up we caught Hero on there eating the food we'd put out for the badgers. We still thought it was a wolf but Bear's friend Kristoff is a vet and a wolf specialist and he said there were differences and that he is probably a malamute-husky-German shepherd cross. So the next night Bear and me camped out to see if we could meet him and he was really friendly and I was able to feed him by hand and stroke him. We didn't catch him that night but a few nights later he just walked straight into our home and we fed him and washed him and then took him to the vet and he didn't have a microchip. So we put some posters out to see if anyone recognised him but no one did so we kept him.'

'What a great story. I think he wanted a home with you because he knew you and your daddy would look after him and love him forever,' Evergreen said.

'We do. And Bear and Mummy too. We all love him.'

'He's a very lucky doggy,' Evergreen said.

Star stood transfixed by the wolves for a few minutes

and then they moved on with the intention of visiting the flamingos.

The whole of the zoo had been decked out for Christmas, with garlands strewn across the path and fairy lights twisted around the trees. With only four days left to the big day it seemed they had pulled out all the stops. When they went to see the bears, the animals had been given Christmas boxes with their food in, which they had to open. Star had great pleasure in seeing the bears destroy the boxes to get to the food instead of delicately removing the wrapping paper. There were a lot of pop-up stalls around the zoo selling hot chocolates with lashings of whipped cream, gingerbread men and mince pies. There was an elf trail throughout the zoo too, where you had to spot the hidden elves either in the enclosures or hiding behind trees in the public areas. Star had managed to find them all so far.

They walked through an archway strewn with tiny fairy lights and Star suddenly stopped.

'Look, there's Cally.'

Evergreen's heart leapt in her mouth as she followed Star's finger. She felt her breath catch in her throat because there was no doubt in the world that the person Star was pointing at was her little sister. She was older, more beautiful, but it was definitely her. She had her hair in two plaits wrapped around her head and she was laughing with one of the other zoo staff. She looked happy.

'Why don't you go and say hello to her,' Heath said to Star.

Star ran off and Evergreen's heart thundered in her chest. Cally would see Star and then look over here towards Heath and spot her. Panic flooded her body but Heath was already on the case, moving her behind a tree before Star could even reach Cally.

'I take it from the fact you've just gone white as a sheet that that Cally is yours?'

Evergreen nodded. Star must have reached Cally because Evergreen watched as Heath smiled and waved.

Heath turned his attention back to Evergreen. 'You don't have to see her today, we know it's her, we can go back home and make a plan from there. There is no pressure to do anything today.'

Evergreen nodded. Despite having all of the night before and this morning to plan what she was going to do if and when she saw her sister again, none of that seemed appropriate now.

She cursed herself. She was such a coward. She should be grabbing hold of Cally and telling her she loved and missed her. But she couldn't do it and she knew why. What if Cally didn't feel the same way?

She had spent the last eight years telling herself she didn't need a family, that she preferred to be alone, and that had worked just fine for her – but the truth was she did need her family, she needed someone to love her. She'd told herself that Cally and the three youngest children, Noah, Oliver and Lucy, were too young to really understand what had happened when Suki had been killed and it wasn't their fault that Rob had kicked her out. But what if what he'd said that night was true?

I hate you, they all hate you. We don't want you here.

We not *I*; he'd spoken for them all.

If Cally hated her, rejected her again after all this time,

the heartbreak and devastation would be as hard as the first time.

'I can't do it,' Evergreen whispered.

Heath nodded. 'And that's totally understandable.'

'I wrote her a letter. It's not long, there are no great explanations or big declarations of love, I just say who I am, and I've left my mobile number and my email if she would like to talk. I figured if she wasn't working today I'd give it to one of her colleagues. You could give it to her for me.' Evergreen fished out the envelope from her bag.

'I'd be happy to.'

'But don't tell her it's from me and maybe tell her to open it at the end of the day.'

'OK, I will. Just stay here out of sight.'

She held onto the envelope for a second. This was ridiculous. She felt like a silly little girl hiding from something scary. She was a grown-ass woman, she didn't need to be afraid any more. What was the worst that could happen? If she was rejected again, it couldn't be any worse than the first time. Life would continue as it always had, with Evergreen being alone. Except now she had Heath to support her through this. She could do this. She could go and say hello to her sister for the first time in eight years.

She took a deep breath. 'On second thoughts, I'll go and give it to her myself.'

Heath smiled. 'And I'll come with you. If there's an opportunity for you two to properly talk, I can take Star off for ice cream or a visit to the dreaded gift shop where she will no doubt want to stock up on more cuddly toys.'

Evergreen nodded. 'Thank you.'

197

Heath held out his hand and Evergreen took it. They walked out from behind the tree and down the path.

Cally was chatting happily to Star as they approached. She glanced up at them as they drew closer, a big smile on her face.

Evergreen watched as the smile fell from Cally's mouth, her eyes going wide, the colour draining from her cheeks. She clearly felt the way Evergreen had a few moments ago at seeing her sister again after all this. But at least Evergreen had had some warning, whereas Cally had been given no hint her day was going to include a long-lost relative.

Evergreen licked her dry lips and forced a smile on her face. 'Hi Cally.'

'Ever… what are you doing here?'

'I'm friends with Heath and Star and when they told me about their tour of the zoo with a woman called Cally, I wondered if it was you. So I came to see you for myself.'

Cally stared at her in horror. 'I don't know what to say. I don't know why you would come and see me after all this time.'

Evergreen swallowed down the lump of emotion stuck in her throat. 'Rob made it very clear that I wasn't ever to come back. I wrote to you, sent you cards for the first few years. I still wanted to be part of your life. But after you moved I didn't know where you were.'

Cally's face clouded with confusion. 'That's not what he said—'

'Cally!' A woman standing further down the path dressed in the same purple t-shirt as the rest of the staff called her with some annoyance in her voice.

Cally looked over her shoulder and nodded at her, then turned back to Evergreen.

'I have to get back to work.'

'Listen, I understand this is a lot to take in but if you wanted to talk to me once you've had a chance to think about it, my mobile number and email address is in here.' Evergreen held out the envelope. 'It seems like you might not know the full story about what happened after Suki died, so if you'd like to hear my side, I'd be happy to tell it. And if you don't want anything to do with me,' her voice broke as she said that. 'Then I want you to know that I only want you to be happy and I hope you have that.'

Cally stared at the envelope as if she really didn't want to take it but she did, stuffing it into her pocket before walking away.

Evergreen stared after her, the tears burning the back of her throat. That had definitely not been the big happy reunion she'd been hoping for.

'I didn't know you knew Cally,' Star said.

'She's my sister but I haven't seen her in a long time,' Evergreen said.

'Why?'

'Because... our stepdad made it very difficult to see each other.'

Star stared at her with wide eyes. 'Bear is my stepdad. I don't think he would ever stop me seeing Tierra or Alfie.'

'No, I'm sure he wouldn't because Bear is lovely.'

Star clearly thought about this for a moment and then her eyes fell to where she was holding hands with Heath. 'Are you two boyfriend and girlfriend?'

If Evergreen thought questions about her and Cally

were hard to answer, questions about her relationship with Heath were even harder.

'Yes we are,' Heath said, simply.

Evergreen looked at him, wondering why he would say that.

'I knew it!' Star said. 'Can we go and see the flamingos now?'

'Yes sure,' Heath said and Star ran off quite happily with this news.

'Why did you tell her that?'

'Because it's true, we're dating, how else would you like me to describe our relationship?'

'You probably shouldn't describe our relationship at all until we have it figured out ourselves.'

'What's there to figure out? We're dating, if it doesn't work out, we'll no longer be dating. No big deal. And I'm never going to lie to her. I can't imagine how she would feel if I denied it now and she found out we were at a later stage. Also, if I want to kiss you, I'm going to kiss you – I'm not going to hide it like we're doing something wrong.'

She stared at him.

'I'd really like to kiss you right now,' Heath said, softly, cupping her face.

She felt herself melting against him, 'I'd like that too.'

He leaned forward and kissed her gently and she felt some of the tension from her shoulders drift away. He pulled back and leaned his forehead against hers. 'I think what you did was really brave.'

'Cally hates me.'

Heath shook his head. 'It was just a surprise for her, give her some time to get her head round it.'

'And what if she decides she still doesn't want to see me?'

'Then she would have lost out on knowing one of the most incredible women I've ever met.'

She gave him a small smile. 'Thank you for being here.'

'That's what boyfriends and girlfriends do.'

She smiled and shook her head. 'You're impossible.'

'Let's go see some flamingos.'

CHAPTER TWENTY-ONE

As Heath approached the end of *'Twas the Night Before Christmas*, he couldn't help looking over at one of the little boys who had sat there listening to the stories, wiping tears from his eyes the entire time.

He finished the poem and all the children and parents gave a little clap.

'Did you all enjoy the stories?' Heath asked.

The children all cheered.

'Well, if you go with Twinkletoes, you can all write a wish to go on the Christmas tree,' Heath said, gesturing to Lindsay, who glowered at him for using the stupid name he'd come up with. He'd told her Lindsay McGhie did not sound like an elf name and had taken to calling her Twinkletoes in front of the children, much to her disgust. He would have to come up with something more obnoxious for the following day. Lindsay quickly plastered on a big fake smile as the children came over to her and she escorted them all over to the tree.

'Theo, before you go, can I have a word?' Heath said, addressing the little boy who'd been crying the whole time.

Theo approached him, still wiping the never ending tears from his eyes. Theo's dad came over too.

Heath crouched down. 'I couldn't help noticing that you were a little sad while I was telling the stories. Is everything OK?'

Theo nodded and then burst into tears. 'I want to spend Christmas with Mummy but Daddy said we can't and she was supposed to be here today but now she can't come and I miss her so much.'

With that Theo threw his arms around Heath's shoulders, little sobs wracking his body. Heath put an arm round him and held him tight.

'Can you make Mummy better, Santa?' Theo asked.

Heath's heart sank.

'That's not something Santa can do,' Theo's dad said. He looked absolutely exhausted.

Theo pulled back to look at Heath, tears filling his eyes. 'Can you?'

Heath shook his head. 'I'm so sorry. I can do lots of things but I can't do that. But why don't you go with Mrs Christmas and see Twinkletoes, she has little gifts for all the children so I bet she has one for you and probably one for your mum too. Then when you see her you can tell her it's from Santa. Go and ask Twinkletoes and I can have a quick word with your dad.'

Theo snuffled and then took Evergreen's hand and they walked over to the tree.

Heath stood back up.

'I'm sorry about that,' Theo's dad said.

'Please don't be. What's your name?'

'Eli.'

'Eli, is there anything I can do to help?'

Eli shook his head. 'Lara, his mum, she's… really ill. She's in hospital right now but it's so far from where we live, we're only seeing her at weekends. We come all this way, stay in hotels or guest houses just to spend a limited few hours with her and it's not enough. I've been trying to sort my work so I can work from home after Christmas and I thought about renting round here. Theo isn't at school yet so it won't make any difference to him but the rent is really expensive so I'm not sure what we will do. And everywhere round here is fully booked or closed over Christmas so we're not going to be able to see her on Christmas Day either and Theo is gutted. So I booked this place for a few days so we could at least see her just before Christmas. She has good days and bad days and the last few days have been good so we were hoping she could come here today to bring Theo to see you but this morning she was really bad again so she couldn't come.'

'I'm so sorry to hear that. The hospital, it's near here?'

'Yes, fifteen minutes away. We don't normally stay here though – no offence, but it's a lot more expensive than a normal guest house. I just wanted to do something special for Theo because he wouldn't see her on Christmas Day.'

'I'm sure we could find a way for you to stay here,' Heath said.

'What?'

'Over Christmas, you could stay here and then at least you'd get to see Lara on Christmas Day.'

'You're full and the prices over Christmas Day were way more than we could afford anyway.'

'We have a lodge here. It was my brother's actually, but he moved out of it a few months ago when he got married. We haven't been renting it out, we weren't sure what to do with it really, people come here for the treehouses and the lodge is nothing special, although it's sturdy and warm enough. We could give it a good clean, add some Christmas decorations. It has two bedrooms so Theo would have his own room and no stairs for Lara to struggle with if she did come.'

Eli stared at Heath in surprise. 'We could stay here? Really? But we couldn't afford it.'

'No charge. Family is important. Stay in it until the New Year as a gift from us, and then if you decide you'd like to stay there long-term next year then we can come up with some kind of arrangement, a monthly rent that you could afford. Say, three hundred pounds a month?'

Eli let out a noise of disbelief. 'That's a quarter of what similar properties round here are charging.'

'We're not doing anything with it right now so any money we make from it will be a bonus. Look, let me talk to my brothers about that, they should have a say in it too, but you can certainly stay here in the lodge until the New Year. No kid should be without their mum over Christmas.'

Eli stared at Heath in shock. 'But, why would you do that?'

'Why the hell not?'

Tears filled Eli's eyes. 'You have no idea what that means.'

'I do. My parents were absent for most of my childhood, not because of illness or work, but by choice, and spending Christmas without them really hurt. Let me do this. Let me give Theo Christmas with his mum.'

To Heath's surprise, Eli burst into tears, his body heaving with sobs, and the other parents and children looked over. Heath quickly put an arm around him and guided him into the bedroom out of view but Theo came running in.

'Santa, did you make my daddy cry?' Theo said, angrily.

Eli picked him up and propped him on his hip. 'They're happy tears. Santa has said we can stay here at Wishing Wood over Christmas so we can spend Christmas Day with Mummy. He has a special house that we can stay in until the New Year so if she is well enough we can see her every day for the next week or so. What do you think of that?'

Theo started crying then too and he reached out an arm for Heath. Heath leaned in for a group hug.

'Thank you,' Eli said.

'Thank you Santa,' Theo said.

Heath couldn't help but smile. At least he'd made them happy, though he wasn't sure how Bear would react when he found out he'd given away his old home.

Evergreen walked back to Wisteria Cottage with Heath for dinner, though she was planning to go back to Christmas Tree Cottage afterwards. She knew that Star was staying at Heath's that night and, while Heath had made it very clear that Evergreen would be welcome to spend the night with the two of them, making Christmas tree decorations, Evergreen wanted to make sure that she didn't monopolise Heath's attention and that he still got quality time alone with his daughter. She didn't want that to change because they were dating and make Star feel pushed out. Cally used to sleepwalk when she was stressed about school and, while Evergreen knew that sleepwalking could have nothing to do with stress, she did wonder if Meadow being pregnant could be a worry for Star. If so, it might be the reason for the sleepwalking. And now Star knew that Evergreen was dating Heath, she didn't want that to cause any extra worry for her.

They walked inside Meadow's part of the treehouse and Evergreen smiled to see Star sitting on Bear's lap as they read a book together about wolves. Hero was cuddled up next to them on the sofa, also appearing to look at the book as if learning all about his ancestors. Meadow was curled up on the oversized armchair, sewing some flowers onto a what appeared to be a cloak.

Meadow smiled at her as they walked in. She held up the miniature cloak. 'I have you to blame for this. Tierra has been talking about your cloak ever since she first met you, so I thought I'd make her one for Christmas.'

'Wow, that's beautiful,' Evergreen said, running her fingers gently over the tiny flowers. 'I'll have to get you to embroider mine too.'

'Oh, I'd be happy to do it.'

'Meadow makes clothes and sells them on Etsy, her speciality is embroidery. She even made her own wedding dress when we got married a few months ago,' Bear said.

'That's brilliant, I'll have to have a look at your site.'

'Oh thanks, there's a few different dresses on there right now. Most of them are party dresses which are proving popular at this time of year.'

'I bet. Every woman wants to wear something individual and unique. Nothing worse than turning up to a party wearing the same dress as someone else.'

'So true. How was your bedtime story session tonight?' Meadow said.

'Heath made one of the dads cry,' Evergreen teased.

'Wow, that's some talent,' Bear said, dryly.

'Yeah, well I need to talk to you about that,' Heath said, awkwardly. 'I don't think you will be too impressed when I explain why.'

'What have you done?' Bear said.

'One of the little boys there tonight, Theo, his mum is in a nearby hospital but Theo and his dad don't live anywhere near there so they weren't able to spend Christmas with her. They came to stay here for a few days but his mum hasn't been able to join them. So I sort of offered them use of your lodge until the New Year so they can at least spend Christmas with her.'

Bear's eyebrows shot up. 'That place is a mess, I've barely been back in it since I moved in here. When are they checking out?'

'Tomorrow.'

'Crap, that doesn't give us much time to sort it out.'

'If we all work together on it tomorrow we should be able to get it in reasonably good condition,' Meadow said. 'And a few Christmas decorations could cover any bigger problems.'

'I think the place is sturdy enough, it just needs a lot of tidying and cleaning,' Bear said.

'I can help with that,' Evergreen said.

'Thanks. I think the more hands the better,' Bear said.

'And he said he'd been looking for somewhere round here to rent for next year, but everywhere is too expensive so I kind of said he could stay in the lodge long-term and we could come to some arrangement on the rent, something he could afford,' Heath visibly cringed.

Bear shrugged. 'Fine by me, we're not using it for anything, and we're not making any money on it, so as long as we cover the money for the added electricity and gas, then we're not running at a loss.'

Evergreen smiled. They were good people.

Meadow stood up and stretched, patting Heath on the shoulder with a smile as she walked past. 'You and your charity cases,' she said, fondly.

Evergreen felt her stomach lurch. Was that what she was to Heath?

'Heath is always collecting waifs and strays,' Bear said. 'He brought a homeless teenager back here one winter, put him up in one of the empty treehouses for a week.'

'And there was that Italian nun he found wandering around Tenby having lost her coach party, she didn't speak a word of English and he drove her around for hours trying to find her party again,' Meadow said, from the kitchen.

'And let's not forget Bluebell RoseGold,' Bear said, his eyes alight with amusement.

Heath groaned.

'The pop star?' Evergreen said.

'Yes, you know the one who is worth millions of pounds,' Bear said.

'In my defence, she dresses like she's been living on the streets for a few years,' Heath said.

'That's called fashion,' Bear said.

'What happened with Bluebell?' Evergreen said, sitting down on the sofa. 'Although knowing her reputation, I can guess how the story ends.'

Bluebell was extraordinarily beautiful and she also had a reputation for sleeping with hundreds of men. Every time Evergreen saw her in the news or on social media it was because some other man had sold his story to the paper about his hot night of passion with Bluebell RoseGold.

'Star, can you give me a hand in here?' Meadow called.

Evergreen smirked; clearly the story had some not so clean elements to it.

Star clambered off Bear's lap and went into the kitchen.

'I found Bluebell sitting on the side of the road one night when I was coming back from the pub, she was crying after a row with her boyfriend,' Heath said.

'Apparently she had been playing a gig in Cardiff so she was staying near here for a few days,' Bear said. 'She wanted to get away from it all somewhere quiet.'

'I had no idea who she was, she was just an upset woman who was possibly under the influence of alcohol,' Heath said. 'I asked her if she had anywhere to go and she said she didn't so I brought her back here. It was winter, we weren't full, so I said she could stay in one of the tree-houses for the night. When we got back here, she started trying to kiss me and undress me, which I stopped. She was an emotional mess, I wasn't going to take advantage of that. She was furious. No man had ever turned her down before. She started shouting at me, asking, "Don't you know who I am? I'm Bluebell RoseGold." I'm leaving out the multiple swearwords she used but I had no idea her middle name began with an F and rhymes with ducking. I told her I was flattered but I wasn't going to sleep with her because she was drunk and upset. She told me she was always drunk and upset and it had never stopped any of the other hundreds of men she had relations with. Anyway I left her to it. Came back the next morning and she'd gone but had completely trashed the place, cups, plates smashed, TV pulled off the wall, really classy stuff.'

'Tell Evergreen the best part,' Bear said.

Heath sighed. 'Three weeks later she released a song about me.'

Evergreen gasped. 'Oh my god, "Treehouse Man". That's about you?'

'Yeah, I guess. I'm not sure if she didn't remember my name or was attempting to be discreet, which is not like her.'

'My favourite lyrics were, "*Who do you think you are, you think you're better than me, say my name bitch, I'm Bluebell ducking RoseGold*," Bear said.

Evergreen felt her eyes widen. 'Wow, that's some over-inflated sense of entitlement.'

'We thought that might put a stop to him collecting strays, but a few weeks later he brought back an old man who was sleeping on the streets, gave him some food and a bed to sleep for the night. There's always someone Heath has to help.'

And now he'd turned his attention onto her.

'I think it's nice that you want to help so many people,' Meadow said.

Evergreen nodded. 'I think what you're doing for Theo and his dad is lovely.'

Although she couldn't help worrying that he saw her as another charity case. It suddenly made her think that their relationship might have its roots in pity, too.

CHAPTER TWENTY-TWO

Evergreen walked back to Christmas Tree Cottage holding Heath's hand. She knew he wouldn't stay because he was keen to get home to spend some time with Star but it was nice that he wanted to walk her back.

They reached her front door and she opened it, stepping inside before turning to face Heath.

He leaned in for a kiss but she stopped him with a hand on his chest. 'Heath, can I ask you something. Am I a charity case to you?'

He stopped in surprise. 'I'm not going to deny that I want to help you. If I can help people I will. There's nothing wrong with that. But what are you worried about here?'

'I worry that this…' she pointed between the two of them 'is some kind of pity date.'

He stepped back, his eyebrows shooting into his hair. Then he took her hand. 'Evergreen Winters, you have no idea what this means to me. Me helping you has got nothing to do with our relationship, I didn't offer you this house in the hope that something would happen between us. And I'm not dating you because, "Oh hey, she's had a crap time, maybe a shag will make her feel better."'

'I didn't mean that.'

'I've never had a relationship with anyone, so I have no idea what it looks like, but this just feels so right, more so than anything I've ever experienced before. I know it's early days for us, but I really bloody like you and that has nothing to do with pity or charity. We share a connection that feels like it could be something wonderful. Don't you feel that?'

She nodded. 'I do but…' she trailed off.

'But what?'

'When things seem too good to be true, they usually are.'

'I'll give you that. But sometimes, very occasionally, the stars align, fate does her job and two people who are destined to be together actually meet.'

She smiled. This man had really got under her skin. This wonderful brilliant man who always knew the right things to say.

'You know that's a bit heavy for two people who haven't even gone out on a first date yet, don't you?'

He stepped forward, a big grin on his face, cupped her cheeks and kissed her. 'You're totally right, I'll dial it back.'

She couldn't help smiling against his lips.

'Are you sure you don't want to spend a night making Christmas decorations with me and Star?' Heath said.

'I do, but you should spend some time alone with her too.'

He nodded. 'Thank you for giving me that. But just

putting it out there that she'll be in bed by half nine. So if you wanted to come back for more of this…' he kissed her again. 'I wouldn't mind.'

'I'll probably get an early night actually. But I'm very much looking forward to more of this tomorrow.'

He grinned. 'Oh me too.'

He kissed her on the forehead, lingering for a moment before he stepped back. 'OK, I'm going. I'll see you tomorrow.'

'Yes, I'll come and give you a hand with Bear's lodge.'

'OK.' He stepped back again as if he couldn't take his eyes off her. Then, finally, he turned and walked away with a big smile on his face.

Evergreen lay in bed refreshing the emails on her phone for the umpteenth time. There had been no texts, calls or messages from her sister. Maybe it was too soon, maybe she needed time to digest this new development. Maybe she was never going to contact her at all. She needed to get to sleep. The message, if there was one, would still be there tomorrow.

She put the phone down on her bedside drawers just as it buzzed with an email notification.

She quickly scrabbled to open it, knowing it was probably some junk mail and nothing of interest, but her heart leapt when she saw it was an email from Cally. Her eyes scanned over the words way too fast, trying to pick out whether it was a message of hate or love or something in between, but she stopped herself, took a deep breath and read it from the beginning.

Dear Ever,

I have rewritten this message to you a hundred times and I still don't know what to say to the sister I haven't seen for eight years.

I'd gone to bed and cried myself to sleep after Mum had died and I woke up the next morning to find out that you had gone too. Just packed your things and left, so Rob said, and I could never get my head round that. You were always there for me and when I needed you the most you weren't there, and you never came back. I never heard from you again.

I was so angry at you. I had no one to turn to. Celeste was cold and distant and Rob was the same. I felt betrayed and alone.

Seeing you today brought all those feelings back but what you said just didn't ring true with my version of events. I never received any letters or cards from you. But what you said about Rob not wanting you to come back kind of made sense. Whenever your name was mentioned around him, he was always so furious and hateful and it wasn't about you leaving. What happened between the two of you? Did he throw you out?

I know you are not at fault for Mum's death. I was old enough to follow the story on the news, to read the verdict in the papers, even if Rob didn't want to talk

about it, so if you left over some misplaced guilt then you have no reason to feel that way.

I want to hear your side, there's a part of me that wants to know every single thing about you. I've missed you so much but I don't think we can ever go back to what we had although maybe we can move forward.

Could we chat through email or text to start with? I need time to think about my replies and not react badly and instinctively. I'm also working a lot between now and Christmas so, if I don't reply straightaway, don't think I'm ignoring you.

Cally

Evergreen read it through a few times. It hurt her knowing that Cally had been so alone after Suki's death and Rob hadn't been big enough to explain the truth about why Evergreen had gone. Cally had felt let down by Evergreen and she couldn't help feeling guilty about that. Maybe she could have done more to reach out to Cally and the others. But Rob had taken her phone off her when he'd booted her out, as it was something he and Suki had paid for, so she hadn't even had a number for Cally. But perhaps there was something more she could have done.

But Cally was clearly open to hearing more from Evergreen, even if it was only through email for now. And Evergreen clung onto the little ray of hope in that email. *Maybe we can move forward.* She couldn't help feeling excited about that.

She was suddenly wide awake and she wanted to share this exciting news with Heath.

She got up, threw her cloak over her pyjamas and left Christmas Tree Cottage, quickly making her way through the glittering woods to Wisteria Cottage.

She ran up the steps and glanced through the door at Meadow's house to see if Heath was in there but Meadow and Bear were lying together on the sofa, her head on his chest, looking up at him with complete love in her eyes, his hand on her belly as they chatted. There was no sign of Heath.

She moved across the rope bridge to Heath's side of the house and saw him walking around the kitchen wearing only pyjama bottoms with dancing snowmen on them. His body was so divine, he was so broad and muscular, his arms so strong and protective. She wanted those arms around her right now.

It was odd that something she hadn't had for so long, she now wanted and needed so much.

As if knowing she was there, he suddenly looked over towards the door and his face lit up in a huge smile at seeing her.

He quickly crossed the space between them and opened the door.

'Hey, you OK?' Heath said, ushering her inside.

'Yes, she sent me an email.'

'Oh that's great,' he paused and frowned. 'Is it great?'

'Yes, I think so, it's not a big happy email but it's not filled with hatred either. Here, see for yourself.' Evergreen handed him her phone and she smiled when he looped one arm round her shoulders and pulled her into him as he read the email with the other hand. She slid her arms around him too.

'That's positive, I think. She says she'd like to move forward, that's got to be good,' Heath said.

'I picked up on that too. I feel we have so many bridges to mend, she needs to know my side of the story and then she needs to decide how she wants to proceed. Maybe she won't want anything to do with me but at least she will know that it wasn't my fault I wasn't there after Suki died and maybe she can find some peace in that.'

'I agree. Are you going to send a reply tonight, do you want me to help you?'

'I think I need to write a reply when I'm not so tired so I can get it right. I just wanted to share this with you. I know it's not the most positive message in the world but she's hardly going to welcome me back into her life with open arms after all this time. It feels like a small step forward.'

'It is, definitely, and I'm happy you wanted to share it with me.'

He bent his head and kissed her. It was sweet and gentle, not expecting anything more, but every time she kissed him she felt her heart opening up a little bit more to Heath Brookfield.

He pulled back to look at her.

'I should probably go, I was in bed ten minutes ago,' Evergreen said.

'Well, I was just heading there myself. Why don't you stay here tonight?'

Her heart leapt.

'Just to sleep, I promise,' Heath said.

God, she wanted nothing more than to do that with

him, to go to sleep wrapped in his arms, but all these cuddles and naps felt a lot more intimate than kissing and sex. Although she had already been brave once today, she could be brave again.

'OK.'

He grinned. He let go of her to turn off all the lights then took her hand and led her up the stairs.

'Star is on the floor above us, just in case you hear any movement from upstairs,' Heath said.

Evergreen faltered. 'Are you OK with her seeing us in bed together?'

'I know I said that I wouldn't ever want to bring a woman into my home because of Star but she knows you, she's comfortable with you and us being together. I don't think this will be a big deal for her. Besides, she's not going to walk in on us in the throes of passion, we're just sleeping together, in the literal sense of the word.'

She smiled. He seemed so blasé about it all, so laid-back. Maybe she needed to stop worrying about things being too intimate, or too fast, and just relax and enjoy the ride.

He climbed into bed and she slipped out of her cloak and shoes and crawled in beside him, cuddling into his chest. He moved his arms around her, holding her tight.

He stared at her and stroked her face, then leaned forward and kissed her. She melted against him, his kiss bringing her to life. He ran his fingers through her hair and she cupped the back of his neck, making him moan softly against her lips. She knew, if she let it, this kiss could very easily turn into something more. And she wanted that. But just as she felt the kiss change into something a bit more heated, Heath pulled back.

'Sorry, I promised you we were only going to sleep.'

'But I don't mind a goodnight kiss,' Evergreen said.

He grinned and kissed her again and, though he didn't take it any further than that, she knew sleep would be a very long way off that night.

CHAPTER TWENTY-THREE

Evergreen woke the next morning still wrapped in Heath's arms. It had been a long time since she had slept so deeply. She gazed up at him and smiled to see he was asleep with a big smile on his face. He looked so beautiful and peaceful sleeping. She had an overwhelming desire to kiss him awake but it had been very late by the time they'd got to sleep.

Sensing she was awake, he stirred and then smiled to see her there.

'Good morning, beautiful,' he said, sleepily, stretching beneath her.

'Hey, I was just thinking the same about you, how beautiful you looked.'

'Well, that's lovely. I could get used to waking up next to you every day. What a perfect start to the day.'

She smiled. 'You know all the right things to say.'

'It's true.'

She leaned up and kissed him and he pulled her tighter against him, his hand slipping under her pyjama top to stroke her bare back. She gasped against his lips at his touch.

'Heath, I want you so much,' she said.

He groaned. 'Christ, Evergreen, I want that too, so badly. But we have about five minutes before Star comes barging in here demanding breakfast. Trust me, five minutes is nowhere near long enough to do what I want to do and that's certainly something I need privacy for, too. But we have our first date tonight.'

'Can our first date be in bed?'

'It absolutely can be, if that's what you want, but I had something special planned. You can stay here again after and I promise to make it a first date to remember.'

'God, that sounds very exciting.'

Just then they heard footsteps charge across the floor upstairs and the pitter-patter of claws as Star and Hero woke up and came downstairs.

Heath didn't relinquish his hold on her although he did remove his hand from underneath her pyjama top.

Star burst into the room. 'It's three days until Christmas!' She stopped when she saw Evergreen. 'Evergreen, I didn't know you stayed here last night.'

'I needed a cuddle from your dad.'

'He does give the best cuddles,' Star said, before climbing into bed on the other side of Heath.

He kissed his daughter on the head and slid an arm around her. 'Good morning, munchkin.'

Hero, not wanting to miss out, launched himself onto the bed too, curling up at their feet.

Evergreen felt her cheeks ache from smiling so much. She could definitely get used to this.

Curled up on the sofa with a hot chocolate in one hand and her phone in the other, it was the perfect time to send Cally a message, explaining what had happened all those years ago.

Heath was sitting next to her, giving her the space she needed to write the message while he was reading his book, but also the support of just being there when she wrote it.

She opened up the text message screen, added the number Cally had left on the bottom of her email and took a deep breath.

Dear Cally,

Thank you for emailing me. It's probably a lot more than I deserve. I hate that you were alone with your grief. I should have been there for you. I should have tried harder. But let me tell you my side of the story and then you can decide if you want to talk to me any more.

When Celeste picked me up from the hospital that fateful night she barely said a word. We were both numb with shock so I didn't really think anything of it. But when we pulled up on the driveway we both sat and stared at the house, neither of us wanting to go in because Suki wouldn't be there. Then just before she got out the car Celeste told me she hated me and that she

would never forgive me for this. I sat in the car and cried.

Eventually I went in the house and you and all the children were in bed. There was no sign of Celeste or Rob so I went up to my room and there he was throwing all my clothes into a suitcase. He told me he wanted me out of the house and he never wanted to see me again. He said that he and Suki never wanted me here in the first place and that she only allowed me to stay because she pitied me, not because she loved me. He said he should have told me to fuck off years ago. Then he said he wished I'd died instead of Suki, that it should have been me that died. He took my phone off me as he paid the bills for it and practically manhandled me to the door. I said I wanted to say goodbye to you and the others but he told me that you all hated me and wanted me gone, then he pushed me out into the street and slammed the door. It was four in the morning and it was raining. I stood outside for ages, too numb to move, before I finally checked myself into a hotel for the night.

I stayed away for a few weeks but I needed things that he never put in my suitcase that night, my passport, stuff for my university course. So I snuck back in one day, using the key Suki always left under the flowerpot. No one was at home so I took what I needed and left a note for you on your pillow telling you where to find me. But as I was coming back downstairs Rob came home. He was furious, I honestly thought he was going to kill me. I ran out of there but I never dared come back after that. I'm guessing he found the note and destroyed it before you saw it.

I did send cards for birthdays and Christmas too but I think they must have gone the same way of the note.

I did come round on your eighteenth birthday two years later – Rob's car wasn't in the drive so I thought I might be safe. That's when the new owners told me you'd all moved out but they had no idea where you'd gone. I didn't even know where to start looking for you, I couldn't even find you on social media. Maybe I should have tried harder to find you all but I wasn't sure if I'd be welcome. I told myself maybe I was better off alone.

But I have missed you every single day, I wondered what you were doing and if you were happy. I love that you are now working in a zoo, that was always your dream. I would love to meet, have a coffee and a chat with you, but I totally understand if you would prefer to keep it to emails and texts right now or if you don't want to take this any further.

At least now you know the truth.

Love always

Ever x

She sat back and checked it through a few times and then handed it to Heath.

His frown deepened as he read it and he put an arm round her and pulled her to his chest.

'I understand now why you were worried that you were just another charity case for me. Rob made you feel that Suki pitied you instead of loving you and that's a hard pill to swallow. This makes uncomfortable reading but she needs to know the truth,' Heath said. 'I'm surprised she never had this conversation with Rob but it sounds like he held onto that bitterness and anger for a very long time.'

'Yeah, it does, and she had to grow up surrounded by that. Even if it wasn't directed at her, it can't have been easy. She didn't deserve that.'

'No.' He turned to her, stroking her face and kissing her sweetly on the lips. 'But you didn't deserve any of this either.'

'No, I didn't. I've spent a long time thinking maybe all of this – my parents abandoning me, Rob kicking me out – that maybe it was my fault, that I somehow brought it on myself, that maybe I did deserve to be treated badly. But talking it through with you, writing it out here, it's been quite cathartic. I feel like I can let go of this guilt now.'

Heath gave her a small smile. 'I think it's time.'

'Shall I send it?'

He gave her an encouraging nod.

She took the phone back off him and, before she could doubt herself, she pressed send.

CHAPTER TWENTY-FOUR

The transition from Bear's old bachelor pad to clean family home was well underway. Bear had removed all his old things, River and Heath had been busy fixing anything that needed it, Indigo was replacing all the old kitchenware with new cups, plates, bowls and cutlery, Evergreen was cleaning, Meadow and Bear were busy hanging Christmas decorations, and the girls were happily decorating the tree. The effect was startling. The lodge had certainly been liveable when they'd all arrived there earlier that morning but now Evergreen thought it looked wonderful.

She stopped mopping and scanned around. Fairy lights hung from the ceiling in the middle and trailed out in a star shape to the corners and sides of the room. The tree sparkled with gold and red ribbons and baubles. The leather sofa was in fairly good condition anyway but had been covered with a large red Christmassy throw. The place looked clean and homely.

Meadow flopped down on the sofa and Evergreen went and sat next to her.

'This place looks great,' Evergreen said. 'You guys make a good team.'

'Well you're part of that team.'

Evergreen smiled. She hadn't been part of anything for a long time. 'I like being part of the team.'

'Seriously, I've never seen the floor looking so shiny,' Meadow said.

'Hey!' Bear said indignantly. 'I kept this place clean when I lived here.'

Meadow grinned at him.

Just then Tierra came over with Star, they were both giggling.

'Were you in bed with Heath this morning?' Tierra said, boldly.

Evergreen smirked. 'I was. We were having a cuddle.'

'Is that what the kids are calling it nowadays?' River muttered as he climbed down a ladder, having just replaced one of the light bulbs.

'Hey, we were actually,' Heath said.

'Maybe then,' Bear said.

'Daddy and Indigo cuddle in bed and sometimes they kiss too. Were you kissing Heath?' Tierra went on.

Evergreen looked over at Heath for some help. They had already told Star they were boyfriend and girlfriend but did she fully understand that that would involve kissing? And what was appropriate for Tierra?

'Yes we were,' Heath said, without batting an eye.

'When Daddy and Indigo cuddle and kiss in bed, sometimes I hear them make other noises too, the kind of noise you make when you eat something really nice and you go, "Mmmm," that kind of noise, and also Indigo makes noises like when you step in the bath and it's too hot and you go, "Ah, that's too hot." She makes that "Ah" noise a lot too when they cuddle. Were you and Heath making those kind of noises?'

Heath snorted, Meadow suppressing a laugh. River had frozen halfway down the ladder and Indigo had buried her head in the cupboard to focus on putting away the last plate. Evergreen bit her lip to stop herself from laughing.

'Well, we're definitely going to invest in soundproofing now,' River said.

'Heath, you haven't answered the question?' Bear said, innocently.

'Bear and Mummy sometimes make weird noises when they cuddle in bed,' Star said. 'Bear makes grunty growly noises and Mummy makes a weird breathing panting noise like she's been running really fast.'

Meadow cleared her throat awkwardly.

'I'll take an order of soundproofing too,' Bear said.

'Oh well, this has been a thoroughly entertaining conversation,' Heath said.

Evergreen had tears in her eyes from trying not to laugh. She had missed this, children saying whatever the hell they wanted.

'I didn't hear those kinds of noises when I came into Daddy's bedroom this morning,' Star said. 'They were just cuddling. There was no growling or panting.'

'See, at least *I* have nothing to be embarrassed about,' Heath said.

'Maybe you need to try harder,' River said. 'Poor Ever-green having a mediocre cuddle.'

Evergreen let out a bark of laughter and then clamped

her hand over her mouth. Heath looked over, watching her with amusement.

Meadow turned to Evergreen. 'Still want to be part of our team?'

Evergreen grinned. 'More than ever.'

Heath knocked on Evergreen's door later that night and she rushed to answer it.

'Wow, you look gorgeous,' Heath said, appraising her.

'Thank you,' Evergreen looked down at the red-wine-coloured velvet dress she'd teamed with some silver sparkly snowflake hairclips. 'You don't scrub up too badly yourself.' She stretched up to kiss him.

'Are you ready for our date?' Heath said, wrapping his arms around her and holding her close against him.

'I am, come in for a second.'

He followed her inside and she grabbed her phone and her purse and threw them in her bag. 'I've been thinking about tonight all day. I've been so looking forward to it.'

He grinned. 'The date or… after?'

She laughed because, if she was totally honest with herself, she had been thinking a lot about what it would be like to have sex with Heath Brookfield.

'I'm excited about our date and spending time with you but, as I don't know what you have planned, it's been hard to picture it in my head. However, my imagination has got a bit carried away with thinking about… after.'

She moved to grab her cloak.

He laughed. 'Me too. I haven't been able to stop

thinking about it all day. What it will be like to touch you and be with you. I don't think I've ever been so excited about anything in my life. I feel like I'm going to be rushing through the date just to get to the end, which is a shame as the place I'm going to be taking you to is beautiful.'

She turned round to face him, her heart suddenly roaring in her chest at what she was about to suggest. 'That would be a shame. Maybe we can push the date back slightly.'

His eyes widened, a slow smile spreading across his face. 'We could do that. Only I don't want you to think that our relationship is just about sex. I want to date you, do things properly.'

'Oh no, I definitely don't think that. I know you respect me,' Evergreen teased. 'And you said you wanted time to get to know the women you date. You know an awful lot about me, from my disastrous childhood, to living in a horse-drawn caravan doing zombie make-up for a living. I've met your family, you've met my sister and we've already slept together twice; I think we're ready for this next step.'

He grinned and nodded. 'You're probably right.'

They stared at each other and for the longest time neither spoke. She wasn't sure if he moved towards her or she moved towards him but suddenly they were kissing, their bodies clashing together hard. He started shuffling her back towards the bedroom and, as they moved across the lounge, she pushed his coat off his shoulders and set about tackling the buttons of his shirt. He pulled her dress up round her hips, only taking his mouth off hers for the briefest of seconds to tear the dress off. His shirt fell off as

232

they reached the bedroom and as the kiss continued they tumbled onto the bed. Her underwear were the next items of clothing to be flung across the room and, after he'd removed a condom from his pocket, his jeans followed suit. She moaned softly against his lips at the feel of his hands on her body, caressing, stroking, adoring her. His hands were desperate for her, as if he was a man who'd walked through a desert and was now quenching his thirst.

'How long has it been since you've had sex?' Evergreen said.

'A long time, how about you?'

'Even longer.'

She guessed that they wouldn't be that late for their date after all, this was probably going to be over very quickly, her body was already humming with need for him. But that was OK, they could take the time to really get to know each other intimately later.

He ran his hand up the inside of her thigh and she arched up against him, desperate for his touch, desperate for him.

'You don't need to pull out all the stops for me,' Evergreen said, attempting to push his boxers off his hips.

He stilled and pulled back to look at her. 'Do you honestly expect our first time together to be a quick fumble?'

'I don't mind. We have our date and then we can do this properly later. I just need… you.' She wrapped her hand around him, feeling how much he wanted this too. He sucked in a breath through his teeth and then caught her hand and removed it. Kissing her palm before pinning her hand above her head, his fingers entwined with hers.

'We're doing this properly now,' he said, firmly. 'But if you need a release I can help you with that.'

He slid his other hand back up her thigh and touched her in the perfect spot, caressing her with his thumb, applying the exact amount of pressure there that sent sparks through her body until the sparks built into fireworks and then explosions.

'Oh god Heath,' Evergreen shouted out, as wave after wave of pure pleasure rolled through her body.

'There, you can relax now, while I take care of you,' Heath said, kissing her, catching the last breaths of her orgasm on his lips. He moved his mouth to her throat and then her shoulder and she lay back on the pillow to watch him adoring her body with his mouth. Her thirst was well and truly quenched now. Nothing was going to top that.

Heath slipped her breast into his mouth and she cried out again. Christ, he was going to kill her with sex and they hadn't even done it yet. He had the audacity to laugh against her skin, he knew exactly what he was doing to her. He moved his mouth across her stomach and very slowly down her legs, kissing on the inside of her knee, before trailing his hot mouth to her feet. The tension started coiling inside her body again, slowly building with every kiss. Christ, what was he doing to her? Every single other sexual experience had already paled in comparison to this and they hadn't even got to the main event yet.

He trailed his mouth up her legs, slowly up the inside of her thigh. Surely he wasn't going to—

She cried out again as he kissed her there, and that feeling that had built in her stomach was suddenly spreading out to her arms, her legs, taking her higher and

234

higher until it exploded through her with such force she was gasping for breath.

She was utterly spent, feeling like she had just run a marathon as he moved slowly back up her, kissing her stomach again and placing a tender kiss right over her heart, before kissing her on the lips, his whole body weight pinning her to the mattress. He carried on kissing her, seemingly in no rush, and she moved her arms around him, holding him close.

He pulled back to stare at her as if drinking her in. She stroked his face and he kissed her thumb.

'It's funny isn't it, how sex is so different with different people,' Heath said, leaning over to grab the condom. 'I've slept with a lot of women.'

And in that one sentence she suddenly felt completely inadequate, her little bubble of bliss popping.

He dealt with the condom and then settled himself between her legs. He stroked her hair and kissed her as he slid very gently inside her.

He pulled back to look at her again. 'But I've never made love to a woman before. I'm not even sure I knew the difference... until now.'

Tears filled her eyes, her doubts and insecurity vanishing in an instant.

'*This* is different, I'm different,' Heath said. 'I want to make love to you.'

She swallowed the emotion clogging in her throat. 'Heath, you promised you wouldn't fall in love with me before the year was out.'

'I never promised that, but it's OK, I can make love to you without being in love.'

She stared at him. 'Can you?'

'You don't need to worry about me,' Heath said. He kissed her again and very slowly started moving against her. She wrapped her arms and legs around him, relishing the feel of his gentle movements, his body against hers… it was wonderful.

She knew this was different for her too. It wasn't just that he was being so slow and careful, it wasn't that he really wanted to take his time with her instead of rushing to the end goal. It was different because it was him and because, despite her best intentions, she knew she was falling in love with him.

That feeling very slowly started to build again, but this time it wasn't an explosion, it was a wonderful feeling of pure and utter bliss that bubbled and then cascaded through her like a waterfall and as she clung to him, tumbling over the edge, she felt him fall with her too.

CHAPTER TWENTY-FIVE

'Best first date ever,' Evergreen said, as she lay on Heath's chest, stroking her fingers across his heart.

'Oh hell no,' Heath said, gently pushing her off him and climbing out of bed. 'We can do a lot better than amazing sex for our first date.'

'I'm not sure anything will ever top the incredible sex,' Evergreen said, as she sat up to watch him get dressed. She was mildly disappointed that her plan to stay in bed with this wonderful man for the rest of the night and maybe even have a repeat performance was clearly not going to happen now.

'Get dressed. You lying naked in bed is testing my willpower to take you out.'

'Then let's stay here and you can make love to me again and again,' Evergreen said, deliberately letting the sheet fall to reveal more of her body.

He gazed at her, his eyes filled with need. 'Very very tempting, but I'm going to do this relationship with you differently to any other woman I've been with before. We're going on a date.'

She sighed theatrically and got out of bed, walking past him to retrieve her clothes. He caught hold of her, kissing her hard as his hand slipped down to her bum.

'When we get back from our date, I promise, there'll be a lot more of this,' he kissed her again. 'And a hell of a lot more of that,' he nodded towards the bed.

She smiled. 'I'm going to hold you to that.'

She kissed him again and then moved away to get dressed. He watched her as he fastened the buttons on his shirt.

'We're going to be outside so you might want to put on some warmer clothes,' Heath said, as she threw on her dress.

She grabbed one of her jumper dresses and pulled it on over her dress before walking out into the lounge to pick up her cloak and put on her boots.

They stepped outside and she smiled when she saw that snow was gently falling. 'Well snow is going to be very romantic for our first date, you definitely get points for that.'

'Just you wait for the rest of it,' Heath said.

'You've brought me to a castle ruins for our date?' Evergreen said in confusion. She loved a bit of history and during the day this would totally be the type of place she would visit, but it was dark so they weren't going to be able to see a lot. Although lots of people were pouring up the hill towards the castle too and there was an eerie glow coming from the inside so something must be going on.

As they walked under the large archway into the court-yard, she gasped at what she saw. The castle was a lot bigger than she'd expected, stretching as far back as the eye could see, as did the extensive grounds, but the thing that everyone had come to look at were the illuminations. Hundreds of huge lanterns filled the grounds of every shape and colour. She walked past a sculpture of three life-size running unicorns with rainbow manes and tails, which she could see was made from a wire frame with silk stretched over the top of it with hundreds of tiny lights inside, causing the lantern to glow against the inky sky.

'This is beautiful.'

'I thought you might like it. I brought Star here last week and we both loved it, I wanted to share it with you too.'

She looked around at the castle walls, which were lit up by trails of fairy lights while projections of reindeer drawing a sleigh across a starry night sky were being played against the stony walls. Lanterns of every possible flower from giant orchids to roses, to lilies and tulips, were growing out of the grassy banks leading up to the castle. It looked magical.

They walked on to the next sculpture and Heath took her hand, which made her smile. This place couldn't be more spectacular or romantic; it was the perfect choice for their first date.

They passed Neptune with his trident, surrounded by other mermaids and mermen and hundreds of tiny fishes. There were fairies sitting on oversized toadstools reading books, a gigantic dragon fighting against a knight on horseback, a flying horse, a centaur, witches, wizards and so many other creatures from myths and legends. Evergreen loved the giant golden phoenix seemingly flying straight from the fire. Each lantern was so beautifully made with incredible attention to detail.

She stared in wonder as a large ship glided along the castle moat and then a giant octopus – or was it a kraken? – appeared from the water and brought the boat under the waves.

They seemed to be moving into a different theme as this part of the castle grounds had lanterns shaped as things from the future, like flying cars and robots that actually moved. It made her smile to see ones like children playing on flying skateboards, just like in the film *Back to the Future.*

Next they walked into a jungle-themed zone with green lanterns shaped like tropical trees. There were cheetahs, elephants, zebras and birds of paradise flying through the leaves.

Heath bought her a burger and chips and they sat on a bench in a land of dinosaurs.

'This place is magnificent, thank you for sharing it with me,' Evergreen said, eating her chips.

'They do it every year but the lanterns are always different. I love taking Star and just seeing how enchanted she is when she sees every sculpture.'

'I can see why. I'm a grown-ass woman and I'm enchanted by it as well.'

'I've loved watching you see it too.'

She tore her eyes from a large brachiosaurus leaning up

to eat leaves from the trees to look at him. He smiled and stroked her face. 'I like making you happy.'

She smiled and shifted forward to kiss him, tasting the salt of the chips on his lips. 'You make me very happy.'

They seemed to be taking a longer route on the drive home and Evergreen wasn't sure why until Heath stopped his pick-up on the clifftops. From there they could see the towns, beaches and woods that stretched for miles down the coast, and she couldn't help but smile. The view was incredible, the lights of the houses and buildings twinkling over the perfect millpond sea. The snow had stopped and the sky was clear, millions of stars sparkling in the sky, the moon bright and full casting silvery ribbons over the waves.

But to her surprise, Heath reversed into the space on the side of the road so the windscreen was facing away from the view.

He climbed out. 'Come on, we need to be quick.'

He grabbed two large duvets and a flask from the box behind the seats and walked round to the back.

Evergreen frowned in confusion and climbed out the cab too. She watched as Heath laid a duvet on the bed of his pick-up.

'Did you bring me out here to have sex? Because the view is amazing but it's way too cold for that.'

He laughed. 'No, but there's something else I want you to see, and I thought the duvets might help keep us warm while we see it.'

He offered out a hand and helped her to climb up into the bed of the pick-up. They sat with their backs to the cab and Heath placed the second duvet over them. He poured out two mugs of hot chocolate from the flask and handed her one.

She took a sip and looked out on the view. 'This view is wonderful, the little houses and towns so far below us, it looks like a tiny model village.'

'I know, I love it up here, especially late at night, it's so peaceful. No one ever comes up here. And look over there, see that glow on the horizon? That's the castle we've just been to see. The collective light of all those lanterns can be seen from miles away.'

'That's brilliant, I love that. Thank you for taking me there tonight.'

'Just you wait for the finale.'

Evergreen sipped from her mug and suddenly the sky beneath them exploded into a riot of colour as fireworks erupted from one of the tiny towns below them.

'Oh!' she said softly. 'That's beautiful. I've never seen fireworks from above before.'

'I know, it's quite unusual, isn't it.'

'It's spectacular.'

Golds, silvers, reds, blues and greens glittered like over-sized flowers beneath them, sparkles cascading down to the sea. Whistles, pops and booms echoed across the bay, as the fireworks reflected off the mirror-calm waters perfectly. As one gold glittery explosion faded into the darkness it was replaced immediately with another.

Finally it came to a deafening crescendo with a huge display of rockets all exploding at once and, as the bay fell quiet and the only thing left in the sky was coloured smoke, Evergreen could hear the cheers of the townspeople from all the way up here.

'Heath, that was magnificent. You were right, tonight's date was way better than staying in bed.'

He laughed. 'I think I should be mortally offended at that.'

She smiled and leaned her head on his shoulder. 'I don't think you have anything to worry about in that department. You were undoubtedly the best sex I've ever had.'

'Really? I was just thinking I was going to have to pull out all the stops when we got back, make fireworks of our own.'

'Why don't we make our own fireworks right here?' She looked up at him.

'Here? I thought you said it would be too cold?'

'I think we can generate enough heat to warm us both up.' She shuffled out of her knickers and then straddled him.

'Christ you're serious,' Heath said.

'I want to see if it lives up to the hype.'

'I'm not sure there will be much hype in this weather.'

She laughed loudly. 'We can keep most of our clothes on.'

'I don't need a lot of persuading,' He leaned forward and kissed her hard, his hands at her hips as he pulled her tight against him, but as the kiss continued she noticed him drawing the duvet back over her shoulders, keeping her warm, and she couldn't help her heart filling with love at that gesture.

He slipped his hand between her legs and she laughed

against his lips as a big cheer from the town below echoed out across the bay. 'My sentiments exactly.'

He smiled as he kissed her. 'Let's really give them something to cheer about.'

She gasped as he increased the pressure, clinging onto his shoulders as that incredible feeling burst through her like a wrecking ball.

He wriggled around to retrieve a condom from his pocket and after a few moments he lifted her hips and guided her down on top of him. She felt her breath shudder on her lips at the feel of him inside her.

'Are you cold?' Heath asked, rubbing her shoulders.

She smiled. 'Not one bit.'

He grinned and they started moving together, their bodies in perfect sync as if they had known each other for years. They stared at each other and the way he was looking at her was more intimate than anything else he was doing to her, it was as if he could see right inside her. He wrapped his arms around her, so she was impossibly close, and she cupped his face, kissing him hard.

She pulled back to look at him again and the complete adoration in his eyes floored her. A feeling in her chest bloomed so big and so sudden, an ache for him, a need to be with this wonderful man always. She tried to push it away but, as he placed a kiss right over her heart, that feeling swelled even more, like it was too big for her heart to contain.

'Heath, stop,' Evergreen said.

Heath stilled immediately, his face clouding in concern. 'Are you OK?'

'I just… you make me feel things I've never felt before.'

He studied her face. 'And that scares you?'

She nodded.

'If it helps, I'm scared too,' Heath said.

She thought about that for a moment. 'You are?'

'Yeah, these feelings for you are not something I've experienced before either. Maybe we can hold each other's hand, figuratively and literally.'

She smiled. 'I'd like that.

He held up a hand and she entwined her fingers with his, feeling that connection between them burn even brighter.

'Would you like me to carry on?' Heath said.

She grinned. 'Yes please.'

They carried on moving together, staring right at each other. That feeling in her chest seemed to spread out to every single part of her so her body felt like it was fizzing under the surface, like dynamite ready to explode.

She leaned back to look at the stars, the heavens stretching on for miles. It was hard to believe that in this big wide world she had met the man who could be her soul mate, her happy ever after.

She'd never believed such a thing could exist, at least not for her, but she also knew what was happening here. Heath tipped her head forwards so he could kiss her. This was something incredible. For the first time in her whole life she could see forever. And it was that thought that sent her hurtling over the edge.

'You've broken me,' Evergreen muttered sleepily as they got out of the truck and headed back into the woods.

Heath couldn't help the grin spreading on his face as he looped an arm round her shoulders.

'I'm not even sorry.'

'You're a sexual beast.'

He laughed and started guiding her back towards his house.

'I think I better go back to my cottage so I can sleep. If we go back to yours, you'll just force me to have sex again.'

'There was hardly much forcing going on when you straddled me in the back of my truck.'

'Oh come on, you have to take some responsibility for this. You just have to flash me one of your charming smiles and my clothes fall off.'

'This charming smile?' He gave her his best smouldering grin.

'No, not out here, people will see me naked,' Evergreen said, breaking away from him and making a run for his house.

He chased after her and caught her. She quickly closed her eyes.

'No, no, if I close my eyes, I can't be dazzled by it.'

'That's going to make climbing the stairs a bit difficult,' Heath said, bending down and throwing her over his shoulder.

She gave a shriek of laughter. 'You're a monster.'

He walked up the stairs to his house and then carried her up to his bedroom before depositing her on the bed. He laughed when she quickly wiggled out of her clothes.

'See, this is the power you have over me.'

He got undressed and pulled on his pyjama bottoms, passing her a t-shirt to put on.

She stared at it. 'Are we not having sex?'

'Not tonight.' He climbed into bed.

'Too tired?' she teased.

He smiled. 'I figured that as you were dozing off in the car on the way home, I might let you have a rest… for a few hours.'

She pulled on the t-shirt and snuggled up in bed next to him, her head on his chest, an arm round his stomach. It was the most wonderful feeling in the world. He had never wanted a woman in his bed before, all the other women he'd been with he'd slept with them at their house or somewhere else, never here. But this felt so right. He'd never shared a bed with a woman without sex being the main reason either. But cuddling Evergreen, just holding her while they slept, was more than enough.

'Wake me up when you've regained your strength,' Evergreen muttered sleepily.

'Oh I intend to.'

He watched her smile, then her eyes closed and he kissed her on the forehead. He felt her breathing change as she dozed off. 'I want to stay like this forever,' Heath whispered.

There was no response and he thought she'd fallen asleep but then she spoke. 'Me too,' she said softly.

He closed his eyes and went to sleep with the biggest smile on his face.

CHAPTER TWENTY-SIX

Evergreen woke up the next day with Heath curled around her from behind. His warm breath on the back of her neck was the best feeling in the world.

How had she ended up here, in bed with such a wonderful man she had only met a few days before? That wasn't her style at all. And it was more than just casual sex, she knew that. She never thought she'd would ever be saying this but with Heath it felt like it could be something amazing, something life-changing. In fact if it all ended now, she knew he had already transformed her life forever. Ordinarily, with any other man she'd slept with she always wanted to get out of there either straight after or very early the next morning, she'd never been big on cuddling. But this felt different, she could stay here wrapped in his arms all day.

She gently rolled over and the movement woke him up. She smiled when she saw a big grin spread across his face at seeing her.

'Good morning, beautiful,' Heath said, leaning forward

to kiss her briefly. He stroked her hair from her face. 'How are you feeling today?'

She grinned. 'Tired but ridiculously happy.'

'Well that makes me happy.' He kissed her again. 'Come on, let's get up and we can have breakfast with the others. As tomorrow is Christmas Eve, the girls are going to be high as kites but we have time to take a shower together if you want.'

'Are you going to take advantage of me again?'

'Absolutely.'

She laughed and then watched in delight as he got out of bed and stripped naked.

'Well that's a lovely thing to wake up to,' Evergreen said, unashamedly staring at him.

'It's all yours baby.'

She smiled and stretched, then picked up her phone. Her heart leapt to see that there was an email from Cally.

'Oh Cally replied,' Evergreen said, sitting up so she could read it.

'What does it say? I mean, don't tell me if you don't want to.'

'It's OK, you've been through this with me from the beginning. I want to share it with you. I'll read it out.'

Dear Ever,

Reading your email made me cry. I can't believe Rob would do such a thing. Well actually I can. He never got over Mum's death, he was a very angry and bitter man. I

249

moved out as soon as I was eighteen and I hardly saw him after that. He died four years ago and his sister looked after Lucy, Noah and Oliver and I'd still go and see them regularly. I know it's horrible to say but I think they were a lot happier after he died, it was such a toxic environment for all of us. Suki would have hated how he behaved towards us after she died.

I hate that you were alone too for all this time. At least I still had Lucy, Noah and Oliver, although I haven't spoken to Celeste for years. But you had no one. Life could have been so much easier for all of us.

But where do we go from here? You don't know the woman I am now and I don't know you, although I would like to. So let's start from there. Tell me about your life and I'll tell you about mine. The bullet points I guess, eight years is a lot to catch up on.

After I left college I travelled for a while and ended up working in a zoo in Austria for a year which I loved. Zoos in this country have much stricter qualification requirements so I came back home and took a diploma in management of zoo animals and then got a job at the zoo where I've worked ever since. I love it, every day is different and the animals are complete characters. I'm not married and I don't have any children. I recently broke up with a long-term boyfriend, we were together for nearly four years. It was quite amicable in the end, we just didn't love each other any more.

What about you, married, divorced, any children? What have you been doing all this time?

Cally x

. . .

'That's hugely positive,' Heath said. 'She wants to know you and she believes your side of the story. You two may never be as close as you were but at least you might be able to have some kind of relationship with her.'

'I know, this makes me really happy,' Evergreen said, scanning through the email again. 'I might just take a few minutes to reply to her if that's OK.'

Heath leaned forward and kissed her on the forehead. 'Take your time.'

He disappeared inside the bathroom and a few moments later she heard the shower running.

Evergreen stared at the screen of her phone for a moment, wondering what she could say. She hit reply and started writing.

Dear Cally,

I'm so sorry to hear about Rob, I know that the last few years of his life were not easy on any of you but he was still the only dad you've ever known.

I'm so pleased to see you have a job in a zoo and it makes you happy.

I'm working as a make-up artist for film and TV, I mainly do monsters, zombies, wounds, all the graphic, horrible stuff, I love it. I also do the occasional background artist acting work. Mostly crowd scenes, so you're unlikely to have seen me in anything. I live in a horse-drawn caravan. It's small but has everything I need, plus I get to travel around the country. I bought a

Clydesdale horse called Thunder and he takes me every-where I need to go.

I've never been married and I don't have any chil-dren either but one day I'd like to.

Evergreen paused, wondering how to form into words that she had never put down roots, never trusted anyone to have a relationship before, because what had happened after Suki died and after her own parents abandoned her – in her dad's case, twice – had scarred her for life. Maybe there was no need to go into details about how broken she was.

I'm dating Heath, Star's dad, but things are very early days for us right now. Although I feel really good about it.

It would be lovely to meet up for a coffee sometime and we can have a proper chat.

Love

Ever x

She read it through a few times and then pressed send.

She got out of bed, undressed and joined Heath in the shower. He immediately enveloped her in his arms and kissed her deeply.

'All done?' he said, his hands wandering down her back towards her bum.

'Yes, it wasn't long. Like she said, how can you

summarise eight years of our lives in an email? I've asked if we can meet up for a coffee, so let's see if she agrees to that. She definitely seems open to having some kind of relationship.'

'I'm so pleased for you. Now would you be open to the kind of relationship where we have hot shower sex?'

She laughed. 'I would definitely be open to that.'

Heath was lying on the sofa in his house reading a book. They were set to go to the Christmas market later that day, but Star had insisted she wanted some time with Evergreen alone. He wondered if his daughter wanted to grill his new girlfriend and if Evergreen could cope with the inappropriate questions, although the alone time was over in Meadow's house so he knew Meadow would step in if it got too awkward.

Just then the door opened.

'Daddy, I fell over and hurt my leg,' Star said.

'Oh no,' Heath said, getting up to inspect the cut and then his stomach lurched with horror at the state of her leg. Blood was pouring down from just below her knee and the bone had quite obviously come through the skin, it was horrific. He was just about to pick her up and rush her to the nearest hospital when he realised that Star was biting down on a grin and he spotted Evergreen lurking in the doorway too. Relief gushed through him.

He decided to play along.

'Oh my god, we're going to have to operate,' Heath said, scooping her up and carrying her to the dining room table.

He laid her down and Star let out a giggle. Even up close the wound looked real, the red blood thick and shiny. 'Evergreen, I'm going to need your help. We're going to have to chop it off.'

'Noooo,' Star howled through her laughter.

'I'm sorry, there is nothing that can save this leg. Evergreen, can you get me a big knife?'

Evergreen rushed into the kitchen and, obviously not knowing where anything was, grabbed the nearest thing to hand. 'Will a spatula do?'

'It will have to,' Heath said.

He took it from her and started sawing away at Star's leg with the plastic implement, much to Star's delight as her laughing went up an octave.

'This is no good, we need bandages, lots of them,' Heath said.

Evergreen grabbed the roll of kitchen towel and Heath started wrapping it around both legs, going all the way up to her body and then rolling it around that too so she looked like an Egyptian mummy. Star was in fits of hysterics by now as he finished wrapping the kitchen towel around her head.

'Why are you bandaging my head when it's my leg that's hurt?' Star said through her laughter.

'Can't be too careful,' Heath said. He carefully tore open gaps in the kitchen towel so she could see and breathe.

'Now what?' Evergreen said.

'Medicine to stop the bleeding. Grab me that brown bottle from the fridge door, that's a miracle medicine, it cures everything.'

Evergreen hurried to the fridge and looked in the door,

snorting when she saw the brown bottle in question was a bottle of chocolate milkshake. She passed it to him and Heath helped Star sit up and take a few sips, although she was laughing too much to drink properly.

'Do you feel better?' Heath said.

Star nodded.

'Well let's see if you can still walk.' Heath lifted her down from the table and put her on her feet. The kitchen towel wasn't done up that tight but it was restrictive enough that, after a few shuffly steps forward, Star toppled over.

'Oh no, she's feeling faint after losing all that blood,' Evergreen said.

Heath nodded gravely as Star tried and failed to get up, giggling so much she was crying.

'Help me move her to the sofa.' He grabbed hold of Star under her arms, the paper towel tearing as he lifted her and Evergreen took her feet. 'Don't drop her,' Heath said, doing a few fake drops but not letting her hit the floor.

They manoeuvred her to the sofa and laid her down.

'We need to prop her legs up,' Evergreen said, gathering up all the cushions.

Heath grinned. The number of cushions she was collecting was enough to practically lift his daughter upside down. They started stacking the cushions up, raising Star up higher and higher until she was almost vertical. Star was still laughing helplessly.

'OK, we'll just leave her like that for a few hours. Although that's a shame because Meadow was making her world-famous incredible chocolate brownies, and Star will miss out.'

'I think a brownie might help,' Star said, wriggling to get down and tearing some of the paper towel in the process.

'Well OK, if you're sure, but if it doesn't fix all the bleeding we might have to do all this again,' Heath said.

Star ripped off the paper towel and looked down at her cut. 'I thought the make-up would be smudged after all that, but it's stayed there?'

'My make-up doesn't smudge, you're stuck like that for life,' Evergreen said.

'Cool!' Star said, reverentially.

'Hang on a minute, are you telling me the cut wasn't real?' Heath said.

Star laughed. 'You knew it wasn't real? But when I first came in I thought you believed it.'

'I did, for a few seconds,' Heath said. 'But then I saw you laughing so I knew it wasn't. It's very convincing though. Is that why you wanted to spend time with Evergreen?'

'Yes, I wanted a fake arrow through my leg but Evergreen persuaded me to go for the bad leg break instead. She said getting an arrow through my leg wasn't that realistic.'

'You're a monkey.' Heath tickled her and she let out another squeal of laughter as she tried to get away. He picked her up and threw her over his shoulder. 'And you, Evergreen Winters, you're in big trouble.'

Evergreen grinned, totally unabashed. 'It was worth it.'

Star wriggled down to get on the floor. 'Come on, we need to go to the Christmas market, Mummy says there's a man who sells crêpes and churros.'

She ran out the door and across the bridge and Heath slid his arms round Evergreen.

'She likes you,' Heath said.

'The feeling is very mutual.'

'Although I'm definitely going to have to get you back for this little stunt.'

She reached up and kissed him. 'I look forward to it.'

CHAPTER TWENTY-SEVEN

Evergreen was loving the Christmas market. All the hard work from the Brookfields and the staff, which she had contributed a small part to, had paid off. The place looked magical. The little huts looked like fairy dwellings, their rooftops sparkling as if they were part of a winter wonderland. The abundance of fairy lights, inside and outside the huts and hanging from the trees, completed the enchanting festive look. Someone had placed oversized animal statues around the area so there were deer, foxes, badgers, rabbits all presiding over the proceedings to give it a natural, whimsical look. Red ribbons were arranged between the huts and periodically there were even old Victorian-style lamps placed between the huts too, draped in garlands or with ribbons wound around them. And with Greta's wreaths hanging from every door, it looked perfect.

There were lots of gorgeous foods and sweets to try, stalls selling delicious chocolates, chutneys, jams, as well as the churros and crêpes that Star had been so keen to eat. There were candles, soaps, smellies of every scent and colour. Star had gone off with Meadow and Bear on a mission to smell every single one. There were so many stalls selling beautiful handmade decorations Evergreen was tempted to buy the lot. Only the fact that she had led a minimalist life for the last eight years was stopping her. Although maybe she didn't need to any more if she had her own home like Christmas Tree Cottage. She could fill every inch of space with Christmas paraphernalia if she so wished. She smiled at that thought.

There were lots of benefits of living in Christmas Tree Cottage. Although it had been a throwaway comment from Heath, she loved the idea of face painting children at the weekends to help pay her way. Despite the common phrase in the film industry of never working with children or animals, she'd always found children fun to work with. As Heath said, they were easily pleased. She also loved the idea of being part of a team, contributing to all of this.

If she lived here, she could just take work at the Cardiff film studios and Thunder could retire. She had no idea how old he was as she'd bought him third- or fourth-hand and, while she felt he still had a few more years on the clock, it would be nice for him not to have to pull her caravan up and down the country any more.

She looked up at Heath holding her hand as they walked through the market. She had to admit he was the biggest reason for wanting to stay, which she knew was a foolish basis for her decisions. But this connection between them was not like anything she'd experienced before and she wanted to see how things would develop.

He stopped in front of one of the huts, where there were a few tables outside to tempt people to browse before coming in. Heath ducked his head to go in and Evergreen stopped outside to look at the Christmas decorations.

And that's when Amelia swooped in, taking her arm and escorting her away before Evergreen even knew what was going on.

'So, my little plan of getting you two together seems to have worked,' Amelia said.

Evergreen laughed that she was somehow taking credit for their relationship.

'And how is this your doing?'

'Reverse psychology 101. Push two people together and they repel apart, take a step back and they come together. I played my hand by asking you out on a date on behalf of Heath, guaranteeing you would run in the opposite direction, but that was merely setting the wheels in motion. Once I visibly lost interest in you two, you were naturally drawn together. It's the old double bluff.'

Evergreen didn't bother to correct her, though the truth was that she and Heath had already been technically dating when Amelia had asked her out on Heath's behalf.

'Do you see marriage in your future?' Amelia went straight in with the big guns.

Evergreen smirked. 'It's probably too early to tell.'

'I don't necessarily mean with Heath, but is that the dream: marriage, kids, the little white picket fence?'

'I don't think I've ever dreamt about what kind of fence I would like in my future. Also, not much call for a picket fence around my caravan.'

'You know what I mean. Do you want the picture-perfect future or do you have more… whimsical fanciful dreams of travelling the world or putting your career first?'

Amelia's tone of voice gave away what she thought of the second option.

Evergreen decided to have some fun with her. 'I know I don't know you, Amelia, but I always thought you were a bit of no-nonsense feminist. Someone who would respect a woman's decision to make the right decisions and choices for herself and not kowtow to the patriarchy by taking part in ancient traditions that have no meaning or relevance in today's society.'

Amelia stared at her, her mouth falling open. 'Of course I'm a feminist. I have two brilliant great-granddaughters and I wish for them the biggest, most colourful dreams. I want them to travel the world and then change it brick by brick. But that journey doesn't have to be one they take alone, they can change the world with a loving husband by their side, supporting them, joining forces with them. Everyone needs someone to love and to be loved themselves.'

'I'm only pulling your leg, Amelia. You have to admit that talking to me about marriage when I've been on one date with your grandson is a bit weird. But to answer your question, I've always wanted to be part of a big family but I never thought that dream was meant for me. And I know it's ridiculously early days for me and Heath and we've obviously not talked about marriage but, for the first time in a long time, I've thought maybe that dream can come true. And not necessarily with Heath, he's a wonderful man but I have no idea if what we have is for forever, neither of us know that. But he's made me realise that that dream is a possibility for me now, one day.'

Amelia looked delighted with this news. 'I knew it, I

knew you two were meant to be together, you're soul mates, I can see that.'

Evergreen shook her head with a smile. Amelia had conveniently bypassed the bits she didn't want to hear and embellished the rest.

'Maybe, just give us some space to screw this up on our own,' Evergreen said.

'I couldn't agree more,' Heath said and Evergreen turned to realise he'd caught up with them. 'Can I have my girlfriend back now?'

Amelia grinned, completely unabashed. 'She's all yours.'

Heath took Evergreen's hand and led her away. 'I'm sorry about her.'

'She's fine, she obviously just wants to see you happy so we're on the same side in that regard.'

He smiled and kissed her on the head. 'Have you given any more thought about whether you might spend Christmas Day with us? No pressure but I'd love to wake up with you in my arms on Christmas morning,' he said. 'And I'm sure Star would love to have you there for the big day too.'

She smiled. 'I would love that too.'

'Really?'

She nodded. 'I was thinking that I'd like to stay here for a bit longer after Christmas too. I'm enjoying spending time with you and I don't want that to end any time soon.'

Heath's grin lit up his face. 'That's the best news I've heard all day.'

'Don't get excited, it's just for a few more weeks. It's not like I'm committing to forever.'

'I'll take it but, look, if things between you and I end, the house is still yours, we can be adults about living in the same place.'

'In a rose-tinted world, of course we could. But if you break up with me I'm not sure I could live with seeing the thing I wanted more than anything every day knowing I couldn't have it. And if I break up with you I wouldn't want to put you through that either.'

'Then let's just agree to never break up,' Heath said, not taking it remotely seriously. He stopped and kissed her briefly on the lips. 'Although I do like the part where you said I'm the thing you wanted more than anything.'

She laughed against his lips. 'It was hypothetical.'

'Shush, don't burst my bubble.' He kissed her again.

They moved on and stopped by a stall selling Christmas jewellery: beautiful little pieces made from resin or clay that depicted intricate leaves of holly, ivy or other pretty sprigs of Christmas foliage with berries or leaves that glittered with snow or frost. They were beautiful. One necklace had a gorgeous small Christmas wreath made to look like ivy, bay and yew leaves mixed with red and white berries, which glittered as Evergreen held it up to the light.

They moved on to another stall selling ornaments that looked like ice carvings: polar bears, penguins, foxes, rabbits, all jutting out of a block of ice glimmering in the twinkling lights.

At the next stall they bought some hot mince pies served with a big dollop of brandy cream and sat down on a nearby bench to eat them.

There was a couple at the far end of the bench too and after a few moments it was very evident they were having some kind of argument, although the market was noisy with lots of people and Christmas music playing out of nearby speakers so Evergreen couldn't hear the specifics. She tried to focus on her mince pie to give them some privacy but the woman suddenly got up and walked away. The man looked absolutely crushed.

'Are you OK?' Heath asked him after a while.

The man shook his head. 'Not really. She just broke up with me. We'd been together for two years. I thought something wasn't right between us for a long time, but we've both been so busy with work that I thought it was that. I can't believe it. You'd think after two years that you'd be safe, that you'll be together forever, but it's not true, is it? No relationship is safe.'

He got up and walked away, his shoulders hunched like he was carrying the weight of the world on his shoulders.

'Poor bloke,' Heath said. 'Break-ups are hard.'

Evergreen stared at her mince pie. What the man had said was true, no relationship was safe. Even Cally had broken up with her boyfriend after four years because they didn't love each other any more. Things were going great right now between her and Heath but were they really going to last? Was she setting herself up to get hurt, if not now, at some point in the future?

She looked at him. Her feelings for him made her want to run away to try to protect herself. She so wanted to throw all her fears out of the window and fully embrace this wonderful thing that was happening between them but her lack of trust, her fear of getting hurt ran so deep.

Just then Star came running over to them, carrying a round sparkly ball. 'Look at this unicorn bath bomb,' she said, excitedly. 'You put it into the bath and it fills the water with glitter and it smells amazing.'

Evergreen pushed away her fears. 'Does it smell of unicorns?'

Heath laughed.

'Of course it does, and magic,' Star said, bubbling over with excitement. She held out the bath bomb for Evergreen to take a sniff. It smelt sweet, maybe sugar and strawberries which maybe, all things considered, was what unicorns and magic should smell like.

'That does smell good.'

'There was one called Christmas magic, I bought that for you,' Star said, rooting in her bag and handing it over.

Evergreen stared at it, a huge lump forming in her throat. 'You bought me a present?'

'I was going to give it to you on Christmas Day but I'm not sure if you'll still be here then so I thought you should have some Christmas magic now. Daddy said you don't have a bath tub in your caravan so you should use the bomb in Christmas Tree Cottage while you're staying there.'

Evergreen had no words at all.

'That's very thoughtful of you,' Heath said.

'Thank you, this is… wonderful, thank you so much,' Evergreen said.

Star shrugged, not realising the magnitude of what she had done with this simple gesture. 'I hope it brings you Christmas magic,' she declared dramatically, waving her imaginary magic wand like a tiny fairy godmother.

Evergreen smiled as she looked at her and Heath. 'I think it already has.'

CHAPTER TWENTY-EIGHT

Evergreen was lying on Heath's sofa waiting for him to come down from putting Star to bed. The girl had been fizzing with excitement all evening but as Christmas Eve was tomorrow it was no surprise.

Her phone beeped with a notification and she reached over and grabbed it, her heart leaping to see it was a message from Cally. She quickly opened it.

Dear Ever

Just a quick message, I've just got home from work and I'm heading out with some friends.

Your job sounds like a lot of fun and I'm glad things are going well with you and Heath right now, he seems like a decent man. And I love the idea of you travelling round the country in a horse drawn caravan.

I've finished work for a few days now and don't go

back until the day after Boxing Day. I have no plans for Christmas as I was going to spend it with Jake and his family but, as we're no longer together, I'm not doing that. I know this might seem too soon as we haven't seen each other for eight years so I won't be offended if you say no but would you like to spend some or all of Christmas together? Maybe we can get together tomorrow, Christmas Eve, if you want. I know that's very short notice so I totally understand if you have plans. I could come to you if that works.

Love Cally x

Evergreen's heart soared. Cally wanted to spend Christmas with her. The thought of being with at least part of her family at Christmas made her feel giddy with excitement. Maybe she could finally put the past behind her and move on once and for all.

Heath came downstairs whistling a Christmas song. 'Star pretty much went out like a light after I read her a story, I think the excitement is finally catching up with her.' He paused. 'You OK?'

'Yes, I just got a message from Cally. She wants to see me over Christmas, she's offered to come here tomorrow if that's OK?'

'Of course it is, she can stay here over the whole of Christmas if she wants. I think all the treehouses are full but she can stay at Christmas Tree Cottage and you can stay here.'

She couldn't help the smile spreading across her face at the thought of spending Christmas Day with Cally. 'Are you sure? This is our first Christmas together and I know you wanted to spend it with me. Are you really happy to share me with my sister too?'

'I still get to spend Christmas with you and I get to see this big beautiful smile on your face because you'll be with Cally as well. Our Christmases are always big noisy family things, Indigo's sister Violet is joining us Boxing Day, so why not add one more member of the family to the menagerie.'

She leapt up to hug him. 'Thank you.'

'You have nothing to thank me for.'

'I'll just send a quick message back.'

Evergreen wrote her sister a message saying she'd be very welcome Christmas Eve and Christmas Day if she so wished. She suggested a time and gave her directions to Wishing Wood, then she turned back to Heath.

'Thank you for giving me this.'

He shook his head. 'Family is important. Sometimes family are the ones you're born with and sometimes it's the ones you choose for yourselves.'

'That's so true and I'm so glad I get to spend Christmas with your family this year.'

'I am too.' He kissed her, deeply. 'And not just because I'll get to hold you in my arms on Christmas morning and do this.' He kissed her again.

She slid her arms around his neck. 'What else will you be doing to me on Christmas morning?'

'You want me to show you?'

'I think we need a dry run.'

He kissed her and, without taking his mouth from hers, he suddenly scooped her up. She laughed against his lips as he carried her up the stairs into his room. He laid her down on the bed and was immediately leaning over her, kissing her as his hands wandered across her body, caressing and undressing at the same time, touching her skin with complete reverence. She pulled his t-shirt over his head, pushed his jeans off his hips, and soon they were both naked. Although Heath was in no rush to take the next step, he was clearly more than happy just kissing her, his hands adoring her body with gentle touches until she was trembling with need.

He finally moved his hand between her legs, still kissing her, and when she came not long after, he captured her moans on his lips.

He pulled back to grab a condom and after a few moments he moved inside her, his eyes locked on hers. She gasped softly at the feel of him, they fitted so perfectly together as if made specifically for each other.

She stroked his face, hooking her legs around his hips, pulling him tighter against her. He kissed her throat, her shoulders, as he started moving against her before kissing her hard on the mouth. She caressed her hands down his back, playing her fingers across his spine and up to the back of his neck, making him moan against her lips.

Every touch of his hands, his lips, the feel of his body against hers made sensations of pure bliss start to spread through her, this was complete heaven.

As the feelings started to build in her body, she felt Heath's breath catch and he pulled back to look at her.

'Christ, why is this so good between us?'

'Maybe because the stars aligned,' she said, using his words.

He smiled. 'I think in our case they really did.'

She looked up at him and knew he was right. She was in love with this man and, while in the cold light of day she knew it would scare the hell out of her, right now she could find nothing but joy at this feeling that was burning through her. For the first time in her life, she was in love.

Suddenly that blissful feeling built into an explosion of pleasure, need and love and she clung onto him as she roared over the edge.

CHAPTER TWENTY-NINE

The morning of Christmas Eve had arrived with a fresh dusting of snow. It wasn't the thick blanket that was really needed at this time of year but it was enough to cover everything with a thin layer of sparkly icing sugar and make everything look magical.

For the first time in years, Evergreen was beyond excited about Christmas. Not only was she going to spend it with Heath and his wonderful family, but she was going to see her little sister as well.

She'd barely been able to concentrate during the last breakfast with Santa session. Cally had messaged back the night before to say she'd be there by ten so chances were that she was already here waiting for her.

Lindsay, or Twinkletoes as Heath was so fond of calling her, was still hot on her time-keeping as she helped to wrap up the session, encouraging the children to write a Christmas wish on the tree before ushering them out. Heath stood at the door offering handshakes, high fives and hugs where appropriate, and then finally it was just the three of them.

'Well I'm off now until the New Year,' Lindsay said, pulling off her jingly hat with great relish. 'Is there anything else you need from me before I go?'

'Oh well if you're asking, another jolly rendition of "Jingle Bells" wouldn't go amiss,' Heath said.

'You don't pay me enough for that kind of shit, Heath Brookfield,' Lindsay said, yanking off her jingly shoes. 'So you can stick these where the sun don't shine.'

Heath laughed loudly and then gave Lindsay a hug. 'Thank you for all your help, you have been a brilliant elf. I hope you have a wonderful Christmas.'

Lindsay grunted her displeasure but Evergreen could see the smile forming on her lips. 'Happy Christmas to you too.' She pulled away from Heath and gave Evergreen a big hug too.

'Happy Christmas,' Evergreen said.

'And to you, will I be seeing you in the New Year?' Lindsay said.

Evergreen glanced at Heath and smiled. 'I should think so.'

Heath grinned.

'Right, I'm out of here.' Lindsay gave them both a wave and left.

'OK, let's get out of these clothes and make-up, I know you're desperate to go and see Cally,' Heath said, quickly stripping off right there in front of her, almost distracting her from wanting to see her sister. Almost.

She quickly removed Heath's make-up and hair and then did her own before running into her bedroom to get changed. She didn't have a lot of clothes so she suddenly had a little panic about what to wear to see her sister again. Heath came up behind her, still half undressed, and wrapped his arms around her, kissing her neck. 'You'll look beautiful in whatever you wear.'

She smiled and grabbed a bright blue dress, quickly pulling it on and turning to face him.

'Will I do?'

'You'll more than do. Are you going to bring her back here so you can chat?'

'Yes I think so, but we'll probably join you all for dinner later tonight.'

'If you want to. If you're having fun here then don't worry. You have a lot to catch up on.'

She leaned up and kissed him. 'Wish me luck.'

'You don't need it, you're an incredible woman and she will see that.' He kissed her. 'I'll see you later.'

He turned to get dressed and she gave him a wave and ran out the house. She quickly hurried over to the reception area and burst through the door.

'She's not here yet,' Meadow said. 'She might have got a bit lost trying to find the place, it can be tricky to locate. Why don't you give her a call?'

Evergreen looked at her watch; it was only half past ten. It was a bit disappointing that she wasn't here already but Cally might be one of those people who were bad at time-keeping, or maybe she'd got stuck in traffic or got lost as Meadow said. It didn't matter. They had the next few days to catch up with each other.

'Oh you're probably right, I'm sure she'll be here soon.

Thank you for letting her stay and for letting us both join in with your Christmas.'

Meadow smiled easily. 'It's no big deal. The more the merrier at Christmas. And I've met Cally, she seems really nice.'

'Still, spending a day with her as a tour guide is a bit different to inviting her into your home on Christmas Day.'

'Evergreen, you're important to Heath, so you're important to us. If this makes you happy then I'm all for it. I know what it's like to have a crappy family, as does Heath. If we can give you a tiny bit of normal family life back then of course we're going to do it. One extra person among all of our chaos isn't going to make any difference.'

'Well, two extra people. You didn't account for me, too.'

'But you're already part of our family.'

Evergreen stared at her in surprise and then cleared her throat awkwardly.

'Where's Bear and Indigo today? They're normally here on reception too, aren't they?'

'Bear is hanging out with Star until Heath gets back from the breakfast session and Indigo has taken River and Tierra to do some last-minute Christmas shopping.'

'Ah, I see.'

'Does it scare you being part of our family?' Meadow said, clearly not letting this go.

Evergreen paused. 'A little bit. I haven't had a family for so long, I find it hard to trust in it.'

'That part is the hardest. Letting go of your fears, taking a step into the unknown. But Heath will be by your side the whole way.'

'Until he's not and I'm scared of how much that will hurt.'

Meadow's face softened. 'You're in love with him.'

It wasn't a question, she'd said it as a fact.

'I'm scared of my feelings for him too, I feel like my body is in flight or fight mode. It knows that pain is imminent and there's a big part of me that wants to run away from it. But I also know I have never felt this way before and I want to stay and fight for it. Right now, I'm not sure which survival instinct will kick in first but I fear it will be the former. And I really don't want to hurt Heath or Star but I don't know if I'm emotionally or mentally ready for a big love story.'

Meadow nodded. 'I get that, I do. I avoided love for eight years because I felt like I was unlovable – mainly because my dad treated me so badly – but I was missing out on the biggest, most wonderful love story all that time. Love doesn't have to be painful. And I do think Heath could be your big love story.'

'Really?'

'I'm pretty sure Heath is in love with you too.'

Evergreen's heart leapt at that thought.

'This is all moving so quickly I feel like I haven't had a chance to draw breath. And Heath has been so respectful about trying to take things slow but I just never expected to fall so hard and so fast. I thought we'd date and get to know each other and it would be a slow build, but that hasn't happened at all.'

'There is no timescale when it comes to love. Bear asked me to marry him twenty-four hours after we finally got together. I know we had known each other for most of our lives, but when you meet the one that makes your heart sing, why wait?'

Evergreen nodded. 'Everything you've said makes sense and if I was talking to me I'd say the same thing, but it doesn't stop me feeling scared.'

'Being scared of getting hurt is a perfectly healthy response, whether that pain is emotional or physical. Running away from something scary is also perfectly normal. I was watching some silly little video on Facebook the other day about how to survive a zombie apocalypse. It said when the zombies come our gut instinct is to run and that's fine. But it's how you handle yourself after that will be the thing that keeps you alive. You can either keep running or try to stay calm so you think rationally and make good decisions, find somewhere safe and make a plan, and I think that rings true for lots of things that happen in our lives. Take the time to think things through.'

Evergreen smiled. 'That's good advice.'

'And no matter what happens between you and Heath, you will always have a home here.'

'Thank you.' She checked her watch again. 'I think I'll go and wait down by the gate for Cally to arrive.'

Meadow smiled. 'OK, I'll see you later.'

Evergreen walked out and made her way towards the entrance so Cally would see her and wouldn't go flying past in her car. Now all she had to do was wait.

And think.

CHAPTER THIRTY

Evergreen bit her lip. It was coming up to twelve o'clock and there was still no sign of Cally. Maybe she'd got completely lost. She'd phoned her once already half hour or so before and it just rang and rang before going through to her answerphone. She decided to give her another call, if she was lost she could perhaps help with directions. She dialled her number again but just like last time it rang for ages before going through to the answerphone. This time Evergreen decided to leave a message.

'Hey Cally, it's me, Ever. Just wondering if you've got lost or delayed? Let me know if you need any help.'

She disconnected the call and looked out onto the resolutely quiet road. Snow sparkled from the bushes and trees; there wasn't a lot, certainly not enough to cause any traffic hold-ups, but then Cally was coming from an hour away. What if the weather was a lot worse where she lived? Her heart leapt. What if Cally had an accident while trying to get here? What if she had driven her car off the road? No, she was catastrophising. She would call her and just ask her to call her back.

This time there was no ringing and the call went straight through to voicemail, as if Cally had turned the phone off.

Evergreen left another message. 'Cally, I just want to make sure you're OK. The weather isn't great today. If you're having trouble getting here because of the snow and you need to reschedule that's fine, but can you just call me and let me know you're OK?'

Evergreen hung up. Why would Cally turn the phone off? It was nearly twelve o'clock, nearly two hours after she was supposed to be here. If it had been anyone else, they would have called by now to say they were lost or delayed, and clearly her sister had her phone on her because she'd just turned it off. Had she listened to Evergreen's first message and then turned it off so she wouldn't have to talk to her? Was she not coming? Had she had a better offer and didn't even have the decency to call and tell her? Or was this revenge for all those years before when Cally felt betrayed and alone after Evergreen had been forced to leave home?

She felt suddenly cold. Cally wasn't coming and she had been foolish enough to stand there for two hours hoping she would show up.

She turned away from the entrance and started walking back towards Christmas Tree Cottage. Tears welled up in her eyes. Tears of anger, tears of grief for the family she had well and truly lost. If Cally couldn't even phone her to tell her she wasn't coming then what hope did they have for any kind of relationship? Maybe her sister's hurt that

Evergreen hadn't been there for her after Suki's death ran deeper than Evergreen realised but clearly Cally wasn't willing to move past that.

She'd had such high hopes for this reconciliation, that she could be part of a family again and finally put the hurt of the past behind her and move forward, not just in her own life but with Heath. She wanted that life with him so much but now it felt like it was slipping from her fingers.

As she walked through the woods she stopped when she saw Heath, Meadow and Bear playing with Star outside Wisteria Cottage. The perfect family. And she'd been kidding herself that she could be a part of that. If she couldn't trust her own family to love her and be there for her then could she really trust Heath to love her?

This had all been a silly fantasy. She'd stupidly let herself fall in love with Heath but she had to get out now before these feelings got any deeper, because when it came to an end it would devastate her. And it always came to an end. She wasn't the sort of person someone loved forever.

She quickly strode off towards her cottage, throwing herself through the door with tears in her eyes. She headed into the bedroom and looked around. She hadn't unpacked because she never did. She was always moving on. And now it was time to move on from here. She quickly went into the bathroom, grabbed a few of her toiletries and threw them in her bag. Then she walked out into the lounge to gather up her make-up, just as Heath arrived.

'Evergreen, I saw you in the woods, you looked upset. Did something happen between you and Cally?'

'She never turned up, that's what happened, and she didn't even bother to call me to tell me.'

'Oh shit, Evergreen.' Heath moved to hug her but she sidestepped him. She didn't want him being nice to her now, she wanted to get out of here before this love story caused her any more pain. Trusting someone, loving them, it just led to heartbreak. She really was better off alone.

He paused, clearly seeing how upset she was. 'I'm presuming you've called her?'

'Several times. At first it just rang and then after the first two times it went straight through to voicemail. She clearly didn't want to speak to me. All these years I've thought my family didn't want anything to do with me and now I find out I was right.'

She threw her make-up into the toolbox.

Heath watched her like she was a bomb about to go off. 'So… you're leaving?'

She turned to face him. 'What's the point of all this? We had a good time and it was fun but it was never going to last. I'm just not the sort of person anyone could love. Even my own family don't love me so I don't stand any chance of being loved by anyone else.'

'But I do, *I* love you.'

She paused in gathering her make-up to look at him, her heart in her mouth. This wasn't real, she couldn't let herself believe in a happy ending because it wasn't going to happen.

'Come on Heath, a week ago you were in love with Scarlet, now you're in love with me?' she said in disbelief.

'Me and Scarlet shared great sex, that was it. What we have is different and you know that. We have something special.'

'We have great sex too, you're overselling it,' Evergreen

said, hating herself for hurting him. But she had to push him away before he got too close. She was no good at this kind of thing; relationships, people. She'd been on her own for far too long.

'Maybe that's all it was to you, but don't dismiss what I feel for you. If you walk away from this, then you can walk away knowing you are loved, that someone does love you and that you left that behind because you got scared.'

'I told you not to fall in love with me, I told you I was never going to be the big love story you were looking for.'

'I can't help the way I feel for you, falling in love doesn't happen at convenient times. And the frustrating thing is that I'm pretty sure you're in love with me too. That's why you're running, because being in love means it will hurt even more if it comes to an end. But not every relationship comes to an end or causes you pain. Some relationships endure and bring years of happiness. Isn't it worth the risk to find out?'

Tears filled her eyes. 'I can't stay.'

'Do you think it will hurt less now than in six months' time just because we've only known each other a short while? A broken heart hurts no matter how long you've known the person. Why put yourself through that pain now when things are going so great for us?'

She shook her head. Everything he was saying made sense but it just made her want to run even more. She needed space away from him now, this wonderful, amazing man who she clearly didn't deserve.

She moved to the door.

'I knew you'd leave,' Heath said.

She turned to face him. 'You didn't trust me to stay?'

'I hoped I was wrong, I hoped I was enough for you, but I knew you'd leave eventually.'

'Then why get involved with me if you knew I was such a flake?'

He gave her a sad smile. 'I have no regrets. As I said before, it's better to have loved and lost than never to have loved at all. It's better to be fleetingly happy, no matter how briefly, than to miss out on this gloriously wonderful ecstatic feeling of pure unadulterated love. I will always remember you as the first woman I ever loved and what that felt like, although I have to say you've set the bar impossibly high.'

'Stop. Stop being nice about this. You deserve someone better than me, someone who will stay, someone who fits in with your family, someone who is emotionally mature enough to handle a relationship. I'm not her.'

'It's not about being emotionally mature. If you had claustrophobia or arachnophobia, no one would judge you for being scared. You have a fear of love and that's pretty understandable based on everything that's happened to you.'

'I told you before, I'm broken, you can't fix this. You need to aim higher, find someone who is worthy of your love.'

She pushed open the door and stepped outside. She hurried down the steps with her stuff and managed to hold the tears in until she got to the shelter and sobbed into Thunder's neck.

Evergreen hadn't got far down the road. Thunder had been really reluctant to leave and she knew he'd loved the children visiting him every day with apples and carrots and giving him fuss and attention. He was definitely moving a lot slower than he normally would, as if he didn't want to go at all.

Suddenly the white stag burst from the bushes at the side of the road, bounced across the tarmac in three large leaps and disappeared into the trees on the other side. But the animal had clearly spooked Thunder as he flinched and abruptly turned round, heading back in the direction they'd just come, practically running down the road. She pulled him to a stop, not far from the entrance to Wishing Wood, and got down to comfort him.

'Hey it's OK,' Evergreen stroked his nose. 'It was just a deer.'

Although not just any deer, the fabled white stag, coincidentally coming along just in time to stop her from leaving, if you believed in such nonsense. The last time he had appeared, supposedly to guide her to where she was meant to be, he had taken her to Heath's house.

She looked back at Wishing Wood as she stroked Thunder and a sick feeling of dread crashed through her. Because if the legend of the white stag was true he'd taken her to exactly where she was supposed to be. Not just that night, but always. She was supposed to be with Heath. What the hell was she doing here? Heath was the best thing that had ever happened to her and she'd thrown it away.

She remembered what Heath had said before, that sometimes family were the people you chose for yourself. She was so hung up on her real family that she had ignored

283

this perfect family that Heath had brought her into. The ones who had taken her into their hearts and homes and she had walked away from all of that. In actual fact she had run.

But Meadow was right. After the panic of getting hurt had gone, now she'd had time to think, Evergreen knew she had to make a plan. She had to find the right words to say to Heath to show him she wanted to fight for him. But at the moment she couldn't find anything to say that would make this better.

CHAPTER THIRTY-ONE

Heath walked into Meadow's house to find Star snuggled up to Bear watching *The Muppet Christmas Carol* again and Meadow pottering about in the kitchen. He moved over to Meadow.

'Hey, how was Evergreen? Was she OK?'

Heath shook his head. He still felt numb over what had happened. In his heart, he'd always been expecting it. He felt like their relationship had always been standing on the precipice, he'd known that no matter how close they were getting, he wasn't going to be enough. He'd waited in her house for a while, hoping she would change her mind and come back but she hadn't and, when he'd headed over to his house, he'd gone via the reception and saw her little red caravan had disappeared. He'd replayed their conversation a hundred times in his head, things he could have said to make her change her mind, but in reality he had nothing more he could do or say.

'She's gone,' Heath said, his voice choked.

'What?'

'Cally didn't show, didn't phone her, didn't answer the phone when Evergreen called her, just didn't bother to turn up. Evergreen took it really badly, she thinks she's unlovable, that if her own family don't love her, then no one can. I told her I loved her but it didn't make any difference. She packed her things and left.'

'Oh Heath. She loves you, I know she does.'

'Did she say that?'

'When I told her that I thought she loved you she didn't deny it. She told me she was scared by her feelings for you and she felt like her body was in fight or flight mode because she knew pain was imminent. She said she was scared she might end up running away and she didn't want to do that.'

'Christ, I don't know what to do. There was no getting through to her.'

'When Cally didn't show, she panicked. Her worst fears coming true and she wanted to get out before she lost you too. When she calms down and thinks about this rationally she'll realise she's made a mistake.'

'What do I do?'

'Go after her, fight for her. Cally gave up on her without even trying, show her that you won't.'

'She's gone.'

'She's in a little red caravan, probably travelling no more than two or three miles per hour, she can't be that hard to find.'

Just then the door was pushed open and River, Indigo and Tierra walked in. Tierra actually bounced in full of excitement. Seeing that *The Muppet Christmas Carol* was on TV, she immediately went over and snuggled into Bear's other side. Bear slung his arm around her, kissing her head.

'It was this that scared her off,' Heath said, gesturing to Bear. 'Our tight little family unit. She's never had a proper family, not really. She didn't feel like she belonged here. We need to show her that she does.'

Indigo came over. 'Is Evergreen OK? We just saw her caravan parked outside the drive. It looks like she was on her way back in but has stopped. We were going to pull over and see if she was OK but Tierra was desperate for the loo.'

Heath looked at Meadow.

'Go,' Meadow said.

Heath tore out of the house, down the stairs and ran full pelt through the woods.

Evergreen was sitting on her bed, curled up in the corner with her arms wrapped round her legs. She was an idiot. She still had no idea what she could say to Heath. What if he didn't want to hear her apologies? What if he didn't want her back? She had proved without doubt that she was a complete flake, that when the going got tough, she would run and not even because of anything that Heath had done. Why would he want that kind of person to be part of his family, to be around Star? That would be very unsettling for a little girl who was already going through some changes. Heath needed someone dependable and reliable in his life, not someone who would run at the first sign of trouble.

Just then there was a noise outside the front of the caravan. It sounded as if someone had just climbed up onto the front seat. The door was closed but she could see movement through the curtained window. She could hear talking but she couldn't make out what they were saying, though it was definitely a man. Was it Heath?

Her heart leapt with hope. There was a knock on the door and then it opened slowly and Heath was standing there.

'Heath, what are you doing here?'

'I've come to take you home but your engine is refusing to start.'

All the words she wanted to say disappeared. She quickly scrambled off the bed and threw herself into his arms. He held her tight, kissing the top of her head, and relief flooded through her, tears pouring down her cheeks.

'Why are you here, after everything I said and did?' she said into his chest.

'Because I love you, and that love doesn't go away because of a silly fight. Why are you here, parked just outside the entrance? I thought you were running away?'

'I saw the stag again, it ran out into the road as I was leaving and it scared Thunder enough to make him run back to here, and that's when I realised. If the stag was trying to guide me to where I'm supposed to be, it was here, with you, that's where I belong. But I've been trying to think of what I could say to you to apologise. I was too scared to come and find you in case you told me you didn't want me any more.'

'Love doesn't work like that. Love is unconditional and

irrevocable. It means to forgive and forget. It means that I will always be here for you. Always.'

She cried harder against him.

'I'm so sorry, I'm such an idiot, I don't know why I let my sister's no-show get to me so much. I always wanted to be part of a family and suddenly I was not only dating the perfect, most wonderful man I've ever met, but he came with this perfect family. But when Cally didn't turn up I started thinking that I could never have that life, that somehow I didn't deserve it.'

He pulled back slightly, stroking the tears from her face with his thumbs. 'You definitely deserve it. But listen, things moved very quickly for us. You arrived and these feelings for each other exploded out of nowhere. We were making love, spending every waking second together, you were spending time with my family, my daughter. Any other woman I'd have dated would never have started off like that. We can slow things down if you want, we can just be friends until we get to know each other properly. Or we don't have to have any kind of relationship at all if you don't want. But Christmas Tree Cottage will always be your home.'

She shook her head. 'It's not. It's a lovely house but it will never be home.'

He frowned.

'You are my home, Heath Brookfield. I love you so much and if you're willing to take a chance on a flake like me, then I want to take it and I promise I will never run from you again.'

His face lit up in a big smile. 'I love you with everything I have and I want this chance with you more than anything.

However, you can't promise that you won't get scared again and I don't want you to bottle up your emotions. But if you want to run, if you need some space to think, you can run to Christmas Tree Cottage or your caravan, you don't actually have to leave.'

'You're right, I do have safe places I can go to, but actually I'm pretty confident in promising that. In my life when I lost the ones I loved, when my dad left, when my mum kicked me out, when my nan couldn't cope with me, when Suki died, when Rob kicked me out, these were all circumstances beyond my control. Today I nearly lost everything that was important to me and the man I loved and it was all my fault. It was my actions that nearly took those things away from me and, when I stopped and had a moment to calm down and think things through, I realised that I was my own worst enemy, that I was self-destructive, and I didn't want to be that person any more. You said I needed a thing to fight for, something that would make me leave my past behind once and for all and give me the determination to move forward. You hoped it would be Christmas Tree Cottage, I thought it might be Cally, but it was you, you are my thing. I want a life with you more than anything and I'm going to do anything I can to make that possible.'

He smiled, cupped her face and kissed her. She slid her arms around his neck, pressing herself up against him.

She pulled back slightly. 'Do you want to make my caravan rock?'

He laughed loudly. 'I'd like nothing more.'

CHAPTER THIRTY-TWO

Evergreen smiled as she looked around Wisteria Cottage the next day. Right now she couldn't be happier. She had woken that morning in Heath's arms, he'd made love to her and then they'd got up and had pancakes for breakfast with everyone else. They'd spent a while opening presents together, or rather watching Star and Tierra opening their massive haul of presents. Both Tierra and Star had been given beautiful cloaks which Meadow had made and they both loved. And now they were all chilling out together watching Christmas TV programmes while the turkey was cooking. Evergreen was snuggled up against Heath's side and Star was snuggled up against his other side.

It had been so long since Evergreen had celebrated Christmas properly and she felt so comfortable and so at ease, like she just fitted here with this wonderful family.

Meadow's phone suddenly rang and she got up to answer it. She said a few words to the person on the other end and then hung up.

'Heath, can I borrow you for a second?' Meadow said.

Heath frowned and got up, walking into the kitchen with his ex-wife where they talked quietly for a few moments. Something was up.

Heath came back and kissed Evergreen on the head. 'I'll be back in a few minutes.'

He walked out the house. She tried to concentrate on *The Snowman* that was playing on the TV when Star shifted over and snuggled into her instead. It was so unexpected that Evergreen didn't know what to do for a moment, but after a second she put her arm around her and leaned her head on top of hers. She couldn't help the huge smile that spread across her face at this simple act.

'If you could fly for one night, Evergreen, where would you fly to?' Star asked.

'Oh, that's a good question. I've never actually left the UK before so there's nowhere I've visited before that I'd like to see again but I've always wanted to see the northern lights so probably somewhere far up north where I could see them, Finland or Norway maybe. Somewhere with lots of mountains and snow and lots of space, no buildings or people, just miles and miles of beautiful hills and forests and the northern lights dancing over it all.'

'That sounds nice. I'd like to see the northern lights too,' Star said, sleepily.

'Where would you fly to?' Evergreen asked.

'Africa to see the giraffes and rhinos and lions. I'd swoop really close to the ground but high enough up so that the lions couldn't eat me.'

'Good plan.'

Heath walked back in and his face lit up at seeing Evergreen and Star together. He gestured for Evergreen to come over to him.

'I've got to go and see your dad, I'll be back in a second.' Evergreen gave Star a little squeeze then got up to see Heath.

'So Cally is here,' Heath said and her heart leapt. 'She was in a car accident yesterday – nothing serious, she's absolutely fine. Her car just hit some ice and slid off the road into a ditch. She wasn't hurt but she was trapped in the car for a few hours. Her phone fell into a puddle of water and eventually stopped working so she wasn't able to call you or anyone else to get help. She was finally found after five hours and the paramedics were worried she might have hypothermia so they kept her in overnight and just discharged her an hour ago. I'm not sure if you wanted to see her as you were so upset yesterday so I've asked her to wait outside for a moment while I checked with you, but I do believe she's telling the truth.'

'Oh my god, I did wonder at first if something had happened, the roads are a bit narrow and windy round here. But her phone rang to begin with and then when I called back and it went straight to voicemail I just assumed she'd turned it off so she wouldn't have to speak to me. Jesus, the poor girl. And now that makes my reaction to her not turning up yesterday even worse.'

Heath smiled and kissed her on the head. 'Forgive and forget, remember.'

'I'm going to go and see her. Is it OK if she stays for lunch?'

'Of course. River bought a bird that is bigger than me,

we'll be eating turkey for months, she is more than welcome.'

'Thank you.' She leaned up and kissed him and then rushed outside.

Her sister was waiting at the bottom of the steps and she looked worried.

'Hey,' Cally said. 'I'm sorry about yesterday I...'

'You have nothing to apologise for, you were trapped in a ditch for Christ's sake,' Evergreen said, hovering halfway down the stairs. She didn't know whether to hug her, give her a handshake or a friendly pat on the back.

'Heath said you were upset.'

'I was but only because I was so looking forward to seeing you. You're here now, that's all that matters. Happy Christmas Cally.'

'Happy Christmas.'

They hovered awkwardly for a moment.

'Can I give you a hug?' Evergreen said, suddenly realising how much she needed that.

Cally smiled. 'I'd really like that.'

Evergreen hurried down the last few steps and took her little sister in her arms, holding her tight. Tears pricked her eyes; this Christmas was just getting better and better.

Heath poked his head out the door. 'I'm sure you two have loads to catch up on but, before you do, Meadow has hidden a load of gold chocolate coins around the house and we need your help to find them all.'

Evergreen and Cally gasped with delight.

'Oh I'm definitely up for that,' Cally said. 'Let's see if Evergreen is as good at it as she used to be.'

'Oh I bet I am.'

Cally laughed. 'We'll see.'

They both went up the stairs and Cally went inside.

Evergreen wrapped her arms around Heath and kissed him. 'Thank you for this, what a lovely idea.'

'It's my pleasure. Happy Christmas Evergreen.'

She smiled. 'I have a feeling this might be one of my happiest.'

EPILOGUE

One year later

Evergreen smiled as she watched Star, sitting under the Christmas tree unwrapping the last of her presents from her and Heath. It was a horror make-up kit and Star's expression of excitement was wonderful to see. She hadn't grown out of her fascination for horror make-up and, at Halloween, Evergreen had really gone to town in making her into the most hideous zombie she'd ever created. Tierra was less keen, so she had given her a cat makeover, which she'd loved. Now Star could practise doing her own.

Evergreen looked around the room. Alfie, now just over a year old, had taken his first steps a few days before and she was delighted that she'd been there to see it. Since then he'd been practising every chance he got and even now he was toddling around the room. He'd land on his bum every few seconds, but it didn't deter him. River, Indigo and Tierra were cheering him on.

Bear was feeding his daughter, Rose, her bottle and she

was watching the fairy lights dance across the tree. Meadow was sitting next to Star, taking photos of her excitement and joy at the present she'd been given.

Amelia was sitting on the sofa with her fiancé Edwin, who was wearing the most amazing Christmas waistcoat. They had apparently met the year before at the Dwelling festival and hit it off but never stayed in touch. When he'd returned for the festival this summer, they had met again and this time it was love. He'd popped the question a few months later and they were due to marry on New Year's Day.

Cally was in the kitchen with her new boyfriend, Alec, they were giggling over the mince pies they were eating and getting in a mess. It was early days for them but they seemed very happy.

Evergreen looked up at Heath, sitting next to her, and he kissed her on the forehead. He made her happy every single day.

The last year had been the best of her life. She had moved straight into Wisteria Tree Cottage with Heath and it just felt so right to wake every morning wrapped in his arms. Star had totally accepted that she was now part of Heath's life and hers. Evergreen had met up with Cally multiple times and she'd even seen Lucy, Noah and Oliver on a few occasions. She still did make-up for a living but only out of the film studios at Cardiff and, when she wasn't working there, she worked at Wishing Wood, sometimes doing a shift on reception, sometimes doing face painting for the kids at weekends or in the holidays. It felt good to be part of a team. Thunder had officially retired from pulling her broken-up caravan but was very content giving rides to Amelia, Star and Tierra every day so she knew he was happier here too.

'OK everyone, it's time to find all the gold coins,' Meadow said.

Evergreen smiled that her traditions had now become their traditions. Cally started warming up in the kitchen as if about to run a marathon.

'Only this year, we've had to use gold chocolate bells instead, I couldn't get hold of any gold coins,' Meadow went on. 'There are some hidden inside here but there are also some hidden in the woods outside. There are four trees with red ribbons round them and the square area inside those trees are where they are hidden. Is everyone ready?'

Everyone cheered and Evergreen scrambled to her feet.

'On your marks, get set, go,' Meadow said.

Everyone split up and most people started searching the house first but Heath seized Evergreen's hand and tugged her outside. 'Come on, we can get a head start out here before the others come out.'

Evergreen quickly grabbed her cloak and stepped outside into the glittering snow that had fallen overnight. She spotted the red-ribboned trees marking out the area where the golden bells were hidden.

'Right, you take that corner, I'll take this one,' Heath said and quickly took off in one direction so she ran over to the other corner. She found two gold chocolate bells fairly quickly and a third a short while after that. She looked around and could see that she and Heath were still the only ones out here, but they wouldn't have much longer before everyone else came out here too, having exhausted the supply of gold chocolate bells inside.

She spotted one underneath the red-ribboned tree and quickly made her way over there but this one was slightly bigger than the others. As she grabbed it, she realised it was a lot heavier too.

'You might want to open that one,' Heath said from behind her.

She turned to look at him in confusion and then back at the gold bell, realising it was a box. She could see the little hinges and the tiny catch. She opened it and gasped to see a ring with a beautiful pear-shaped emerald surrounded by diamonds. The shoulders of the ring also had diamonds on them. It was stunning. She looked up to see Heath getting down on one knee in front of her and her heart thundered in her chest.

'Evergreen Winters, I love you with everything I have. You are the missing piece I've been searching for and I thank my lucky stars every day that your friends were unable to come last year and you came here instead. You have changed my life so completely and utterly and I want to spend the rest of my life making you as happy as you make me. Will you marry me?'

Evergreen bent over and kissed him hard on the mouth and he pulled her onto his lap and kissed her back. Eventually he pulled back slightly. 'Is that a yes?'

She giggled and nodded. 'I love you so much. You gave me a home – and I don't mean this place, I mean with you. You make me so ridiculously happy. Every single day I wake up like a kid on Christmas morning because I'm with you. I've been running for so long but I know this is where I belong. Of course I will marry you.'

His face split into a huge grin and he placed the ring on her finger.

There was a huge cheer from Wisteria Cottage and Evergreen looked over to see every member of the Brookfield clan and Cally and her boyfriend all cheering and clapping.

'Finally,' yelled Amelia.

Evergreen laughed.

'Are you sure about marriage?' Heath said, rolling his eyes. 'Unfortunately I come as a package deal with this lot.'

'I love your family Heath Brookfield, every single crazy member of it. I love them because they are part of you.'

Heath grinned and kissed her again, ignoring the cheers and whistles from his family.

Evergreen pulled back slightly as light snowflakes started dusting her cheeks and that's when she spotted movement through the trees. She gasped and pointed to Heath and he turned to look at the white stag watching them, before he turned and walked away.

'Where is he going, should we follow him?' Evergreen said.

'No need, he's heading in the direction of the wedding chapel treehouse, we'll be there soon enough.'

She laughed. 'Happy Christmas.'

'It is now.'

He kissed her again and she knew this was the start of her forever.

If you enjoyed *The Christmas Tree Cottage*, you'll love my next gorgeously romantic story, *The Little Beach Hut Hotel*, out next year.

Sandcastle Bay Series

The Holiday Cottage by the Sea

The Cottage on Sunshine Beach

Coming Home to Maple Cottage

Hope Island Series

Spring at Blueberry Bay

Summer at Buttercup Beach

Christmas at Mistletoe Cove

Juniper Island Series

Christmas Under a Cranberry Sky

A Town Called Christmas

White Cliff Bay Series

Christmas at Lilac Cottage

Snowflakes on Silver Cove

Summer at Rose Island

Standalone Stories

The Secrets of Clover Castle

(Previously published as Fairytale Beginnings)

The Guestbook at Willow Cottage

One Hundred Proposals

One Hundred Christmas Proposals

Tied Up With Love

A Home on Bramble Hill

For Young Adults

The Sentinel Series

The Sentinel (Book 1 of the Sentinel Series)

The Prophecies (Book 2 of the Sentinel Series)

The Revenge (Book 3 of the Sentinel Series)

The Reckoning (Book 4 of the Sentinel Series)

STAY IN TOUCH…

To keep up to date with the latest news on my releases, just go to the link below to sign up for a newsletter. You'll also get two FREE short stories, get sneak peeks, booky news and be able to take part in exclusive giveaways. Your email will never be shared with anyone else and you can unsubscribe at any time
https://www.subscribepage.com/hollymartinsignup

Website: https://hollymartin-author.com/
Email: holly@hollymartin-author.com
Twitter: @HollyMAuthor

A LETTER FROM HOLLY

Thank you so much for reading *The Christmas Tree Cottage,* I had so much fun creating this story and including all the magic of living in a fairytale wood at Christmas. I hope you enjoyed reading it as much as I enjoyed writing it.

One of the best parts of writing comes from seeing the reaction from readers. Did it make you smile or laugh, did it make you cry, hopefully happy tears? Did you fall in love with Heath and Evergreen as much as I did? Did you like the little treehouses in Wishing Wood? If you enjoyed the story, I would absolutely love it if you could leave a short review on Amazon. Getting feedback from readers is amazing and it also helps to persuade other readers to pick up one of my books for the first time.

If you enjoyed this story, my next book, out next year, is called The Little Beach Hut Hotel. You'll meet Fern and Fletcher and stay in a gorgeous little beach hut overlooking golden sands. I've absolutely fallen in love with Fletcher already and I know you will love him too.

Thank you for reading.
Love Holly x

ACKNOWLEDGEMENTS

To my family, my mom, my biggest fan, who reads every word I've written a hundred times over and loves it every single time, my dad, my brother Lee and my sister-in-law Julie, for your support, love, encouragement and endless excitement for my stories.

For my twinnie, the gorgeous Aven Ellis for just being my wonderful friend, for your endless support, for cheering me on, for reading my stories and telling me what works and what doesn't and for keeping me entertained with wonderful stories. I love you dearly.

To my lovely friends Julie, Natalie, Jac, Verity and Jodie, thanks for all the support.

To the Devon contingent, Paw and Order, Belinda, Lisa, Phil, Bodie, Kodi and Skipper. Thanks for keeping me entertained and always being there.

To everyone at Bookcamp, you gorgeous, fabulous bunch, thank you for your wonderful support on this venture.

Thanks to my fabulous editors, Celine Kelly and Rhian McKay.

To all the wonderful bloggers for your tweets, retweets, facebook posts, tireless promotions, support, encouragement and endless enthusiasm. You guys are amazing and I couldn't do this journey without you.

To anyone who has read my book and taken the time to tell me you've enjoyed it or wrote a review, thank you so much.

Thank you, I love you all.

Published by Holly Martin in 2022
Copyright © Holly Martin, 2022

978-1-913616-41-0 Paperback
978-1-913616-43-4 Large Print paperback
978-1-913616-42-7 Hardback

Cover design by Emma Rogers

Printed in Great Britain
by Amazon

12214363R00180